A Cuban Girl's Guide to Tea and Tomorrow

A Cuban Girl's Guide to Tea and Tomorrow

LAURA TAYLOR NAMEY

A̶ Atheneum   New York   London   Toronto   Sydney   New Delhi

An imprint of Simon & Schuster Children's Publishing Division
1230 Avenue of the Americas, New York, New York 10020

For information about special discounts for bulk purchases, please contact Simon & Schuster
Special Sales at 1-866-506-1949 or business@simonandschuster.com.
The Simon & Schuster Speakers Bureau can bring authors to your live event. For more
information or to book an event, contact the Simon & Schuster Speakers Bureau at
1-866-248-3049 or visit our website at www.simonspeakers.com.
The text for this book was set in Adobe Caslon Pro.
Manufactured in the United States of America

2 4 6 8 10 9 7 5 3
Library of Congress Cataloging-in-Publication Data
Names: Namey, Laura Taylor, author.
Title: A Cuban girl's guide to tea and tomorrow / Laura Taylor Namey. Description: New
York : Atheneum, [2020] | Audience: Ages 12 up. | Audience: Grades 10-12. | Summary:
Seventeen-year-old Lila Reyes, furious when her parents send her to the English countryside
to recover from grief and heartbreak, unexpectedly falls in love with a teashop clerk—and
England, itself.
Identifiers: LCCN 2019055585 (print) | LCCN 2019055586 (ebook) | ISBN 9781534471245
(hardcover) | ISBN 9781534471269 (eBook)
Subjects: CYAC: Loss (Psychology)—Fiction. | Cuban Americans—Fiction. | Bakers and
bakeries—Fiction. | Dating (Social customs)—Fiction. | Love—Fiction. | England—Fiction.
Classification: LCC PZ7.1.N3555 Cub 2020 (print) | LCC PZ7.1.N3555 (eBook)
| DDC [Fic]—dc23
LC record available at https://lccn.loc.gov/2019055585
LC eBook record available at https://lccn.loc.gov/2019055586

For Hildelisa Victoria, my brave and beautiful mother

✳

*If you find undissolved sugar in the bottom of your teacup,
someone has a crush on you.*

—Superstition

*Mañana, by the way, does not mean tomorrow:
It means not today.*

—Billy Collins

1

Call it whatever you like. A vacation. A high school graduation present. Maybe even an escape. All I know is I'm as far from Miami as I've ever been.

I'm here because the Cuban Remedy failed. It's forever ancient and reads like a recipe. Though the ingredients may vary from family to family, the goal is always the same: suffer heartbreak and your family will fix you. Except no amount of food and family could heal my heartbreak, so like a plotline from one of Mami's telenovelas, they tricked me instead.

"Next, please." The London Heathrow customs officer waves me forward. "The purpose of your visit, miss?" he asks after I hand over my passport.

Two seconds pass, then four, then my blatant lie. "Vacation."

I keep quiet because one of my summer hosts, Spencer, is waiting, and me getting hauled into secondary screening sits right up there with teeth pulling and gyno exams. But *Dios*, how I want to go full force on this officer and this entire day. I barely resist leaning close to his dapper blue customs uniform and snarling, "I. Am. *Here*. Because not only did my most beloved abuelita die, but within two months of her death, my best friend abandoned me, and my boyfriend of three years dumped me right before prom. I call it the trifecta. Apparently, I wasn't getting over it all fast enough so my family sent me here to 'cool down.' I didn't want to come to your England, but my mami pulled out her greatest trick of all, even more powerful than guava pastries and other common Cuban heartbreak remedies. She pulled out Abuela. So to answer your question, *I* have no purpose for being here."

Thwack. The officer stamps my passport and slides it toward me. "Enjoy your stay."

Not bloody likely.

Two hours later, after a near-silent bus ride followed by a totally silent cab ride, the driver drops us off at a place I've only seen in pictures. Unfortunately, they forgot to add sunshine. I'm shivering under a bland sky as Spencer wrestles my two large suitcases from the trunk.

So this is Winchester, Hampshire, England.

I cross the narrow street and approach the Owl and Crow Inn. Like many of the buildings we passed in town, the Owl and Crow looks like something straight out of a Jane Austen novel. The massive wedding cake of orangey-red brick towers over the neighborhood. Climbing ivy twists from the portico, traveling around the three-story inn with avenues of green veins. History—this place bleeds it.

Nothing in Miami is this old. Not even Señora Cabral, who still hobbles into my family's bakery every Monday and was tan vieja before my parents were even born, is this old.

Spencer Wallace rolls my bags under a rose-draped arbor. Seeing Spence here, instead of in Miami when he's visited with his wife and son, makes me realize how much his entire look blends into his brick-and-mortar inn. Newly graying red hair. Tight goatee and moustache combo. He even wears a heavy tweed blazer. And it was *this*, the first glimpse of my distant family member at the airport, that made my journey even more surreal than when I boarded my flight. Mami and Papi have sent me to a foreign country where men wear tweed blazers. In *June*.

"Come along then, Lila," Spencer says from the doorway.

"Cate should be back from the physio by now. Nice and toasty inside." He bumps into my shoulder when he shuts the door behind us. "Sorry," he says, and casts another concerned glance at my traveling outfit, the same one he's been side-eyeing since I exited customs. As I discovered all throughout Heathrow Terminal Five, my white jeans, gold sandals, and flimsy hot pink tank aren't typical choices for England vacations, even in early summer. But it's *perfectly normal* for my Miami. Whether I'm cold or not makes no difference.

Inside the inn, the air is warm but not stuffy, and scented with butter and sugar. I breathe in the elements and try to keep them there. The familiar smells are as much home as I can have right now.

Tía Cate appears at the bottom of a polished wood staircase.

"Ah, here she is." She approaches, looping her arms around me. "Sorry I couldn't come with Spencer to meet your plane, and I had to hijack the car, too."

"The shuttle bus was fine," I say into her itchy wool shoulder. Her blond low bun is the same as I remember, but her accent sounds flatter than ever. Is this what twenty-five years in England does to a Venezuelan woman, born Catalina Raquel Mendoza? Here, in this Hampshire medieval town, with this husband, she is Cate Wallace.

"Look at you. Almost eighteen." Cate steps back, furrowing her brows. "Let's get you into the parlor for tea while Spence takes up your bags. There's a fire going and I can get you a sweater before you unpack. That thin blouse—we don't want you to catch cold."

My chest tightens around my heart and then . . . it happens. Here in the cozy Owl and Crow foyer with weathered wood planks beneath my sandals and tall canisters filled with pointy umbrellas at the door. It didn't happen at Miami International when I wore an unbreakable scowl, even as I gave obligatory kisses to mis padres and my sister, Pilar. It didn't happen as I watched the stardust lights of my city disappear behind the jumbo jet wing. I didn't cry then. Wouldn't. But Catalina-Cate Wallace gets me good right here and I can't stop it. My eyes well, and my throat closes over a memory that won't ever let me go.

¡Ponte un suéter, que te vas a resfriar!

Put on a sweater or you'll catch a cold! The Cuban mantra of all mantras. Tattoo it on our foreheads. Write it in indelible ink on our violet-scented stationery. Yell it at impressive volumes from windows to children eating Popsicles on Little Havana streets. My abuela threw out stacks of virtual sweaters left and right. Until that cold March morning she couldn't. The coldest day of all.

My hand flies up to the golden dove charm hanging around my neck, Abuela's gift from four years ago. Cate notices, her refined features wilting. "Oh, your sweet abuelita. She was such a wonderful woman, love."

Love. Not mija. Not for English Cate.

"Abuela practically raised me, too." Cate meets my swollen eyes. "I hated that I couldn't come for the funeral."

"Mami understood. It's a long way." Four thousand, three hundred and eighty miles.

Cate webs both of her hands over my cheeks. It is a gesture so like Abuela's that tears want to flow again. "Tell me the truth," she says. "Even though I'd just had neck surgery, your mother still found a way to blame me, right?"

I laugh. England hasn't stolen everything. Her pursed lips, cocked hip, and challenging eyes hail straight from the Cate I remember from the Wallaces' last Miami trip. "How did you guess?"

"I love your mother dearly. But telenovela mujeres could take lessons from that one."

Soap opera drama. Mami never went to college, but she majored in drama, anyway, with a minor in extra. She also majored in doing the opposite of what's best for me.

"Find a seat in the parlor while I fetch the tea Polly made for us," Cate says and gestures to the archway before scooting off.

I remove my black cross body purse; the customs form peeks out from the front pocket. *Enjoy your stay.* I crumple the slip into the smallest ball I can manage. No so-called vacation is going to fix me.

2

I can see why Owl and Crow guests rave about the afternoon tea served in the parlor, but there's too much sugar in this scone. Although the texture is nearly perfect, sweetness level is where many bakers fail. Flour, butter, and sugar are only platforms for other flavors—spices and extracts, fruit and cream and chocolate. A pastry never needs to be overly sweet. It only needs to be memorable.

Not that I'm a scone expert; in fact, I've never made one. The last one I ate was four months ago when Pilar wanted to celebrate her twenty-first birthday with afternoon tea at the Miami Biltmore Hotel.

Like that historic space, this parlor, with its icy blue walls and brocade fabrics, seems more like a painting than a room. Here, I'm a figure drawn into someone else's life.

I'll call it "Cuban Girl with Over-Sugared Scone in Not-Miami."

"...and walks, and the countryside is so close. You can ride one of the guest bicycles everywhere and really, really get some rest. City center has cafés and little shops I know you'll love." Between sips of strong black tea, Cate has spent the last five minutes trying to sell me on Winchester like some real estate agent.

I smiled stiffly through it all, as if she *could* sell me. "Sounds nice. And thanks for letting me stay." The imaginary space between wanting to drown all my words inside the rose-covered teapot and showing respect to this woman whom I've known since birth—that's where I sit.

"No bullshit," Cate says. "You can be straight with me."

"Fine." I set down my teacup with an undignified clank. "I don't want to be here." Family or not.

The words don't even pierce her gaze—cool like the white marble sky outside the windows. Cate traces the rim of her teacup. Her oval-shaped nails shine with black cherry lacquer. "Of course you don't. No need to pretend. But your parents think some time away will help—"

"What about what I think? How *I* feel?" I'm a broken record, repeating the script I've been reciting since my flight was booked. All the help I need lies four thousand miles across the Atlantic. It's the place where, weeks ago, I had everything I wanted. It's the home of our bakery that I will take over and grow—the one that would always rest on Abuela's roots. Panadería La Paloma. Her memory and spirit are still inside those walls and now, I'm not.

I don't need England. Miami is my charm city. The home where I have won so often in seventeen years. It calls me, blood thick and marrow deep. *You are mine*, it says. *You can win again.*

But not here. Not in England.

Miami held my most cherished relationships, the ones I cry for in secret. Abuela. Andrés. Stefanie. My heart and body and memory are not finished with them yet. In eighty-five days in England, too many more things can change and I won't be home to stop them.

"You're hurting, Lila. And you frightened your parents," Cate says. "Your mental health is more important than your taking over La Paloma right away."

Bueno. Well. The no-bullshit rule goes both ways. *But I was handling it.* I need more time, not more talking. Not more space. Why can't Mami and Papi see that?

Cate twists a blond strand escaping her bun. "Just promise one thing, because we both know the wrath of tu mamá."

I flick my eyes up at her use of Spanish.

"Try to find your place here. Maybe even have a little fun. But you'll do it carefully, no?" It sounds like spending the last half hour with me has caused her accent to lean southwest a little. "Don't jog alone at night or do anything . . . reckless."

Reckless. Like what I did two weeks ago? My cheeks flame with ire and regret. *I was so sloppy. Careless.*

But I don't say any of this. I hide the rest of my verbal responses under my last bites of Polly's black currant scone. Yes, too sweet.

Half of the tea remains in my cup when Cate jostles my forearm. "Let's get you settled. Spence should have your bags set up by now." She stands, motioning for me to follow her into the foyer and up the sweeping staircase.

The second floor of the Owl and Crow Inn hosts eight guest rooms. Cate had mentioned all are booked, but right now the paneled hallway is only occupied by rows of brass sconces. Large, golden bird wings flank each fixture.

We stop at a wide, unmarked door with a keypad. "Here are the stairs to our private flat. The door code is the Miami zip code for our old neighborhood." Cate's features soften with nostalgia. When her parents moved to Miami from Venezuela, Cate spent so much time at Abuela's with Mami, it became her second home. Pilar and I never called her cousin. She'll always be our tía.

She motions for me to enter the five digits I know well. After a beep, the lock clicks open, revealing the mouth of another carved-spindle staircase.

The stairs dump us into a sprawling loft-like space. Cate points to one hallway. "Spence and I have our rooms down there." She pivots, leading me across the living room through the opposite wing. "This side has your guest room, one bath, and Gordon's room. He's with a study group at the library."

I have a vague memory of being told school exams run well into summer around here. "I can't believe Gordon's sixteen."

She grins. "And so tall you'll barely recognize him. The last time you saw each other he must've been around twelve. Right before our Key West trip."

"Yeah, he loved running around the kitchen at La Paloma while you and Mami drank cafecito out front." My dark hair falls over my face and smells like airplane. I rake it back. "He tried to steal an empanada from every tray Abuela pulled from the oven. She kept whacking at him with her hand towel, but it didn't stop him."

The burst of memory stings like a rubber band snap.

I look away until Cate squeezes my shoulder. She opens a paneled door and pokes her hand inside. "Here we are. You know where to find me. Supper's at seven."

Alone, the bedroom where I will spend the next eighty-five days has an actual four-poster bed. Not some IKEA special, but an authentic piece fit for the regency period. I drop my purse and slide my fingers along the cherry wood grain. Like the rest of the inn, it feels old.

Spencer left my bags next to a gray velvet bench. I survey the space—dresser with TV on top, gray floral loveseat, writing desk. One wall has a generous paned-glass window, now letting in dusky light from the street. The other outside wall has a wider set window, but with crank mechanisms. I shove back cream silk drapes. The window frames let out a paranormal whine as I turn the handle and inch my torso through. Leaning over the sill, I peer just over treetops into a walled church courtyard that bumps closely against my side of the Owl and Crow. My eyes struggle to adjust, trading palm trees and peach stucco for weathered brick and steepled churches—just like the tiny stone parish next door.

My new room is gorgeous. But it doesn't stop one half of me from wanting to beat my fists against the wall, screaming the feral sounds I've had echoing in my mind all day. All March and April and May. It doesn't stop my other half from wanting to hide underneath the plush down comforter.

I settle for rolling my suitcases toward the door—I'm not ready to organize my new reality. I unzip my large carry-on tote on top of the bed. Miami is inside. Traces of Mami's lemon-vinegar tile cleaner and my gardenia-scented room spray cling to all the contents I'll need tonight. Abuela could've packed this bag.

Because of her, Pilar and I would never dare board a plane without toting a spare pair of underwear and a change of clothes. *After all, the airline could lose your luggage!* Abuela never did trust those baggage handlers.

And I hadn't trusted them with these items. After leggings and a long tee, I remove Abuela's signature white apron. The one I held on my lap during her funeral. Then, a family photo of myself and my parents and Pilar in my great-uncle's garden. And another small snapshot of Abuela I took last year, her slight frame topped with a jaunty crop of graying black hair, smiling over her simple breakfast of café con leche and pan tostado.

Abuela and I were the only ones in the family big on keeping los recuerdos—mementos. Pili didn't get the sentimental gene, and Mami hates clutter. But Mami still hasn't removed the little altar of cards, photos, figurines, and dried flowers from Abuela's dresser. She hasn't turned Abuela's bedroom into a guest room yet, or moved her worn garden clogs from the patio. For now, even my mother is keeping things.

I set up *my* transplanted altar, placing my Miami items on the nightstand. My heart snags on the last item in my tote: a white University of Miami t-shirt I bought for Stefanie. It's un recuerdo of huge proportions, a memento of a best-friend plan I'm not quite ready to stuff into a drawer.

This shirt is the biggest reason I'm here.

Two weeks ago, the back-ordered white tee arrived at Panadería La Paloma on the same day Stefanie's flight left, like a sick joke. Stef wasn't going to UM anymore. My friend wasn't going anywhere in Miami anymore. Not with me.

The beginning of our ending happened two days before the shirt delivery. I'd flopped onto her bed the same way I always had, except now, an enormous duffel bag swallowed Stef's area rug. Her passport and piles of travel documents and the packet from the Catholic Missionary Fellowship of South Florida covered her desk.

The end of our ending happened as I slammed doors and fled from a house I'd been welcomed inside like family for years.

And in the middle, my best friend admitted she'd been preparing for a two-year health aid post since November. Months of training she never mentioned. Stef had traded her University of Miami acceptance for a remote African village without a word.

Two weeks ago, alone in the bakery office, I'd stared at the UM logo on the t-shirt. The words we'd spewed pelted me like hail.

You couldn't tell me?

Lila, I'm so sorry. You would've talked me out of it.

That's not true.

I have to go.

You totally rearranged your life behind my back?

You'd just lost your abuela. And after what happened with Andrés . . . Plus you know you would've fought it. And won, just like always.

Then I ran home and cried over a graduation selfie of us, taken the week before. My brunette mane and her fine blond layers flowed under mortarboard caps tinted the dark color of deceit.

Holding the soft jersey tee in the panadería office only hardened one fact inside of me: My grief had changed, morphing from a line between two throbbing end points—Abuela and Andrés— to a new shape. A triangle.

And this trifecta loomed so large, I couldn't shake it. I couldn't find myself underneath the black emptiness. My heart fragmented and my breathing came like the prelude to a storm. I had to move. I had to run.

Recipe for Being Abandoned by Your Best Friend

From the Kitchen of Lila Reyes

Ingredients: One packed gym bag kept in Papi's office. One pair of Nike running shoes. One neon blue tank. One pair of Adidas compression leggings.

Preparation: Change into your gear and flee out the rear service door. Go to your sweet birth city, your Miami. It's large enough to take you in. Reclaim places and streets that knew *you*, that knew your love and joy before the last three months took so very much. Reclaim it all.

*Leave out rehashing Stefanie with your family. It's your loss and you're going to handle it.

Cooking Temp: 475 degrees—precisely how hot Miami feels when you're running during the afternoon.

That afternoon, two weeks ago, I went to the rear parking lot and locked everything but my key fob and phone into my turquoise Mini Cooper. Bending and stretching, I prepared to do the thing I did second-best of all. I ran farther than ever before, the kind of distance people earn medals and ribbons for. My only prize was the worn-out reward of stubborn defiance. For hours, I pushed past every hazard sign my body threw out, crossing neighborhood boundaries, until dinnertime came and went. One thought cut through the sweat and heat and pain until my limbs finally shut down: If I traveled far enough, I might be able to run right out of my own skin.

Today I wonder if Stef was right, if I actually could have changed her mind. After all, my powers of persuasion hadn't worked on my family.

I sink onto the gray velvet bench and try to be as still as possible. I pretend if I don't move, the place I come from won't either. West Dade will lock into space and time until I'm home again.

3

After twenty-four hours in my room, I have no idea about the outside temperature, or the number of steps between the inn and Winchester city center. I do know every mysterious smudge on the ceiling, and that it's six steps from my doorway to the bathroom. Fifteen steps to the loft kitchen and back.

The Wallaces don't comment on my hibernation, and I find meal trays on the kitchen counter—bless them. One had a note:

Rest. I'm updating your family. Mami's only called six times.
—*Cate*

Cate's also said nothing about the suitcases still propped by my door. About my powered-down phone perched on top of my powered-down laptop.

And then there's Pilar. I picture my sister's pert smile and her calm, rational eyes and wonder how many times she's texted. Or did she power down from me, too, knowing I couldn't stay away for long? I glance at my phone, the voice of the most precious person in my life, only twenty seconds away. But no. Not yet. I'm not quite ready for an actual conversation with her. At least one not seasoned with the best swear words I know, in two languages.

A white UM t-shirt may have provoked my run, but my flight to England might as well have been booked by one Pilar Veronica Reyes. Since landing, I've thought about the midnight scene in my West Dade bedroom a dozen times—the one unfolding after I took off running alone for hours from La Paloma. The aftermath was a hurricane. As irked as I am with my sister, I'm more furious with myself for being so sloppy.

My body had paid dearly for my recklessness, too. I remember the way *everything* ached. How the fibers of my gray and white comforter scraped against screaming muscles and sunburned skin.

"Más," Pilar had said that night, holding out the hundredth spoonful of caldo de pollo. I had made this batch of Abuela's magical chicken soup. That plus a generous coating of "Vivaporú"— Vicks VapoRub—could cure any ailment. "I said more, Lila," she told my shaking head and tucked-in lips.

"Enough," I said. My skull housed a bass drum.

Pili huffed and slammed the bowl down on my nightstand. This accounting major moved like an army nurse, stoic and strong, back to our little first-aid caddy.

Her hands rubbed more of the cool, tingling VapoRub onto my calves. I winced when she went in for another round of blister salve.

"Serves you right." More salve on my heels and toes, patches of skin rubbed clean off. "If you never wear those red stiletto sandals again, it's your own fault, hermana."

Yes, my fault. It's what I got for running for over five hours and more than twenty miles, all but crawling at the end. Once I'd started, I couldn't stop. And I just hadn't cared.

Pilar skittered around my bedroom, fluffing pillows and refilling my water glass, poking her head out to see where Mami and Papi were. She muttered hushed Spanish.

Ridiculous girl. Clueless, rash, and selfish. What if I hadn't found you? What then? God, Lila.

This was what I heard.

This was what I saw.

Mami and Papi huddled in my doorway with their courtroom verdict. Papi's head bent low, revealing his salt-and-pepper hair and sand-dollar bald spot.

Mami clutched a wad of tissues. "We just got off the phone with Catalina and Spencer."

Her words came fast and harsh: England. Summer at the Owl and Crow. Cool down. Take some time.

At the end, Mami was crying and my chest was a hollow cavity.

"England? Are you kidding me?"

Papi stepped forward. "This is for your health. This spring was already unbearable for you, and now Stefanie has left."

They just had to leave me alone. Let me fix it.

Mami brushed black waves from her face. "You think we don't see you? Weeping in corners for weeks? Hunched over and almost running into the walls? Papi finding you crying in the panadería walk-in? Alone and freezing. That is not right, Lila."

But it had felt more than right. I remembered the delicious relief of head-to-toe numbness, cooling the flaming loss of Abuela's forehead kisses. And for Andrés, too. The way he used to hold me so tightly, so completely. Warmed from ankles to ears, his embrace was the one place I'd felt both as big as planets and as light as feathers. In the walk-in freezer, I'd only wanted a few moments of quiet relief. But Papi had barged in, worrying and overreacting.

"You can't send me away." Not from La Paloma. Not from my Miami. My family.

"But the neighborhood, también. They're talking about you more than ever. You can't heal when . . ."

When *what?* When my private business was whispered around town? Oh, it wasn't hard to see why. It had been going on for three years. All I had to do was snag Andrés, son of prominent Congressman Millan of posh Coral Gables. Andrés was featured in local magazines and society columns. He'd flashed his movie star face on TV with his family during campaigns. Customers and neighbors and fellow shop owners shipped us; they thought our story was adorable. Four years ago, I'd catered his parents' fundraiser, where he'd tried his first Lila-made guava pastry. For two years, he came into La Paloma every week for more, until he finally asked me out. I was fifteen and head-over-pastelito for the congressman's son.

A West Dade Cuban fairy tale. But Andrés canceled our castle.

My parents faced Pilar, practically turning their backs to me. "Elena from Dadeland Bridal came into La Paloma last week," Mami said. She gulped back a sob. "She told me there was a game between the employees and some of the regular customers. They had a bet on when Lila would be picking out her vestido de boda."

A wedding dress? Seriously? My blood passed through fire. "Mami! Do you hear yourself?" Just cut me open, spread the past three months all over my bedroom like another coat of pale blue.

"But it's true," Mami said. "And I'm so sorry."

"Now the gossip has changed," Papi told Pili. "Why did Andrés break up with her? How could Stefanie leave her best friend without any notice? Horrible. People talk at the bodegas, the grocery, the newsstands."

Pilar sat on my bed. "I know. I hear it too."

Was I even present here? Wasn't this *my* life? Their little trio of oversharing went around and over the top, even right through the apparently invisible me. "Enough, okay?"

Finally, Mami looked at me. "It's not enough because you never say anything to us about your feelings. We can't help if we don't know what's going on."

I straightened, my limbs lumbering and achy. "I don't need to talk about my losses. I need to un-lose them."

"What if that is impossible?" Mami asked.

Impossible. I'd heard this word before and pounded it like a hard coconut shell. Then I used the rich, white flesh to make a cake.

"You lost your abuelita," Papi said softly. "The biggest part of your heart."

"Papi." The word was thick and dark, but I wouldn't cry; they couldn't have my tears. The pain was real and it was mine. Mine to suffer and mine to fix. Discussing my hurts didn't make them theirs to "help" and direct. And now they wanted to "help" even more by sending me away?

"England will be good for you. The chisme will die down and you'll come back refreshed—" Mami's cell phone rang. "That's Catalina." She stepped out with Papi.

I held out wide, helpless arms to Pilar. I needed her to step in and shut down this ridiculous idea. She would. We were a team: las Reyes.

Now that I'd graduated, I was finally ready to step into my role as full-time head baker and future owner of Panadería La Paloma, right alongside Pilar. There would be no college degree for me— I'd already learned everything I needed from Abuela. The business was ours to take over in a year. Our legacy, our future. Abuela had started it, and we were supposed to carry it forward starting this summer. I couldn't do that from across an entire ocean.

"I can't wait to see what you do," I said over a caustic laugh.

Pilar rose, urging another sip of water down my throat. This time I obeyed. "Do?"

"How you'll get me out of this England scheme. We don't have time for this. We need to plan the new business model and menu and staffing changes—"

"Lila." She pivoted, her brown eyes hooded. "They're right. You need this. I love you, but I have to let you go. Just for a little while, no?"

It was as if every footstep I'd left across Miami this afternoon turned back to stomp upon my chest. I shuddered. I could only shake my head. *No. No. NO.*

"I can't."

Pilar grabbed Abuela's white apron with the blue scripted *L* on the front. She placed it into my arms. Hours ago, they had dripped with sweat and salt. "What would she say to this?" Pilar gestured to the disaster of my overworked body.

"Your sister is right, nena." This from Mami, who had returned. "Abuelita left you her skill and drive. More than just her recipes. Honor that, Lila. You, in the walk-in, crying. You, a wreck, twenty miles away, scaring us, not caring for yourself—is that how she would want you to go on?" Tears leaked down Mami's face. "How can you let her look down and see you like this?"

What I wanted to scream: How *can* I? I can because the one recipe Abuela never taught me was the one to make inside myself when she died and left us too soon. The one to make when a boy shattered my heart, and my dearest friend stomped on my trust.

What I actually said: " . . ."

Silent and shaking, I clutched the apron and held on to memory.

"Óyeme, mi amor," Abuela had said months ago, after one of my fights with Andrés. "You love that boy like you love the kitchen." She was stirring a bowl of mango glaze. "But you add yourself like too much sugar sometimes. Too much temperature."

I had scoffed at that then. Brushed her off.

"Mi estrellita, if you shine too bright in his sky, you're going to burn him out. Burn yourself out, también."

That day, I'd burned my entire body out. I had turned up my own heat and lost control.

"Lila, you will go to England," Mami had finally said. "We cannot give you the place Abuela built if you're not well."

And there it was.

But my run—the exhaustion, inside and out—had muzzled my fighting words. As Papi logged in to the British Airways website, I only stared at that *L* on the apron placket.

4

Two weeks after Papi booked my flight, Abuela's white apron sits folded on a nightstand in England. It's been more than a full day since I've landed, but I have barely left my bed.

I glance at the clock—eight p.m., and a cacophony of synths and pounding drumbeat roars from across the hall. It has to be from Gordon's room. I can't see Cate or Spencer blasting eighties rock between entertaining guests and managing the property. Just as I identify the group as Van Halen, the music stops. Not ten seconds later, a bass intro from another tune vibrates through the fine wood paneling, volume set to overload. Then . . . it stops after a few bars. *¿Cómo?*

My eyes find rest and respite on my little altar of mementos— the framed photos and white t-shirt. The swoop of the embroidered blue *L*.

Los recuerdos have a unique kind of power, one of love and history and legacy. Here this memento calls me out sharply, decibels louder than the music, in the language that raised me. Abuela would never stand for me being this idle, barely leaving my bed for more than a day. For her, I will at least get up and unpack.

Just as I peel back my comforter, I'm greeted by a blaring wave of electronic techno-pop. All right, is it the universe's turn, in the form of Gordon Wallace, to say my hibernation time is officially done? Either way, no. Racket this loud is not going to work for me the whole summer. Before I reach the door, the music stops abruptly, just like before. I wait for some terrible reprise, but nothing comes. "Hmm," I tell myself and face my suitcases.

Ten minutes later, after dividing up shoes and clothes between the dresser and closet, I'm into my second bag. My flat iron and cosmetics case rest on top. But underneath my bathrobe I find a square notecard and my sister's familiar scrawl.

> *Hermana, don't be mad, but I know you.*
> *Love you, but miss you more, already.* —P

Don't be mad? One never-fail way for Pili to make me mad is to tell me not to get mad, so I'm extra wary when I pull out a thick parcel. The first item out of the brown paper wrapping is a black merino wool sweater.

I did not pack a single sweater.

And then it gets out of control:

Another identical sweater in gray. Short, black waterproof trench coat. Two running jackets. Pair of dark skinny jeans. Two long sleeve tops, one in blue and white stripes and the other in solid navy. Finally, an oversized scarf in a gray and black abstract cheetah print.

Now I'm suspicious of everything in this suitcase. I rummage through for more evidence of tampering and find the black ankle boots Pilar bought when we visited New York last fall. I want to hug her. I want to throw one of these boots at her round, Cuban ass. Neither is an option, so I break my sister-silence and reach for my phone.

The lock screen lights up, showing four voicemails and sixteen text notifications from Mami. Nothing from Pilar.

"You knew, Pili!" I say when my sister's oval-shaped face fills my FaceTime screen. She's in Papi's black leather chair in the back office of the panadería.

"Well, hello to you, too," Pilar says. "No contact for two days and this is what I get?"

"I texted you and Mami when I landed." I wave the black sweater in front of the phone. "You knew."

"What, that you'd spite pack?"

I blow a single puff of air.

"And," she goes on, "that when I'd go through your suitcase all I'd find would be las camisas pequeñas and sundresses? Of course I knew. And I was right. An English summer is not a normal summer. Mami told you how to prepare, Cate told you, and I told you, pero—"

"I'll wear what I want."

She sighs; I can almost feel the hot breath circling it. "Winchester is not Miami."

I fling daggers into FaceTime.

"Lila, don't you think I know? Me without you is never okay, but it was the only way."

"I. Was. Handling. It," I say through clenched teeth.

"Handling it? You, disappearing and Papi seeing your car in the lot and thinking . . . well what would *you* think seeing that? And when I finally found you . . . what I found? *Dios*, Lila, that is not handling it."

Pilar rarely cries. She considers and dissects. She organizes and compartmentalizes. It's one of the reasons we work so well together. I dream and create with eyes that are too big for everyone's stomachs. Then I make the food that fills them to brims while she finds every way to sell it. But now she's sniffling and dripping like a leaky faucet, and I am so dense to think I was ever the only one broken. The only one who has lost her abuela.

"Stop, Pili. I know I scared you. I just want to be home." Home where I can put it all back together.

She blows a foghorn into a tissue. "Home hasn't been good for you lately. You've proven that, okay?"

"The panadería—"

"—is something we've been over, what, twenty times? Angelina will do just fine."

I don't trust the new baker who's only been training for a couple of months. "Temporarily."

"Claro. It's always going to be you and me. But I need my sister back. Take some time and let Cate take care of you." She blows her nose again then leans in. "So what's it like there?"

"You mean outside? I wouldn't know."

"I should've guessed by that trash heap you're wearing as hair. But two days!"

"I'll . . . tomorrow, okay?"

Music blasts again, drowning out her answer. This time it's a screaming guitar riff. "Gordon," I tell Pilar's puzzled expression.

"Sounds like 'Gimme Shelter,'" she says.

"You'd know." Pilar's penchant for classic rock, especially in vinyl form, is one thing we don't share. "He's been doing this—" Again, the music stops. "No clue what he's doing, but I'm gonna make him quit right now. I'll call you tomorrow."

"Espérate." Pilar holds out a hand. "The new clothes are nice, no?"

"They're hideous," I say. But I can't stop rubbing the soft merino wool.

She snorts a watery laugh. "You've been coveting my boots for months."

"Sí, pero that doesn't mean I'll wear them."

A crack across my sister's face. "But you'll put them in the closet. And the tops and jacket, too."

And then I feel one across mine that I can't control, no matter how hard I try. "Maybe."

Gordon playing yet another jam thirty seconds after I hang up sends me knocking, then pounding. Then pounding and screaming. The noise finally ceases and the rogue DJ swings open his bedroom door. His deep red hair—a mirror of his dad's—gathers into a disheveled ponytail nub at the base of his neck.

"Hiya. You're not *actually* dead, then." He's holding a colored pencil.

I ignore that and lead with, "So, the music."

"What about it?"

"The volume." I'm using my hands to demonstrate. "There's just a lot of it. A lot of volume."

It's like a lightbulb turns on in the middle of his head. "Ahh. We're properly soundproofed up here and I'm not used to having anyone else in this wing."

"That's not my doing."

Gordon employs the flip side of the pencil to scratch his temple. "Right, well the music helps me achieve a certain creative mood."

"Could a quieter version of the same music help with whatever you're creatively *mooding* for?"

"Oh. For this." With a grand flourish, he moves aside.

And . . . wow. His walls are covered with framed pencil drawings of houses in every architectural style imaginable. Intricate details and colorful landscaping touches fill each piece. "You drew all these?"

He nods toward a drafting table topped with measuring tools and a rainbow of colored pencils and a new square of ivory parchment. "I have for years now. A sort of hobby."

I walk the perimeter of Gordon's tiny home neighborhood, past stone cottages and Victorians and English Tudors. Near the window, I find a black Crosley turntable system with speakers. Records stacked in a storage cube wait for Gordon's decibel abuse. "I have found the loud."

He approaches. "Sorry about all the starts and stops. I couldn't find just that right one, you know? I'll try for less."

"Thanks." I pick up a Rolling Stones LP, home to "Gimme Shelter." "Pilar collects these too. She's always looking for rare ones."

"Shocking what some of them go for. We have a record shop here called Farley's. So good, many non-locals travel into town to check it out. In town just off the High Street."

I make a mental note before investigating the rest of Gordon's artwork. Maybe it's the color or the shape, but I'm instantly drawn to a two-story drawing in bright peach with a terracotta roof. Delicate palm tree fronds sway across Gordon's rendered green lawn, and pink bougainvillea vines climb across the bright stucco. I whip around. "Is this . . . ?"

He lifts his chin. "Thought you might go for that one. Straight out of Miami—Coral Gables, if I recall from last visit. I liked the style and colors."

Home. My heart fumbles, like it knows. Then I step back, surveying the entire wall. Next to the Coral Gables model, I find a perfect rendering of the Owl and Crow and a craftsman bungalow. Among brick Federal mansions and thatched roof cottages, the peach stucco house looks totally out of place.

5

I wake too early the next morning for any human who fell asleep as late as I did. After three days, my body is still ignoring all the clocks here, still swinging from the Eastern time zone hour hands I've been under my whole life. My stiff leg muscles protest as I head downstairs. The gold filigree mirror in the Owl and Crow foyer says my eyes look like half-baked death discs.

As it's clear I won't be heading back to Miami anytime soon, I need something in England that's mine. Necesito correr. More like, I *really* need to run.

One thing I did pack was my workout gear. Over my calf-length running leggings and sports tank, I layer a long-sleeved quick-dry top. My closet holds two running jackets (Pilar), but I rarely need them in Miami. I don't need them here, either.

Fellow early risers pass through as I stretch my calves and quads in the foyer. My cell phone juts from the zip pocket on my tights. I've been careful to avoid Instagram for weeks, first because of

Andrés and now, Stef. But after so much silence and homesickness, my fingers itch for one click, one glance at a page that used to be filled with as much of my life as his. *Is Andrés seeing anyone else yet?*

The thought pulls tighter, but my oath to Pilar drags along my runner's lunge.

I swore to Pili I'd cut back on my Insta-stalking. I promised to move on, though forward feels like the last place my feet want to go right now. But my promises to my sister mean something, and I hate that. So the phone stays in my pocket and I move to quad stretches.

Two pigtailed girls squeal as they scurry up the grand staircase ahead of their parents. The family's brisk movement has moved the air, which smells of baked goods. I can't resist. Instead of going outside to the trail, I run toward the opposite service corridor. The carb trail stops at a wide push door with a peek-through window. The kitchen.

Qué hermosa. Beyond the threshold is officially the second most beautiful kitchen I have ever seen. Only the sight of our kitchen at Panadería La Paloma makes my blood pump harder. Rows of industrial hanging glass pendants illuminate a massive space. A large butcher block island marks the center and carries dusty scatters of white rolling flour. My gaze falls over French pins and glass mixing bowls, canisters and open shelves housing dishware, equipment, and pans of all sizes. An open door across the room teases an abundant, walk-in pantry. I step toward the commercial deck oven; four oval loaves rise and tan like Miami sunbathers. The *smell* . . .

I might be forced from my city, tricked into this summer break. I'm desperate for home but *here* I find a faint glimmer of myself. The equipment and ingredients call to me in a voice I've heard since I was little. Measure, mix, season, and simmer—these are my words. And most of all, this warm and yeasty room feels like Abuela and me. No matter what it takes, I will not be just an Owl and Crow guest. I will become one of its bakers.

An exterior screen door creaks open, then slams shut. "Lost, are you?" The voice at my back is brassy with the cries of parrots. "The parlor's across the main hall. Opposite end."

I turn.

"Ah, sorry then. You're that Lila girl." The voice pours from a white woman I'd peg as mid-sixties. The kind of tall that makes my eyebrows notice, her frame scored with creased edges and paper-cut lines. Her unpainted face sits under a squat cap of gray hair, circular, reminding me of a B-movie flying saucer.

"Yes, hi, I'm Lila Reyes."

"Polly. The missus showed me your picture." She beelines to the sink to wash her hands. "If you're wanting breakfast other than what's in your flat, I'll be setting up the usual parlor spread. Shortly." I know a firm dismissal when I hear one.

And, no. I plant myself across from her, the wooden island like gold-rich land between us. "Actually," I say, "I'm here for the summer."

"So I heard."

"My family owns a bakery. Has for more than forty years."

Polly checks a digital wall clock, then the rack oven. "I believe

I heard that, too. Mrs. Wallace mentioned a little Cuban place."

Little. Cuban. Place. I clamp my mouth tight to stop the flames. But as much as I'm prime to detail my extensive baking résumé, I respect the "kitchen." And this one is Polly's. If I want to pass my summer with the butter, flour, and sugar composing the only part of my heart left intact, I'm going to have to watch my approach. Slide in, not stomp. I'm going to have to be . . . nice.

I secure my ponytail. Smile. "Ms., err, Polly, I tried your bread and scones the other day." Too sweet. "And I was wondering if I might spend some of my time here. Maybe help with the baking duties?"

Polly hooks one spindly arm onto her hip. "You, baking for guests? With me?"

"Well, there's an idea!"

Polly and I whip our heads toward the door. Catalina "Cate" Mendoza Wallace is one stealthy Venezuelan.

"Really?" Polly and I say in unison. But I say it with high-pitched glee. Polly barks it out like Cate just handed me the last cookie from the jar.

Cate steps closer, her mint green cashmere poncho winged over black skinny pants. She puts her hand on Polly's shoulder. "I would not trust your kitchen to anyone less. Lila is highly experienced and capable." Cate turns to me. "Hopefully this will help you feel more at home here. But I'll leave you to Polly's charge and direction."

I swear I hear the baker hiss.

"Now," Cate says, peering into the oven, then our faces, "I need to see that Gordon's not late for the dentist, so I'll leave you two to sort out duties."

Polly plucks a red binder from a shelf. "I have five minutes to give you thirty minutes' worth of directives. How we do things." And by *we*, she clearly means *I*.

"I assure you I can handle any recipe in that binder." I'm already washing my hands. "And I'll find my way around the equipment and ingredients."

"We'll see. Mornings, we do a small spread of breads and jams and seasonal fruits. I've got honey orange scones and white toasting bread ready for serving. Then we provide a teatime offering at half past three." Polly opens the red manual to a laminated, typed recipe. "Today calls for Madeira sponge cake and chocolate biscuits."

Chocolate biscuits? Abuela taught me to take big risks with flavor, just like she did. But some flavor mash-ups simply do not mash. "Biscuits with chocolate?" I ask, feeling my nose wrinkle.

"If you're going to even attempt to bake in England, you'd best familiarize yourself with our *basics*." Polly says *basics* like she's already enrolled me in her Baking for Preschoolers class. She shoves the red binder into my vision. The full color photo tells me an English biscuit is a cookie. Ahh. Right.

"I'll see to the biscuits," she says, flipping pages and ensuring I take the book this time. Then she tosses over a clean apron. "I suppose you can prepare the Madeira cake. Can you manage four loaves all right?"

Sometimes respect warrants education—un poquito. I steel

my spine. "When I was thirteen and my parents were stranded in New York, I catered a huge order for our congressman's party. I made more than a thousand Cuban pastries and appetizers, working overnight. The *Miami Herald* even did an article on it." I spot the correct pans and grab them. "I can manage four sponge cakes."

Polly totes a wooden baking peel to the oven. "Hmmph. The finished cakes will tell, won't they?" She opens the glass door and slides the peel under the golden loaves, transferring them to the island to cool.

I scan her recipe for Madeira cake. My eyes immediately latch onto problems. The sugar to flour ratio is off and . . . margarine? Butter is best for these types of dense cakes. Oil, second best. But margarine? No.

"Polly?" *Her kitchen. Not my kitchen. Polly's kitchen.* "After looking over your recipe, I was wondering if I might bake a butter pound cake that's very similar. It was Abuela's—my grandmother's—recipe."

She exhales a quick puff of air. "I see. Still, that Madeira cake is the only one we've ever served here. *My* nan's, in fact. As are all the scone recipes."

Ahh, the culprit revealed. One sugar-happy grandmother and a palate never trained out of it. I tell my running shoes, "That's really special, but—"

"Heavens. I've too many tasks to stand here and argue. I *suppose* you can do your nan's cake." She hoists the serving platter. "Whether you make it again remains to be seen."

Dios. I locate a few key utensils in a cylindrical caddy near the sink. I move the container to the butcher block island, where bakers would actually use it, then introduce myself to the oven. The Owl and Crow deck oven is the same model as ours at the panadería— at least one thing's familiar. I know the ingredients for Abuela's pound cake by heart, but I still check the recipe app on my phone to make sure I correctly convert the measurements to feed a crowd.

But an iPhone in my palm instead of my pocket means Instagram beams, right there in front of me. Maybe it's jet lag, maybe it's Polly weariness, but I can't resist one, teeny-tiny look before I preheat.

My feed usually opens with a baking or cooking account, but not today. Stefanie's bright smile greets me as she poses in front of the University of Ghana, her blond ponytail slung over one shoulder. Her arms are spread wide in wonder and she looks . . . happy. Without me. And more, she had internet access and still didn't reach out. Even just to say she was okay.

The stir of disappointment and regret kicks me right on to another page I vowed to avoid: *Andrés Millan*. And there he is, grinning in a new profile picture by the sparkling canal backing his Coral Gables home. I expand it briefly—olive tan skin and lean muscle and the short, dark buzz cut that always looked best. And still does. I have to minimize him again.

After a week, there's no new picture update, but a scan down his profile glazes my stomach with sick. It's just . . . gone. Andrés deleted one of my favorite selfies of him and me. Other pictures of me remain, but the one of us, waterside at Coconut Grove for his birthday dinner? Poof.

Why did I even look? I click back to the recipe app, but our last conversation echoes:

It's not about love. I need to figure myself out and see who I am.

Andrés's parting words sting again like new wounds. Who he is now is a boy who's slowly deleting me from the pictorial record of his life.

Twenty minutes later, I've got batter in my mixing bowl, multiplied to the correct proportions. Accounting whiz Pilar feasts on all the math I avoid daily, but recipe math is a must for me. And this recipe's ready to show the Owl and Crow kitchen monarch a thing or two about what a girl from a "little Cuban place" can do. Four loaf pans are greased and waiting. Now for one last touch.

A harsh rumble sounds while I'm searching the pantry for almond extract. It's either a mutant lawn mower or a motorcycle with the engine version of a head cold. Moments later, I peek from the pantry to see a raindrop-sprinkled guy, about my age, in my kitchen—er, Polly's kitchen. A white carry box that wasn't there before rests on the counter. Before I can even think *hello*, the guy marches up to the wooden prep island, dips one finger into my batter bowl, and licks.

I launch myself from the doorway. "What the hell are you doing?"

He flinches.

"Your finger! My bowl!"

"Oh. Sorry." Yeah, not even a teaspoon of sorry fills his six-foot-something frame as he leans against the counter. Blond hair—a dark variety his creator dyed in a murky rain puddle—

curls slightly on top of a cropped cut. He's wearing faded jeans and a brown leather bomber jacket.

"We've not met." He springs off the counter but whatever's on my face has him inching back his offered hand. "Orion Maxwell."

I don't want his name. I want his blood sprinkled over Spencer's topiary hedges for his indiscretion. But I still grumble out, "Lila Reyes." I tip my head to the bowl. "And that's for guests. What if that was meringue prep? Even two drops of water from your finger would ruin it."

"Is it for a meringue?" He waggles his brows. "My favorite."

"No, it's not meringue. And your hands. You rode over here on a dirty motorcycle."

Orion nods toward the sink and wiggles his fingers. "Washed them before I sampled. Always do."

"You mean you do this often?" I'm a telenovela of gestures. "Just go around sticking your fingers into people's batters whenever you want?"

He steps closer, so close I note storm blue eyes and a tiny cleft in his chin and the knife edge shape to his nose. He smells like trees and damp leather. "Only if invited."

"I don't remember issuing an invitation."

"I realize that now," he says. "I do apologize. It's a habit. Polly's always encouraged my sampling."

Dramatic snort. "I'll believe that when—"

"Orion. There you are, dear." Polly all but levitates, floating from the swing door to Orion's side. "Our canisters are down to dregs and fumes."

He grins. "Sorry. Meant to get 'round sooner but we had an issue at the shop. How's your sister?"

Snap! Crack! Polly's a glow stick. Orion has broken her right down the middle and she's beaming from gray hair to orthopedic kitchen clogs. "She's faring much better, thank you. Was only a virus."

"Good to hear." He points to the white box. "That should do you. English breakfast, Jasmine green, a double order of Earl Grey this time, like Mrs. Wallace said. Dad threw in a sample of a new Darjeeling reserve he's discovered. Really smooth."

"Oh, I'll have to try it later," Polly says.

"It won't disappoint. See you." He moves to the door, dragging his gaze over me, standing in an ivory apron over running clothes, clutching a bottle of almond extract.

"Wait up." Polly rushes to him with a small brown sack and a wide-toothed smile. "Biscuits from yesterday's tea."

"Thanks, I'll try to make them last the ride back." He sniffs inside the bag. "Lemon! My favorite."

I thought meringue was his favorite.

Now he's not dragging, he's planting his eyes into mine, nodding a stray pigtail curl over his forehead. "Lila."

I make a small, noncommittal noise.

Polly's glow wanes when Orion shuts the door, her face tightening, but she says, "Orion's family owns the best tea shop in Hampshire—Maxwell's. Such a darling boy."

Right. Darling. I pour batter into cake pans.

"Get used to him being around." She huffs as she drops my dirty mixing bowls into the sink, then makes a big show out of moving the utensil canister back to where I'd found it on the counter. "Things here are best as they *were*. And that includes established business dealings. So do, at least, attempt to be pleasant. He always hand-delivers our orders at no extra fee."

Perfect. Even better. Orion sticks his finger into my bowl and he's rewarded with a happy Polly *and* cookies? Bah. I slide on a heat-proof glove, open the oven, and shove in my cake pans. Then I slam the door shut.

6

My first clue is the smell. To say I know a few things about baking is an understatement. I *know* when I've screwed up a pastry or cake. Which is never. Which is also right now.

Rushing through the swing door, I kill the heat on the oven as my belly sinks with dread. Smoke fills the shallow rack area. I have to go in. Coughing, I don gloves and quickly remove all four loaf pans as a sooty cloud—the kind usually following botched magicians' tricks or genie lamp escapes—envelops me.

Even from the kitchen garden, I'm certain Polly can smell the smoke. The guests probably think the inn is on fire. More cough-swearing as the air clears enough for me to see the blackened loaves shriveled into doorstop bricks ¿Qué pasó?

I've been making Abuela's recipe forever, using the same kind of pans, in the same model oven, but . . . *oh*. My mind clicks onto a key fact I've known for years and completely spaced out on when I preheated. England cooks in Celsius, not Fahrenheit. Me, trying to set my temp to 350 degrees Fahrenheit made this UK calibrated oven heat to way over 600 degrees. Standard for pizza. Devastating for cakes.

Polly's footfalls in from the garden slash through my thoughts.

I curl my fingers around my apron hem, bracing for a verbal onslaught to rival that of mis tías, or Mami when Pilar and I used to turn curfew into a suggestion. The tone will be the same, maybe even the acrobatic hand motions. Only the accent and maybe the words will vary.

She sniffs, clears her throat, and briefly leans over my shoulder. "Well then," she says crisply.

I hinge open my eyes. Polly's at the freezer. She swings around with a pyramid of small loaves in her arms. "I had these on hand for such a time as this," she says. "Ginger cakes. They'll thaw before teatime."

Polly drops the cakes on a rack and heads straight for the sink, frowning at my equipment pile-up. "Simply dreadful! Around here, I clean as I go." She gestures broadly to the stacks of bowls and spoons I was just about to wash before my cake fail. "Mrs. Wallace won't like all these piles of greasy, disorganized items. What if she tours a special guest through the kitchen?" Polly stomps to the swing door and barks, "I trust you'll see to it immediately."

Shaking, I scrape my ruined cakes into the trash—or as Polly says, the rubbish bin. Rubbish, verdad. I spend extra time scrubbing pans and cooking surfaces. Furiously.

Well then. The small words taunt as I fling off my apron. Kitchens have always been the one place I could rely on for guaranteed success, but today, this one is the site of yet another loss. I can't spend one more minute inside the burnt odor of my failure. Attire wise, I'm already set for a quick escape. I drink half a bottle of water and exit the side door, deciding on the same route I was going to run two hours ago.

Apparently, the Owl and Crow lives in the St. Cross neighborhood of Winchester. I navigate toward a scenic trail bordering the River Itchen, my steps weighted with jet lag and Celsius. I pant and struggle along a narrow, rain-soaked street dotted with brick and stone homes. Again, the tying architectural theme is: old. As the street forks, I meet the wide mouth of a main access road. Thoughts rush with the wind; I knew they would. This isn't the first time I've handed my frustration to sneakers and sweat.

Well then.

The chef in me realizes exactly what Polly's response, or lack of one, means. Budding chefs often get dragged by superiors who want next-level best for them. Abuela taught me with love, but she still held me to nothing less than the kind of food that makes people happy to line up for it. If I made something mediocre, I heard about it. Then I did better the next time.

In Polly's eyes, I wasn't even worthy of critical words and "I told you so." If I was, she would've at least questioned how or why I'd set the oven too hot. She would've reminded me that professional cooks don't have room to make careless errors. But to her, I'm not anyone to be taken seriously. I'm only a kid, trying on a chef's hat in a costume box, playing "baker" in a make-believe game.

Even kitchens are telling me I don't belong here.

My body is just as confused. Running on UK ground is a different sport. In Miami, the muggy heat slicks across my skin while the sun whips my back with slashes of too bright and too hot. Another kind of pain pulls here. Cold rakes against my face and grabs my lungs, webbing into my sinuses. I tuck my hands into my shirt cuffs. The rain's moved on, but the wind jabs at trees, loosening droplets over my hair.

But then the map leads me on to a pedestrian path carved into acres of pistachio-colored grass. Spencer mentioned the River Itchen between bites of vanilla custard last night. Here, I meet the narrow channel of the famous landmark as it ribbons toward city center. The footpath worms along beside the gently moving water. I'm alone. And I don't know what to do with this quiet.

My Miami life is noisy. I can barely stir together one whole thought without a background track of piano and drums and my neighbor's yippy dog. I live under crowing laughter and jibes in the panadería kitchen. Crashing waves and catcalling tourists. My landscape is thunder and the rustle of birds fighting over flowers, the everyday alarm clock of wild roosters.

But now it's just me and a river and wet grass and what's left of my heart. My brain fills the emptiness, acting out the noises of my home. It's screaming inside my skull that running was the thing Stefanie and I always did together, every Saturday across Key Biscayne Bridge. It fills spaces with people too—how Andrés and I strolled the bustling Miami Riverwalk, sharing ice cream and butter pecan lips, my hand tucked into the back pocket of his jeans. My mind sings the warm alto of Abuela's voice. "Mi estrellita." My little star. "It's time to make the tamales. Ven." Come.

Not today and never again.

Dios, there's nowhere to put it. No way can I trust this alien green and marbled gray with the past three months. No matter what my parents think, Miami knows what to do with me.

And as the trail comes to an end into town, it's even clearer how far I am from home. My steps slow to a brisk walk. Old . . . older . . . oldest. Trade my spandex and sneakers for a corseted gown and court shoes. This place begs for it. When were these painted row houses—red-doored and crawling with vines—even built? Ornate windows and crested emblems jut out everywhere. Many of the stone surfaces have weathered to sharp angles and rough planes; one shove against a wall like that would draw blood.

I inch through streets so narrow that bike riders would brush shoulders. It's all here: coffee houses, shops, little cafés, cars zooming through on the wrong side of the road. By the time I reach a bustling main street, I'm not really exercising anymore so much as sightseeing. I also need to figure out where I am.

"Lila, isn't it? From the Crow?"

Dozens of streets for my Nikes to wander, but I end up right in front of . . . I look up from my phone and confirm. Orion Maxwell's five feet away, plastic safety goggles pushed back over his head. He's shed the leather bomber and is wearing a plaid shirt, sleeves rolled to his elbows, and blue rubber gloves. "Err, hi."

"You're in my batter bowl now," he says and when my brows drop, adds, "my street," and when I feel my nose wrinkle, he smiles and points across the nearest intersection. "Our shop's just there."

I follow his hand to a storefront dressed in white paneled wood. Even from here I can make out the large scripted *M* resting over a stylized leaf. Maxwell's Tea Shop. "If your shop's over there, then why are you . . . ?" More like *what* is he? A spray bottle sits near his rugged boots, along with a filled bucket and a small assortment of brushes and sponges.

A shadow crosses his face. "Victoria's store was tagged." He grabs a brush and points it at what is now nothing more than a watery black blob over a brick wall. "Had to be last night and I wanted to see to it before she opens up. We're finding it more and more around here lately."

I step back, eying the windows. Turned out mannequins pose in various outfits. I read the name etched onto the glass out loud. "*Come Around Again.* Cool name for a secondhand shop. But it's not yours, so why are you on graffiti cleanup?"

He wets the scrub brush and takes to the wall. "Looking out for one another. It's what we do."

Warmth—only a quarter teaspoon—settles over my damp skin. I step to the right when Orion turns from the wall and attempts to step left. He avoids me deftly.

"Sorry," he says and grabs a wet sponge. He uses a circular motion to remove traces of black from grout.

"I've noticed that you, and by *you*, I mean the English, say that a lot." Not excuse me or pardon. Only sorry, sorry, sorry.

"Another thing we do." Eyes trained on paint removal, he doesn't even look at me. But one edge of his mouth jerks up. "You're here visiting, I take it?"

"Yeah, from Florida. Miami." The words, icing on my tongue. "Cate is my mom's cousin, but they grew up like sisters. And best friends."

Now he turns through a single nod. "Gordon's one of mine. You're Venezuelan, then, like Mrs. Wallace?"

First I say, "Cuban." Then I give him the sixty-second version of my summer stay and my role at Panadería La Paloma. I leave out my Celsius oven disaster and Abuela and the rest of the trifecta.

A low chuckle rattles his chest. "And you've already managed to infiltrate Polly's kitchen? I'm impressed. How'd you swing that?"

"It's what *I* do."

Now a smile, the kind where quick lips plus gleaming teeth plus dimpled cheeks equals hazard. For some girls. Not me. Obviously. "Earlier, you looked lost," he says.

"Oh, I was just deciding whether to head back to the Crow, or to check out a vintage record shop Gordon mentioned."

"Yeah—Farley's," he says. "The inn's straight up Kingsgate or St. Cross. About a twenty-minute walk or as fast as you can run it." He tips his head toward the opposite direction I walked in from. "Farley's is a few streets that way. You're into classic vinyl?"

"My sister is." I tuck stray hair under my headband. "Though she helped my parents plan this three-month 'dream vacation,' so I'm not sure she's worthy of souvenirs."

He actually looks hurt. "What's wrong with England? Or are you opposed to Winchester in particular?"

I blow out a sharp breath. "It's not Miami."

"Hardly. But as I see it, you being here for so long against your will is due to one of four reasons." Orion splashes a full bucket of water over the wall. The paint is gone. "Correction, let's make that three reasons. The number four is considered unlucky in China."

"Because England and China are the same thing."

"Can't be too careful." He whips off the gloves. "So, reasons. One, a problem with your passport. Two, a family issue. Three, something to do with your mum and Cate requiring your extended services."

"Mostly the second one."

"Sticky, those family issues. Yours expects Winchester to help?" Storm blue, right into my chocolate brown.

Oh, no. Not now, not this boy. "You ask a lot of questions."

Orion tosses the gloves and the goggles into the empty bucket. "Sorry."

My run ended hours ago. But at half-past eleven, as Spencer—or Orion—would say, my mind is still awake, sprinting to keep up with the new way my life looks.

With a weighty sigh, I reach for the charm I never take off. Pilar wears an identical necklace. Four years ago, Abuela presented them to us when we made one of our Sunday regulars—tamales.

The charm is just the outline of a small dove—a golden replica of the Panadería La Paloma logo. In the dark loneliness, I close my eyes and inhale the memory of Abuela as she fastened the chain around my neck. Her hands were wrinkly-soft, smelling of masa and garlic and fragrant pork filling.

"Un regalito," she'd said to thirteen-year-old me, and seventeen-year-old Pilar. A little gift. "What you both did last month for Congressman Millan brought such honor to our family and business. Your father has to hire another clerk because we're getting so busy from the publicity." Abuela's smile showed off clean, white teeth.

Pilar nodded. "The biggest dollar month in La Paloma history."

All because I hadn't listened to Papi when he'd called, stranded with Mami and Abuela in a New York blizzard. I was supposed to cancel the enormous catering order for Andrés's father. But I wasn't about to let that prestigious job slip away, and Pilar had no choice but to follow my reckless ambition. I'd taken over, wrangling employees and working overnight to make a truckload of Cuban appetizers. And I had won, even garnering the attention of reporters. For years, I'd continue to win, securing my spot as future co-owner, mapping my biggest dream.

But this morning I had failed and lost. Abuela had taught me to feed my city, sharing the best of what we know. That wasn't me in the Owl and Crow kitchen with burned cakes. I rise and go downstairs to feed the inn my best.

An hour later, simmering orange-almond glaze mixes with the scent of warm butter and sugar, filling the inn kitchen. I fill it too, wearing Abuela's apron over my pajamas.

A quick boil, my little pan of glaze bubbles. I remove the saucepan and swing it around as Cate peeks through the door. "Oh. Hi. I hope I didn't wake you," I tell her, wincing.

"Not so much that." She yawns and cinches her fluffy bathrobe tighter. "I needed a pain tablet and realized I'd left them in the office. Had to make sure no culinary ghosts were haunting our kitchen."

"Sorry." Now I'm starting to sound like Orion.

"So what's on the menu tonight?" She moves toward the oven, peeking into the glass door. My cakes are almost done. "Lila. Polly's ginger loaves were fine and she'll think up something else for tomorrow, or I guess for today, now. You made a simple mistake. Nothing you had to stay up to fix."

"I don't make mistakes in my bakery kitchen," I say into the pan of cooling glaze. But the truth is, if I hadn't stalked Andrés's Instagram, I wouldn't have been distracted and forgotten the entire metric system. I hate that Pilar was right. I hate that any part of my screwup was due to a boy.

"I know what you can do," Cate says. "Much of West Miami does. They don't call you Estrellita for nothing. But even little stars need to sleep."

I grab a basting brush.

Cate shakes her head. "You shouldn't stay up late cooking just to wake early to bake with Polly. That's not good for you. I'm responsible for keeping you safe and healthy."

"Yeah, I know. To return me to Miami better than ever," I mutter. Cate's concerned face softens my sarcasm. "Promise this is my last midnight kitchen spree."

"Oh, like you promised to go to see Father Morales, but canceled behind your parents' backs?"

Of course Mami told her. And she's right; I canceled my appointment with our priest and they were furious. I get how counseling or therapy can help people. But I will decide whom I talk to, and when. I couldn't stop Stefanie from boarding a plane to Africa, or rewind Andrés's goodbye speech or . . . Abuela. I couldn't change the hand of God. But I could have control over my words, my heart, my pain.

The oven beeps. I grab pot holders and transfer my loaves to the wooden prep island. Abuela's pound cake, done perfectly. "I'll go to bed when I get these glazed and ready for Polly to find when she comes in. *Promise.*"

Cate leans over the cakes. "So this is about Polly."

No. Sí. "She barely said two words after . . . earlier. She thinks I suck."

"No, she doesn't. Polly's worked here fifteen years and has her routine. I understand you wanting to redeem yourself. But you'll get sick if you keep doing this," Cate says. When I don't respond, she sighs. "I'll be checking to make sure you're back in bed in an hour. And that's *my* promise."

And then I'm alone again.

Redeeming myself? Is that what I was trying to do? Or was I just trying to fix the one crumbled, burned thing in my life I knew for certain I could make right?

Minutes later, the cakes are glazed, plated, and perfectly documented in my own Instagram photos. Minutes after that, I'm at the private apartment stairs.

Cate left a weak hallway light on for me. At my door, I notice something wedged against the base molding. I must've missed it on my way downstairs. I peer down at the framed drawing of a

Coral Gables home. I grab the frame and an attached note and read it on the way in.

I thought you might like this for your room to remind you of home.
Don't get any ideas about stuffing it in your bags. It's just on loan
while you're here. —Gordon

I shake my head and lean the drawing on my nightstand; I'll meet the peachy stucco and tiled roof every time I wake. After a quick scrub, I reach from underneath ivory sheets to touch the tiny white front door behind the glass. I never had a dollhouse as a little girl. I played with wooden spoons and clanging bowls. But here I make-believe my dream home before I close my eyes. I push a doll-sized Stefanie into the door first, dressing her in the University of Miami t-shirt. Andrés comes next, legs bent to sit, drinking lime and Coke on Gordon's meticulously drawn porch. Then mini-Pilar and mini-me, plotting our world domination— family business style—one pastry at a time. I can't forget Mami and Papi, curled up on the couch watching their favorite TV show, *Family Style*. Lastly, I place Abuela. She goes inside the kitchen, where we made tamales and a hundred other dishes. I set her feet by the sink, right where I found her three months ago. I stand her up tall. In this little peach house, there is a heartbeat.

7

Three suppers later, after Spencer's roast chicken (yummy) with a side dish of Gordon's ramblings on Winchester home developments ruining the beloved medieval feel of their town (snooze fest), I close myself in my room. The clock pegs Miami time at early afternoon; Pilar should be done with her summer session class at Florida International University.

My sister's face materializes on FaceTime. Again, she's parked inside La Paloma's back office, which is now looking more like her space than Papi's. Just like the kitchen becomes more mine every single day, even when I'm four thousand miles away. Mami and Papi are letting go of La Paloma matters, little by little, transitioning their efforts into finding a new cake shop property. In less than one year, all the managerial responsibilities will fall onto Pilar and me, and I can't wait to get started. After a quick greeting I have to say, "Take me in."

Pilar knows where *in* is. "But, you—"

"Just do it, yeah?" The *it's half your fault I'm here and I miss it so much* look must be blaring across my face because she huffs and walks her laptop through the rear corridor.

"After ten whole days, the paint's the same and the floor, también."

"Shut up, Pili." On my panoramic tour, I note the wholesale flour and sugar bags piled in the storage room. Closer to the kitchen, rack carts wait in line. Now she pans over fluorescent lights and the huge metal sink area and flour-dusted work spaces.

"¡A ver! Say hello to Lila in England!" Pilar barks. I hear my nickname under today's back room soundtrack of Afro-Cuban jazz. Estrellita. Javi and Marta and Joe rush the screen and blow me kisses.

I return them, emotion scarring my throat. I also learn my parents are on a big catering run. "Angelina around?"

"She's on a break." Pili walks the laptop to a cooling rack heaped with trays of empanadas. Angelina would be responsible for those. "She's doing fine at being you. Better than fine."

"Wait. Bring me closer." I lean into my phone. "I told Angelina to take her time with the egg wash and not just throw it on like abstract art. It doesn't even reach the edges half the time. Do you think we'll ever get nominated for *Family Style* with food like this?" It was our dream to appear on the popular Food Network program showcasing family-run food establishments. But it wouldn't happen with sloppy pastries. "Marta should have caught this."

Pilar resets her screen just in time for me to catch her eye roll. "I had one fifteen minutes ago. Delicious," she says.

"Pili! Tell her." La Paloma cuisine has standards.

"Oh, no. Not my territory. I'll have Javi take care of it or something."

I slump onto my four-poster bed. "But really? The taste was on point and the texture, too?"

"Sí, hermana. Now, tell me you've been at least going out into town."

"I've been . . . running."

"Lila . . ." Pili extends my name, long and whiny—*Leeeeeela*. "Do you think avoiding Winchester will magically change it so you're back in Miami sooner? Is that your game?"

Ugh. I could throttle my sister and all her rightness. My face tells her so. But then my chin crumples and my eyes well into overflow. I could just as easily slide in next to her on our sofa. Our talking spot, late at night with our shoulders pressed tight, eating snacks I've likely made.

Pilar covers her face with both hands. "I'd tell you to go out, make friends or whatever for *me*. Or if I really wanted to be a jerk, maybe even for Abuela. But you won't. I know you have to want to for you."

She means for me to want to go on, move on, carry on. So many *ons*. I glance away for a beat. "When people ask, I'm doing amazing here, okay? A dream vacation."

She frowns. "Your fake-glossy Instagram is one thing. Shots of pasteles and views out your window. But I'm not lying for you."

I wanted Andrés and Stefanie's parents to see my very best. "Think of it more as creative marketing. Of which you're the expert."

She just shakes her head.

"Pili," I say at length. "Angelina's empanadas were good but, you know, not as good as mine, right?"

Pilar's back in the office that will officially become hers soon. She curls her ruby-painted lips inward. "Nothing is ever as good as you and me."

We've hung up, but my eyes are still damp when I reach for the TV remote. Muffled sound fills my room, but I've pressed no buttons. I hear faint voices, happy, laughing voices. It's not coming from Gordon's room, either. At the side window I find a small clutch of bodies hovering in the adjacent church yard.

The window makes a terrible banshee cry when I crank open the panes. Voices halt and all eyes spring onto me. Of course, Orion Maxwell cranes his neck toward the inn side of the courtyard.

"Lila from Florida," he calls while his siblings or friends or brainwashed tea cult members watch.

I manage a small, courtly wave.

"Trade that window for a balcony and you'd pass for Juliet," he says. The melodic lilt of his accent is warm against the cool, black sky.

But Juliet? Only if Shakespeare secretly wanted to pen Romeo's paramour with a messy topknot, costumed in a black tee and boyfriend jeans. "Good*night* Orion and Orion's—"

"Join us."

I steal a fleeting glance back into my softly lit room. Oh, so much to do. Binging a few episodes of *Family Style* on demand, and a moisturizing face mask, and trying to channel the regular sleeping pattern I left back in West Dade. "I. Um." My sister's gone from my screen but I still see her face, can already feel the warm grin she'd send across oceans if I told her I not only went outside, but talked to actual teens.

"Coming down is really in your best interest." The others have gone back to their conversations, but Orion breaks away, stepping toward the wall. "I've been in the Wallaces' guest room. Your bed faces north and I can't begin to tell you what sort of trouble that spells."

It's over—I'm laughing. Can't help it. The Lila variety of laughter has been out of season since March. I've hardly been able to find it. But here, it sprouts up wide and leafy under a yellow moon.

Staying in or going out—it's my choice. On my terms. No one is trying to force me into more than I'm ready to give. And tonight, I won't lie to myself, either. That bright wave of laughter felt the kind of good that baking does. I hold out my hands, conceding.

Orion grins.

I nearly collide with Gordon in our hallway.

He looks up from his phone. "Sorry." Another sorry abuser. "Just going down to meet some mates."

"Me too, actually." By the time we reach the second floor, I've filled Gordon in on my meager Orion history and hangout invitation.

"He told you the one about your north facing bed, then?" He spits out a laugh. "Ridiculous bloke. He's really into superstitions. Keeps a storehouse of them in his head."

The number four is considered unlucky in China. Now it makes sense.

"Interesting," I say, following him down to the foyer. We choose the kitchen side door since it's closer to the courtyard. Dim fluorescent lights are always on, and tonight Polly's bowl of farmer's market strawberries waits for her, or me, to make a compote for filled butter biscuits tomorrow morning. It's been three days since I worked through midnight, fixing my epic pound cake fail. And just as many days since Polly had to admit my redone cake was more than good and that I was somewhat worthy of a spot in her kitchen.

On one condition: "We will be making the recipes out of my folder. And only those recipes," Polly said. If I wanted to work with flour and sugar, I had to comply. But Lila Reyes from Miami was not without ideas. And tricks.

Tonight, I cross through the Owl and Crow side lot with Gordon. A wooden plaque designates the neighboring stone building as one of many Church of England Parishes. Nothing states a group of teens may absolutely and especially not hang out in its walled courtyard after hours.

Orion slaps Gordon on the shoulder, then points at one of my cap sleeves. "You might want to run back up for a jumper."

"A what?"

"Sorry. A sweater."

"I'm fine," I tell him. Truth is, my toes are icicles frozen onto flip-flops and the hair on my arms is standing military tall. Still, no. I mentally channel Miami summer nights. Warm pavement under bare feet and musky breezes still heavy with the heat of the day.

Orion shrugs. "Suit yourself." He swivels around and tells the other three, "This is Lila. She's from Miami and spending her summer at the Crow. After almost two weeks of sharing a washroom with Gordon, she's likely well versed on his cologne abuse."

A few yards away, Gordon texts with one hand and flips off Orion with the other.

Friends are spaced like triangle points. Immediately, a black guy one head taller than Orion steps up and swallows my vision. He pokes out a hand. "Remy."

"Lila."

Remy's smile is seasoned with big, jovial kindness, and the rest of him is decked out in rolled-sleeve plaid, trim jeans, and Euro-style sneakers.

"Hold on, people. I saw her at the window." The nasally voice comes from a wooden bench. On it, a girl lies on the seat and loops black denim legs over the back, dangling fuchsia Converse high-tops. "Almost got it." Upside-down bench girl arranged her curved body into a gray stretchy top and suede fringe vest, accented with a huge turquoise pendant necklace. I could never pull off this look, but it totally works for her, strong against ivory pale skin and white-blond hair.

She shuts a purple notebook, then stands in a one-shot maneuver. "Sorry. I have to get my ideas down or it's like they never were," she says and flutters pages. "I'm Jules. Never Juliana."

Orion's speed drill catch-up reveals she and Remy are a couple, Remy's family owns the best pub in town, and Jules is a songwriter.

Orion adds, "One thing, mind what you say because it might appear in one of her lyrics."

"He's not exaggerating," Remy says.

The slight tug of apprehension surprises me. I try to cover it with a quick smile. "I'll remember."

"No matter what, it can't top me mistaking Lila's batter bowl for Polly's and helping myself to a sample," Orion says, taking a few seconds to detail the whole story, waving his own flag of embarrassment, all by himself. I don't know if this kind of easy, self-deprecating honesty is a British thing or an Orion Maxwell thing.

When he's done, Remy nudges a snickering Jules. "Think you can work Ri's moment of glory into a song?"

"I think I sort of owe it to music itself, a fail like that," Jules says.

"Yeah," I say through a giggle. "My abuela would have been after you with her rubber sandal, asking what kind of manners your mother taught you."

Before my mouth even closes, my words strike faces. Orion's head drops away, nodding slowly. Remy's whipped out his phone but it's as upside down as Jules's posture when I met her. The songwriter studies her lyric book again.

¿Qué hice?

My fault. I did it, but I don't know what *it* is.

After what seems like centuries, Jules chimes in, "You're from Miami, then? A few years back, my parents took me to Los Angeles in July. You know, the typical holiday. Hollywood Walk of Fame, Beverly Hills. There was a heat wave and my makeup dripped off everywhere. I was going for, you know, aloof British rocker, but it came out more like Hampshire skunk face with sweaty pits takes on West Beverly."

I've only just met her, but I have a sudden urge to bake Jules-never-Juliana "thank you" cookies and "you saved my ass" pastelitos.

Remy grins; it steals his whole damn face. Orion steps closer, features starched and ironed, awkward wrinkles a memory.

I realize I'm twiddling my fingers. Actual twiddling and my words race over my own curiosity and everyone's awkwardness. "Miami in the summer is like taking LA and dunking it into a vat of boiling tar topped with a steam sauna and hot rain. Gordon can tell you, he's—" But Gordon has moved to the broad lip of the dormant statue fountain—probably a saint—in the center of the courtyard. Next to him, a girl who looks a couple of years younger than the rest of Orion's friends is chatting with him. "Anyway, why do you hang out in here?"

"We all live close and the Crow grounds are off-limits except for guests," Orion says. "Most of the year it's too cold to hang outside at night." He shrugs. "Winchester summer is short. We catch up here and take in our little season of agreeable weather while we get it."

"This isn't my usual definition of agreeable weather." Cold-edged night wind dashes over rain-soaked pavement from an earlier downpour. Dashes over me. I can barely feel my toes.

Orion's gaze travels up and down my outfit. "This is how Mrs. Wallace told you to pack for England?"

Grumble. "More like how I told myself to pack for England."

"Well." He shrugs out of a gray cable knit cardigan with a wide collar and large buttons. Off his body, it's something a British grandpa might choose. But on Orion, it looked like it had been imagined and crafted just for him. Casual and modern and perfectly arranged about his lanky frame. He holds it out, sheepishly. "Watching you chattering your teeth and gathering goose bumps has made me even colder. So, you wearing this while you're down here would actually benefit me as much as you."

¡Ponte un suéter, que te vas a resfriar!

It hurts worse at night. And in the morning, when I'm blanketing dough with damp cloths to rise. And all of the time.

Still, my limbs betray me. They need more warmth than I've been able to give them lately. The sweater is in my outstretched arms and a smile is on Orion's face and, *Dios*, the wool is so soft. At first I just drape it around my shoulders, but my arms have to tunnel deep and long, folding the long cuffs over my fingers like mittens.

"Thanks." But we're all looking at Jules, who's scratching inside her book.

"Really? That inspired lines? A cardigan and a cold Floridian?" Orion says.

"Never you mind what I'm doing." Jules writes some more. "At any rate, chivalry is far from dead." Her entire face blinks. "Chivalry. Ha! That reminds me about Sunday." She elbows Remy and tips her chin at Orion.

"Right," Remy says to Orion. "My dad's all set on that, um, thing you need for that person at your place."

Jules smacks the heel of her hand on her forehead. "Don't be such a twat! What's wrong with saying Orion's 'entertaining'" — she uses actual air quotes— "a girl and Remy's dad agreed to provide a nice meal he can warm up?"

"It's a good second date," Remy says. "Thoughtful. And you've already done the cinema."

I thought the batter bowl incident provided a solid reference point to Orion's blush. That was only a preview. A red fruit-punch stain, louder than Gordon's music, spills from Orion's cheeks to the patch of exposed chest under his collar. "Will you two kindly shut—"

Movement in the form of Fountain Girl arrowing toward the front gate chops the rest of Orion's thought. Her fairy-like body shoots up into a cute, bobbed cap of blond curls.

"Hold up, Flora," Orion says. "You didn't meet Lila."

Flora rolls her eyes and holds her phone up.

"You can spare thirty seconds." His words cut like a meat cleaver.

She stomps toward us on black Doc Martens and skintight gray jeans.

"Lila, my sister, Flora."

Ahh, sister. Close up, they do look alike, sharing the same curls and clear, peachy skin. Ocean-blue eyes, too, although Flora's hold a storm.

"Nice to meet you," I say.

I get a chin lift. "Yeah. Enjoy England," she deadpans, then tells her brother, "Gotta run."

"Where did you say you're off to?" Orion asks.

"I didn't."

Orion looks left then right before gently tugging Flora by the elbow. Yards away, I hear bits of, "The rules don't change just because Dad's traveling." They volley low whispers and obstinate stares.

The other three have moved to Jules's bench. Gordon and Remy are studying Gordon's phone screen while Jules writes with her head on Remy's lap and her knees hooked over the wooden armrest, feet seesawing.

I sit alone on the fountain lip, cold from the stone surface bleeding through my jeans, until Orion makes my party of one a two-top. He folds himself in half, clasped hands over his lap. "She's fifteen and hates that the four years I have on her make me responsible for her when Dad's away."

"He travels a lot?"

"For the shop. He makes a couple big trips a year to remote parts of the world, trying to discover the latest blends or crops. He's in China now."

What about their mother? She must have more than a little to do with everyone's reaction to my unintentional blunder. But it doesn't feel like my place to ask. It barely feels like my place at all. My mind drifts to what I know, ideas forming. "I could help, too. With Sunday night and your . . ." My face crinkles.

"Her name's Charlotte." Miniscule eye roll over a wisp of smile. "It's no big secret and my friends are ridiculous."

"She lives around here?"

"No, but close. A neighboring town. Her family likes the tea at our shop."

"Looks like she likes more than just the tea."

Orion's face pings with mischief and just a touch of mayhem. Blue eyes train onto something shapeless and distant, not walled inside this tiny courtyard. "About your proposition?"

I tug his sweater tight across my chest, burrowing my nose into tree sap and the remnants of woody-spiced cologne. "Right. An impressive dinner—"

"Tea. That's dinner. And means a meal invitation, versus inviting someone for a *cup* of tea."

Ugh, England. "An impressive *tea* deserves an impressive dessert—"

"Pudding."

Big glare. "No, not pudding. What I was trying to say is that I can make a cake or pastry for your date in the Crow kitchen."

"First of all, no need for all the trouble. Secondly, dessert around here is often *called* pudding. Which makes it even more confusing, I suppose, that various puddings are also commonly served as . . . pudding."

Oh, my head. Not jet lag this time. England all the time. "See, I could use the trouble. Believe me when I say I have nothing better to do. Also believe me when I say my *puddings* are legitimately awesome."

Orion smiles. "All right, I accept. Thank you." He opens then shuts his mouth, fidgeting, shifting his head into various angles. "I have a proposition of my own."

I motion for him to go on.

"Well, it's just that since you're new here, you might need

someone to show you 'round a bit. I've lived here all my life." He jerks a thumb toward his friends. "They have too and their exams end soon. So we could, um . . . we could all . . . err, do that. Show you around I mean."

My Cuban radar beeps. Espérate—something is off. Orion's fingers are skittering across one side of his jeans and his eyes flit around like a deer evading a hunter's footsteps.

"Show me around. Okay. And this is your idea?"

His sneakers must be interesting. He's studying them intently. "Well, I mean, I think it would be helpful—"

I rasp out a laugh. "She got to you, didn't she?"

He snaps up. "What?"

"Your proposition has Latina mother written all over it on Latina paper in Latina ink. It was Cate, right? What, did she come into your tea shop, or bump into you at the farmers' market?" When his chin twitches, I get enough confirmation to press on. "I knew it!"

Orion holds out his palm. "Lila, I'm terribly sorry." He shakes his head. "It's really not as, I dunno, conspiratorial as it might sound. Mrs. Wallace happened to mention you and your stay. It went on from there."

I'm sure it did. Her, choosing what I need instead of letting me choose what I need—right out of Mami's parenting manual— despite twenty years in England. Another thought tumbles in, making me want to hide behind the fountain statue. I glance up to my third-story window. Juliet, my ass. "Guess I made it easy."

He gasps, hands waving like a referee. "No." He cringes. "Shit, I know what it looks like, but Mrs. Wallace had nothing to do with me calling you down to join us tonight."

My brows rise.

"I promise. That was spur of the moment." He sobers. "I'm many things, but I'm not a liar."

I give him a resigned nod. There's nothing here to make me doubt his sincerity. It's as warm as his sweater. And it's not his fault he was trapped by a well-meaning but meddling Venezuelan.

But still, I decide what my days and nights look like here. "About Cate's scheme, we're good. And this has nothing to do with you or your friends. They seem cool. But as for fulfilling some proposal from your friend's mom, don't worry about it. I can read a map. I'll find the sights I want."

Air leaks from his chest. "Fair enough. But you don't need an invitation to hang with us here. Or anywhere."

"Fair enough."

We join the others and I have to admit, I don't have a terrible time.

Sometime later I break from the laughter, from the silver flask Gordon passes around, to head up. I slide out of Orion's sweater, feeling the whole of the temperature setting—*Not-Miami-Degrees Celsius*. I think of how we freeze foods to use later. To preserve them so they don't rot away. Maybe this is what my family wanted. To freeze a flame-star heart, a burn-planet body, while it heals.

8

I pedal two blocks toward town on one of the green Owl and
Crow Pashley bicycles before I give up and circle back, my face in
snarls. I haven't worn any of Pilar's sweaters yet. And I don't even
acknowledge the black warm-up jacket I transfer from my closet
to my freezing body. *¡Carajo!* I refuse to discuss this with myself.

As Polly takes Sundays off after baking extra morning and teatime food on Saturdays, I ran earlier during normal baking time.
And now I'm biking during normal running time. The St. Cross
streets are damp and sleepy; dog bark choruses and the peal of
church bells weave into my path. Air flaps across my face—clean
and sweet—and in minutes, I reach the city center and lock the
bike near the High Street pedestrian mall.

I stroll the commerce-lined lane, letting Winchester blink
me into Sunday. I don't believe in magic or legend. But for a few
moments, this little town becomes big enough to make me forget where I came from and why. It's alien—the not-me who feels

lightweight and not as desperately hungry for yesterday.

This magic is temporary, though. Soon the spell breaks and I'm the me who always remembers too much. I'm heavy and grounded by the time I reach Farley's Records. A bell announces my entrance into a wood-paneled space clouded with the ripe tang of patchouli and old paper. Customers mill around wooden display cases, records packed tight, or browse along walled cubbies filled with more vintage finds.

I do some milling of my own, sifting through punk and jazz legends and British bands I've never heard of. I have no clue what to *maybe* get for Pilar. I'm about to abandon this joint for the market when an ancient brown album cover snags my attention. *Orquestra Epoca*. Salsa music! My insides are already dancing. I flip it around and let lifelong memories of the first listed tune, "Trampas," fill my homesick spaces with percussion and piano and brass riffs.

After a few moments, I open my eyes and notice a black, patch-covered bomber jacket and a blond curly bob. Orion's sister Flora is a Farley's customer too. I'm mostly blocked behind one of the display cases. Flora's checking out a used CD when a tall man—older teen, really—turns into her view. Asymmetrical black hair drops over half his face. He's in peg leg jeans and a moss-green leather jacket. From my spot, I can't hear their conversation. Their faces tense until Flora slaps the jewel case back into its place, shooting through the front door. But the guy follows and Flora slows her pace before they disappear out of view.

Does big brother Orion know about this? Now I'm starting to sound like the West Dade chismosas—let's just say random busybodies—who followed my every move with Andrés. Are they still talking about me in neighborhood shops and salons and restaurants?

No gossip follows me here. I can step outside and walk to the market and no one knows my history. Claro, I'm still the girl carrying a trifecta of loss. I always will be. But as I wander along the pavement, I'm just a seventeen-year-old on her way to buy ingredients for Cuban flan. And that feels like the best part of home.

Cuban flan—this is what I choose to make for Orion and . . . Charlotte? With all of Orion's pudding talk the other night, I decided on what is essentially a fancy custard pudding. Cubans have many puddings: Natilla and arroz con leche are at the forefront. Vanilla cinnamon and rice pudding are simple treats fit for weekday desserts. Comfort food, not impressive date confections.

But flan is smooth and sexy and maybe even elegant. The puddle of caramel sugar syrup on top shines with coppery gold. There are several variations of flan adapted from its European origins. Naturally, I prepare Abuela's Cuban version, which is slightly more dense and sweet. This is one of the few desserts I make where a little more sugar is better. And is it ever memorable.

The Crow kitchen is mine today and happily Polly-less. I've got my ingredients measured and ready. The eggs here are different from home, smaller and brighter. I'm whisking glistening whites and yolks, fiery orange, like little suns.

The rear door swings open and Spencer and Cate enter with a basket of kitchen garden pickings.

"Even on off day, can't keep her out of here," Spencer says.

Cate peers into my bowl. "Flan Cubano?"

I whisk in evaporated and condensed milk. "Sort of a special order for Orion."

"Special is right. Spence and I haven't had good flan in four years," Cate muses.

I point to the two glass baking dishes. "I figured. I'm doubling so there's one for you guys, too."

"Well, that's a fine treat." Spencer adds tomatoes and cucumbers to a wooden bowl.

He leaves, but Cate darts in and out of the pantry for one of the tea tins. I've kept quiet about her little meeting with Orion, wondering if she'd bring it up herself. Or maybe she's been waiting for me to bring it up. And does she think this flan has anything to do with her meddling? "No wonder Orion doesn't mind dropping off your orders. He sure doesn't seem to keep many shop hours, what with all his extra time to play tour guide."

Cate has the grace to look abashed. But only for a half second before her mouth curls to one side. "You know I couldn't help myself."

"I figured you couldn't," I say casually and pick up my whisk. "Of course, I turned him down."

"I figured you would." Well. Our eyes lock until we both relent. Her grin. My head shake and dramatic eye roll.

Cate leans close before she leaves, her long strands loose and feathered from gardening. "When I came in, you were smiling."

"I'm always happy in the kitchen."

"Uh-huuuuuh." Cate extends the last syllable so it lingers even after she leaves the room.

Smiles or not, I'm all business as I return to my flan. The steps unfold into the hour with muscle memory. When the batter is done, I reach for a sheet pan and spy my phone on the back counter. Leaving it out is silly because no one texts or calls me here. It's barely dawn in Florida. Who's going to text me? But Instagram never sleeps.

Andrés Millan. University of Miami. All about Hurricanes football and Marlins baseball. Ice cream junkie.

Once upon a time, his bio could've said pastelito junkie. Lila junkie. Not anymore. Combing his feed is like picking at a scab. I know it won't heal this way. Claro que sí, I should bandage it, keep it out of sight. But I'm not as strong facing memories as I am in front of mixing bowls.

Andrés's page shows a new picture from yesterday, geotagged at South Beach. I can almost feel the glare of strong sun—my sun, not the filtered peekaboo England version. I smell the brine and his favorite Sun Bum sunscreen. It's a close-up shot of his unrolled towel, headphones and Rainbow flip-flops positioned in the foreground. The caption reads: *Saturday has me like . . .*

Saturday has you like what, Andrés?

I can't hide the thought that dangles like a loose thread from Abuela's apron: Andrés never goes to the beach alone. Was he with friends, or?

I drop my phone like a hot potato.

¡Basta! Enough. Last week, these useless thoughts won and I

ruined my cakes and made myself look like a fool. An amateur. I let him into my pound cake, but I won't let him ravage my flan. I pull out the phone and press the little camera icon to make Instagram disappear.

I breathe in and out, holding the moment for a beat before it disappears too. Now it's time to work.

I divide the batter between the two baking dishes already filled with my cooked sugar syrup, then set them inside the sheet pan in my preheated oven. Then the baño maria—the hot water bath. This will make my flan cook evenly and slowly, with no cracking on top. An electric teakettle dings from its hot plate. I pour about an inch of boiling water into the sheet pan and trust the oven to science that feels like magic. The kind of magic I believe in.

After Spencer's pasta carbonara with kitchen garden salad and my (perfect, delectable) flan, I'm folding laundry and staring out the window at dusk. Two hours ago, I sent Gordon, the flan delivery boy, over to Orion's after his sworn oath: *Yes, Lila I will mind the glass-domed plate and not drop it.*

After an alert sound, the FaceTime window flashes across my laptop screen. My parents are at the kitchen table, huddled in front of Papi's computer. Off camera, the TV plays the catchy theme song belonging to *Family Style*. Early afternoon Miami sun lights their backs.

This isn't our first chat, by far. But our opening words are still tentative. We're not *us* . . . we haven't been since I lost my world and they flew me across half of it to try to put me back together.

"There's my beautiful girl," Papi says. But his hooded brown eyes speak another truth. *Will you ever be the same Lila we knew?*

"You guys are looking good," I say. So trite. So shallow. I can smell the kitchen through the screen. Oranges and guava and coffee grounds, but not tamales. Can they hear this through the screen? Can they hear what I'm really crying out? *You won't eat tamales until I return! Pilar and Stefanie and I made them with Abuela on Sundays. Then Pilar and me, and Stef. Now two of those key additions are gone, and Pili won't make them without me.*

Mami asks, "Now that you're settled, do you have everything you need?" *Have you met some new people? Are you finding your way?*

I need Stef to come back from Africa and talk to me. I need Andrés to realize he can find himself and still love me. I need . . . "Send guava paste. They don't sell it in Winchester and it's expensive online. And Cuban coffee. There are a billion coffeehouses here, but espresso isn't the same. And then there's the whole tea thing." I think of Orion.

"Give me until Monday to get the guayaba," Mami says. "Stop and Shop is running a promotion."

It was like Abuela herself had dropped right into our conversation. She always insisted her savings account was built one frugal principle at a time.

"Next week is fine, Mami." A small way to honor her spirit.

Papi chats for another moment then blows me a goodbye kiss, off to La Paloma, but Mami remains. "Anything else you need?"

"A plane ticket."

"Lila." My mother cries at puppy food commercials and adorable little girls coming from church to buy pastries in floofy dresses. Her hands raise, flapping toward her chest like wings. Face contorted, her eyes well and the real words come now, bold with her own pain, strong with mothering. "Still? You *still* think we wanted to send you to Catalina? You think we don't understand how difficult this separation is? We miss you."

But none of that is enough to put me on an airplane. And I don't know why, but it just hits me now: three losses, three months. Was this Pili's idea? Did she plug me into one of her accounting algorithms, reconciling the sister she knows and loves?

"You'll get your ticket soon. I promise." Mami sucks in a breath. "But there's some good, no? Cate told me you've discovered the kitchen."

The word *kitchen* is the only thing that keeps me from hanging up. "Top of the line," I say, remembering Mami was here only two years ago when Papi surprised her with a ticket for her birthday. "Show me outside." *Show me home. My neighborhood, my world.*

My mother is one of those soft dolls where the dress and head can flip to show two opposite emotions. Sad face doll, happy face doll. Crying face Mami can easily switch to mischievous *I have news* face Mami. The latter fills my screen. Then she turns her computer so I can peek through the big kitchen nook window. "Maybe I shouldn't say this."

Inner eye roll.

Not two seconds later I hear, "I saw Angel coming out of Chany's house." She leans forward. "Sí, it was like seven in the morning."

"Interesting." And maybe I'm only half listening to the chatter about my neighbor's ex because I'm staring at our street through the little computer window.

Mami carries on, her update snippets weaving into my memories.

"Óyeme, Señora Cabral had her gallbladder removed . . ."

Kids playing baseball in the street before dinnertime. Wild roosters running loose and never letting me sleep in. Gloria's daughter practicing her saxophone in the garage.

"I saw Stefanie's mother at Dillard's the other day. I didn't go up, but . . ."

The hummingbird feeder and mango trees and Andrés in his silver Camaro, parked three houses away, kissing me.

"Mami, are they," I say quietly. "Are they still talking about me?" About Andrés and Stefanie? How one girl managed to lose so many people so quickly?

"Cariño, do not worry about such things."

"But what have you—" I'm interrupted by oddly persistent knocking. I cut off my thought and the connection with a goodbye, vowing to question Pilar about gossip later. I find Gordon on the other side of my door.

"Jules and Remy are out front. Asking for you," he says. "Well, both of us, but especially you."

Me? I shrug and follow Gordon onto the private staircase. He shoots ahead when we reach the foyer, ushering Remy and Jules out of the evening chill.

Jules sticks her arms out of a snow leopard printed cape, texting furiously while shooting me a little wave.

"Orion just texted," Remy says. "A bit of a mishap at his place."

"Tell me he didn't drop the flan," I say.

"More like his date dropped him," Jules says, wedging her phone into her jeans pocket. "Charlotte canceled. Said she was ill."

"But that's not the worst of it. Teddy—he works at Maxwell's—saw Charlotte going into a coffee shop in Twyford with some other bloke slinking and slobbering all over her," Remy says and turns to me. "That's a nearby town. He told Orion just now."

"Well, that's complete shit," Gordon offers.

Jules notes my overblown cringe and follows with, "Exactly. And that's why we're all going over now. Distraction. Remy's dad sent gigantic portions of Sunday roast with potatoes and veg. And then there's that whole pudding you made for them."

"Which would only remind him of his ruined evening," Remy says gravely.

"Gordon and I already ate. We just had flan too."

"Lila, do you really want your flan to become a symbol of sadness?" Gordon asks then tells the others, "Her flan is bloody spectacular. Besides, we can't let him wallow alone."

I concede but look myself over. I'm a disaster in yoga pants, flip flops, and a long tee. The mirror pegs my hair at bird-nest bun. "Give me five minutes."

Our little distraction posse makes the short walk to Orion's. While Orion shrugged off the idea at first, by the time we reach the nearby street lined with rows of attached narrow brick homes, he's in the doorway, arms crossed over a royal blue sweater. Charcoal socks poke over the threshold.

"Come on in, then." Orion moves aside and his friends barge through. Jules tosses off the cape and helps herself to Orion's home entertainment system. A dark EDM jam fills the living room.

I hang back while Orion locks up, feeling the bass line wedge under the wood plank flooring. "I'm really sorry."

"Thanks." His eyes flit around the room. "But that's the way of it sometimes. Or much of the time," he adds, almost like he's used to disappointment. But then he cracks a smile. "Anyway, welcome."

After two weeks inside the wide and tall spaces of the Crow, Orion's house feels extra cozy. I wander through. A narrow staircase shoots right up from the front door, perfect for someone trying to sneak in, or out, unnoticed. The living room is all soft light and Persian rugs and worn oxblood leather furniture. Clean white walls back overstuffed bookshelves and framed collages. I draw close to one. Black and white photos show the Great Wall of China and an endless bamboo forest. Desert sunsets and abstract sections of bridges and monuments. It's like the world on a wall.

"My dad's travels," Orion says behind me.

"You ever go with him?"

"Not this far." He points to a photo of a gigantic flat mountain. "Table Mountain in South Africa."

"Ri, we've got it all set," Jules calls from the kitchen. "I can only hold off these barbarians for so long."

"Better hurry if your friends are anything like my family," I say.

In less than five minutes Jules and Remy managed to artfully arrange plates of reheated food on Orion's counter. They move around the kitchen like they belong here. Sliced roast beef with a thick, plummy glaze and tiny herb potatoes and roasted vegetables smell almost as good as they look.

Remy hands Orion a plate. "You first and we'll slop up what's left."

"Like farm animals." Gordon hands me a plate and grabs one for himself. "Should we save some for Flora?" He cranes his neck. "Where is she anyway?"

"At Katy's for pizza and whatever else they do," Orion says, piling his plate with Remy's dad's delicacies. "She meant to scram while, you know . . . but she's got curfew."

I'm no part of hungry, but I still take a bit of everything before joining Orion at a round farm table. Jules pulls a spare chair from the wall. She turns it so the spindled back rests against the table, then straddles it like a horse. Does this girl ever sit in chairs normally?

Remy and Gordon are last, plunking down five ice-cold bottles. I read the label—Oldfields Cider—and remember Orion's old enough to buy alcohol here. I'm new to hard cider. My first sip is a burst of hoppy, tart, apple happiness. Not too bitter or sweet or anything. The cider is perfectly balanced, just like any proper dessert.

Doesn't take long for Jules to become heavily acquainted with hers. She traps a belch into silence, but her chest still balloons with it.

"A toast," Orion says, holding up his bottle, "to friends who don't listen when you say stay the bloody hell away, you meddling-arse muppets."

Snickers all around. "To Jules forgetting her song notebook in the rush over here," Remy says and the toasts alternate between sips, with Gordon saluting Remy's dad's delicious food, and Jules acknowledging Remy for putting up with her moody creative spurts.

All eyes fall on me, the new girl with the new cider and old hurts. I try to keep them off the table. They don't belong with friends like these, who drop everything for one of their own. "To having a better option than Netflix," I say.

Four bottles tip toward mine. I drink again, feeling warm with sour apple and fizz.

"But a whole summer away," Jules says after mostly swallowing her roast beef, "without your Miami friends. You must miss them loads."

"I . . ." I'm certain I fail at hiding the wave of bitterness that pulls through me.

"Especially that one girl? The blond who was always around when we visited," Gordon offers.

"Stefanie," I say.

"Right. Couldn't she come here for at least part of the time?"

Couldn't she have told me her life-changing plans? Been honest? "Not when she's in a remote village in Ghana."

Eyebrows raise, forks rest, and once again, no one forces details from my heart. If I talk, it's my choice. Add in the alcohol and the coziness of the small kitchen nook—it opens me. I turn to Orion.

"Not to hijack your night, but still, my friend stood me up for the next two years." I give them a ten-second intro to La Paloma, and how I practically grew up in the bakery kitchen.

"Stefanie was supposed to be right there with me, like we've been since we were kids. Her plan was nursing school and working with us part-time. We were thinking of getting our own apartment next year."

But this plan has cooled and changed into a completely new recipe. I tell the group about her health aid volunteer work.

"That's major," Orion says. "She didn't lead on about Africa at all?"

"I had no idea. Her whole family came into my bakery twice a week, and nothing. Not until I went over and saw the huge duffel bag and Stefanie's passport on her desk. "She said I would have tried to stop her from going. But I would have supported her and given her my blessing." I have to push these last parts out. They want to stick like honey to the back of my throat.

Jules asks, "How'd you leave things?"

"Broken." The only word that works.

Time crawls. I can actually hear the *click, click, click* of the wall clock above my head. It's official. I should hold no part in any distraction posse. I am Lila Reyes, displaced Miami baker and genuine mood killer. Didn't we come here to cheer Orion up? I groan inside at myself and hop up. "Flan?"

Jules beams a clownish grin and the boys sit up straighter in their chairs, eyes bright. Flan, the only word I need.

9

My domed plate of flan sits on the top shelf of Orion's fridge. I uncover and present the round, yellowy cream custard topped with caramel glaze. It smells like calories and sin.

Orion gets the first slice and stares at it dreamily, almost adoringly. I imagine it's the gaze Charlotte is missing right now, wasted on Cuban baked goods. And now it's on me, winter-blue eyes and soft mouth. "This is brilliant. You've known us only a few days and still went through all this trouble."

"It's what I do," I tell him and watch his peekaboo smile grow into a grin.

I pass out the remaining pieces, forgetting Gordon already had two slices at the Crow and prudently remembering my one and a quarter. I can't resist another sliver here, though.

The others eat, and actual moaning floats over the music. "You all need a private room with your flan?" With cold velvet vanilla and sweet caramel syrup soaking into each bite.

Remy says, "Excuse our ecstasy, but . . ."

"*God*, I mean it's similar to our traditional custards." Jules punctuates herself with her spoon. "But it's like you infused the batter with a steamy bout of snogging."

We all laugh. "No snogging or French kisses went into the making of your flan." Sadly, none went into the making of my recent past, either.

But I do enjoy people loving my food. I focus on that until multiple helpings demolish most of the flan. I start stacking empty plates to busy my hands, but Jules stops me. "Enough of that, Lila. Cooks don't clean in my family."

The boys pitch in too, so I rise and poke through the adjacent living room. I'd left my purse on an ebony piano bench. I pull out my phone; it's early afternoon in Miami, but no one's texted me. No crucial e-mails or missed calls either, like the usual state of my phone. I have officially disappeared to England.

"Lila?"

I whip around. Orion's holding out another hard cider as a liquid gold offering.

"I'm good, thanks."

Remy tosses a dish towel to Gordon. "Mum rang. One of the dishwashers at the pub went home sick, so I'm gonna fill in." He points at the cider and tells Orion. "Drink another for me? And chin up, mate." He works the locks and compliments my flan one last time.

Jules slings on a gray messenger bag then swoops the snow leopard cape over her shoulders. "Wait, love. I'm coming to help too. I look amazing in those striped aprons."

Remy holds the door. "She just wants to sing classic rock hits with the cooks."

Gordon's next to rush Orion's threshold, lobbing a broad wave at both of us. "Shit literature exam 'rang,'" he says. I start to follow, but he continues, "You'll see Lila home, then, Ri? Someone's got to stay a bit to make sure you don't dissolve into a puddle of your own salt water."

"Always the optimist," Orion says, then adds, "Hold up, Gordy." He stops his buddy on the porch.

Alone and apparently staying for a while, I study the upright piano against the staircase wall. *Bösendorfer*, the gold scripted logo reads. Faint scratches mar the smooth, matte ebony finish. Brass fittings have darkened, and the keys, while in perfect order, bear a slight yellow tint. This piano is well loved and used.

As intriguing as the instrument is, the series of framed photos lined on top snags my attention. The first photo shows a bride and groom under a floral arbor. The man could be Orion—same wiry but present build under a gray morning suit, same dark blond hair with the promise of curl on the ends. On his arm is a slight woman in a column of ivory lace. Blond hair sweeps back and a posy of roses blooms in her hands. Orion's parents—have to be. Next to it is a studio portrait of the same woman balancing a small boy on her knee and a frilly dressed baby in her arms. Lastly, there's a family photo against a stormy background of grass and craggy seashore. I pick up the large silver frame. The Maxwells huddle together in wool and tweed under a gray sky. Orion looks about ten or twelve and little Flora clings to her mother's side, sunshine curls tumbling down her back.

"Ireland. Cliffs of Moher in County Clare."

I face Orion, his family in my hands. His face tenses like it's struggling under the weight of untold things. Curiosity wins over politeness, and I ask the boy I accused of asking too many questions, "She's your mother?"

He takes the frame. Nods. "My mum."

"Is she . . . gone?" Like Abuela?

I don't expect the way his mouth works, angling wry and off center. "Yes and no."

"She left?" Like Stefanie?

"In a way." He replaces the photo slowly, almost reverently. "But not the way you think."

What is wrong with me? Like I've been the billboard of soul baring, lately? "I'm sorry. I shouldn't have asked," I say through a straggly breath. I hastily grab my purse from the bench. My eyes jump. Pictures. His dad's travel wall. Kitchen. Front door. "I should go. I can see myself—"

Orion steps in front of me and gestures to the sofa. "Please sit." *May I?* speaks from his face as he hesitantly reaches for my black purse, setting it on the bench. "Stay. It's fine, Lila."

I nod and sink into thick oxblood leather.

Orion grabs his cider from a sideboard. "Nothing to drink? You sure?"

"Maybe just water."

He's back with an etched crystal glass. He cuts the music

then sits, one cushion between us. And says nothing.

The silence feels like forever. I raise my glass to the bottle in his hand. "So. Cheers?" I wrinkle my nose. "Or is that weird?"

He evades my reach but the quiet room snaps back into rhythm. "Actually, that could be deadly for both of us, according to the ancient Greeks. The dead used to drink from the River Lethe in the underworld to forget their past lives. So, the Greeks always toasted the dead with water to mark their voyage, via the river, to the underworld." He gestures broadly. "As a result, toasting some-body with water is considered the same as wishing them and your-self bad luck, or even death."

"Wow. Okay. No cheers, then. But all these superstitions you're always rattling off. You don't really believe in them." I narrow my gaze. "Right?"

He flinches, looking royally offended. "Hey, what if I do? Is that so bad?"

"Um, really?"

"Yes, really," he counters.

"There are tons of superstitions from hundreds of cultures." My free hand flails. "Some of them probably contradict one another. If you believed them all, you literally couldn't do anything! I mean wrong facing beds and not stepping on cracks and under ladders and treacherous black cats and that's just a few!"

Orion looks over, a devil on his face. "Your voice rose about two decibels right then."

Well. He led me right into that one. My cheeks are hot candy apples, no mirror needed. "So *you* were just trying to bring out my . . . I won't say *Cuban*, because not all Cubans have volcano tempers." I make a face at him: more overblown smirk than anything.

"No assumptions." Another sip. "Was actually just going for smart-arse on my part. As usual." When my smirk curls into a mock snarl he adds, "And no, Lila. About the superstitions, it's more that I like to collect them. A sort of hobby. I also enjoy the history behind them." His shoulder bone pops up. "I have for years since . . ." He darts to a cherrywood bookshelf, returning with a photo. He keeps the framed subject turned toward his chest.

"I wasn't being evasive about my mum or trying to make you feel bad. It's a long story. But I'll tell you the basics."

I set my glass on a coaster, nodding.

"Seven years ago, she was diagnosed with a type of early-onset dementia called FTLD—frontotemporal lobar degeneration. I was barely twelve and Flora, eight. And Mum was only forty-two."

His revelation drops inside of me, spinning in silent chaos, bumping away the teasing jabs from just moments ago. My words change. "I'm so sorry," comes easily. "Is she here? Upstairs?"

"Not anymore. Dad wanted her home as long as possible. We had caregivers, in and out, for years. And my last six months of school I was on home study so I could help." He stares ahead now. "But about nine months ago, she became too far gone. We moved her into a group home where they take amazing care of her. I visit about every other day."

He places the photo into my hands. "This was one of the last shots Dad took of her before her diagnosis."

I swallow past the lump in my throat. His mother is beautiful in a cream sweater, fairy blond hair dusting over her shoulders. Orion has her eyes and I'm lost at the sight of this woman, his mum, standing under a cherry blossom tree in bloom. "Oh, Orion, she's . . ."

"She's everything." His voice cracks. "The cherry blossom trees in London were her favorites. Flora's named for them. But she doesn't know me or Dad or Flora anymore. She doesn't know her own name anymore."

My mouth opens to offer some kind of consolation, drawing from the place where my own loss grows, when the front door squeaks open.

Flora steps in, dragging a chilly gust behind her. Seeing me, her face goes blank with what could be confusion; I'm clearly not Charlotte from Twyfold.

Orion jumps up. "Hey, Pink, you want some amazing flan custard that Lila made?" he asks like we've been discussing movies or music or anything but their mother. I note Flora's nickname, too. Pink for cherry blossoms? Maybe. But Flora's black and gray getup is the opposite of pink *or* floral.

Flora's already a third of the way up the stairs, just ahead of a *no, thanks.* Orion approaches, whispering over the railing. And then she's gone.

He turns, cocks his head, then grabs the mass of dark gray wool hanging off the banister. It's the cardigan I wore the other night in the churchyard. "Here. You're shivering."

The patches of forearm visible under my three-quarter-length plum top are goose bump–heavy. I realize I'm not so much cold as overwhelmed. But I trade the photo frame for the soft wool and drape it around my shoulders. "Thanks."

Orion replaces the picture, this time on the piano. "This was Mum's. She was an incredible pianist." He rattles his head. "That's actually how she suspected something was off at first. Songs she'd memorized for years and played all the time, well, she began losing the notes."

"Only forty-two, though. It's hard to think of that happening to someone so young."

Orion sits, closer this time. "It's more common than it should be, medically speaking. But you never think it's going to be you or your family. Especially when you're twelve."

"You must've had to grow up pretty fast."

A single nod. "That's why I latched onto superstitions. As a mental escape, not a code of conduct. Dad and the doctors tried to help and inform me—always forthright about what was happening—but there was so much extra inside. Confusion and bitterness. The collecting gave me something to do. Superstitions explain or give meaning to some things we can't understand." Orion grabs the cider, runs his finger around the lip. "Cultures trapped that confusion into relatable objects or notions. It brought people a sense of closure and maybe some control."

Some things we can't understand. How Stefanie can share a past with me but not trust me with her future. How Andrés can say he still loves me but can't be with me. How Abuela went years too soon. "My family tried to help me, too." And counsel and treat and coddle. "But I wouldn't have it, so they sent me here."

Orion leans forward, hands clasped. "Three months, though. All because of your friend?"

"I wish that were it." I bite my cheek.

"I see. Well, the story of my mum seems a thousand years long. But you got the highly abridged version. The simple one, if we could ever call it that."

I peek at him with one willful eye. "You mean I could give you the quick and easy version of mine, like when you make a store-bought cake mix instead of baking something from scratch?"

"You could, yeah." He points at me. "But I'd bet my next pay-check on the fact that you've never used a cake mix. Never will, either."

My mouth springs wide, just for a breath. "All right. I can do highly simplified," I find myself saying. I've been holding all the trauma of last spring so close. But just like earlier with Orion's friends, no one here will make my personal business the next slice of neighborhood chisme. No one's judged me or hovered too closely over my every word and move. Orion just shared his mom with me. We're still inside the small and quiet space of that. One that feels . . . safe.

So I start. "I call it the trifecta. Stefanie's only one end point. As for the other two, my boyfriend of three years dumped me about six weeks ago. And my grandmother. My abuela." I meet him face to face. "She died of a heart attack in March. That was her flan recipe tonight."

"Wow, that's a lot at once." He looks at the floor then up at me. "I'm so very sorry. And those aren't just throwaway words. I get it—loss like that."

"I know. I still have my mom, though. She and my dad are amazing. They raised me." My voice wobbles. "But Abuela . . . grew me."

Unlike my mass of hair tumbling in thick waves, my hands are small and slight. He reaches tentatively for the one resting near his thigh, covering when I accept with a single nod, bending my fingers into a circled fist. A miniature planet inside the tight gravity of his hold. My eyes drift closed. I've missed this. No, not just a guy, alive and warm at my side. But someone, other than family.

Orion listens, too. Upstairs, Flora's lug-soled footsteps stamp the ceiling. Bits of her muffled phone conversations seep through heating vents. Soon, we finish our drinks and find ourselves strolling the St. Cross neighborhood toward the Crow.

Rain fell while I was away. We walk in tandem, feet striking soaked pavement. But it's taking longer than when I walked over with his friends. "Is this another way?"

The outline of his smile shifts under the glow of streetlamps. "Longer, yes. Thought I needed it after two slices of flan."

I toss out a laugh. "You mean three." We both swerve to dodge an extra-deep puddle. "Sorry again about Charlotte."

"Yeah. I fancied her, but I've already brushed that one off. I don't play games."

The word sounds through my head, telling me it's time to forfeit a game I can't win anymore, either. Here, against the dark blanket of tree canopies and the strength of old brick walls, I stop playing one with England. *Fine,* I tell this little medieval town. *You're not so bad. Happy now?*

We round a corner I recognize. Passing the church, then the walled courtyard with its saintly, dormant fountain, we reach the inn. Lights shine behind second-floor windows.

Orion stops me at the arbor gate. "You and the others, but mostly you, made my night un-suck, so thanks for that." He's so close. The kind of close where anyone passing by could mistake us for a starlit couple, moments away from kissing. But we're not. We are Lila Reyes from Miami and Orion Maxwell from Winchester.

"May I ask something of you?" The sweet-sour tang of hard cider rolls off his breath.

I flinch and shiver a little. Maybe it's the cold. "You *may*," I say with my own playful jab at his formality.

He snorts faintly. "What I'm about to suggest—I don't mean to be awkward, Lila."

Usually when people lead with that, it means awkwardness is following right behind them like a puppy. "You could have said you don't mean to be British."

This earns a laugh, both deep and bright. When it fades, he says, "See, even though it's cold right now, summer *is* on the rise and so are the temps. And I'd hoped Charlotte would be around to do things with. There's the cinema and some fun events that come around yearly. And Jules's band, Goldline, plays all sorts of cool gigs."

I tense. "You want me to be your stand-in Charlotte?" I am no one's stand-in anything.

"No. Not at all. I get what you've been through. You just broke it off with that bloke. What was his name?"

"Andrés." Andrés Christian Millan.

His brows jump. "Andrés. Now that's a marquee name." I move to duck my head, but his next words are right there, chinning me up. "Lila, what I'm proposing is more like an arrangement."

"So is prostitution. You're not helping yourself here."

Orion exhales heavily. He rubs his face, forehead to chin. "I understand why you turned down my offer the other night—Mrs. Wallace urging me to show you around."

My bottom lip drops.

"But she was right about one thing. You can't possibly live in that kitchen all the time. You should get out, and not just by yourself. So my very decent proposal is this: I'll show you around, and you can be my plus-one. It's all me asking this time. Not my friend's mum."

It's the same offer, but also, completely different. Tonight, it's genuine. I try out my answer in my head. Miami will still be waiting even if I do a better job at living where I am, right? And so I say it out loud. "Yes."

Orion grins. "Brilliant."

I crack a smile. "Looks like I'm getting a tour guide after all."

"Sure, let's call it that for starters. There are many things about England that maps can't show you. But I can."

I hand over his sweater. "What happens if Charlotte shows up at your door tomorrow?"

"Nothing happens. Not after what I heard from Teddy. See, market cake mixes are fine." He backs away, winking like the stars. "But I like the real deal."

10

I'm trying to wash a morning of baking off my equipment when the oven timer buzzes. And buzzes. But no Polly. Her Jammie Dodger cookies—bah, biscuits—are going to burn and my ears are going to break. I wipe my hands on Abuela's apron then attend to the deck oven.

I have two of the three sheet pans on the butcher block when the Crow's lead baker floats through the push door. "What are you doing?"

I'm painting my nails and tap dancing. I slap the third pan down and the oven door closed. "Your biscuits. I was worried you didn't hear the timer."

Polly slips on her apron again. "Course I did. I'm here aren't I?"

Dios. Not my kitchen. Polly's kitchen. I raise my hands in mock surrender and return to washing the endless bowls and utensils it had taken to make Polly's red recipe binder assignment for the day.

My hands are elbow deep in suds when Orion enters the rear kitchen door in loose track pants and a long-sleeved running tee. Basically the male version of what I'm wearing, minus the bang tamer headband and ponytail.

Polly's stacking cookies on cooling racks. "Well, hello there. We don't have an order for today, do we?"

Relaxed and dopey-eyed, Orion manages to address her via my general direction. "You don't. But if my memory's right, morning baking wraps up around this time, and then Lila does her run. And I've decided to take up jogging again."

Oh really?

Polly cocks her head. "All the more reason to fuel up with something sweet first. Pastries are set up in the parlor."

"They *were* set up." This, from Cate who blazed in with two coffeepots. "We have some bannocks left, but not even a crumb remaining on the tray of Chelsea buns."

I hang my dishtowel, intrigued. Polly made the bannocks—savory, round flatbreads—but I made the Chelsea buns. Currant-filled yeast dough treats similar to cinnamon rolls.

Polly turns to me. "Didn't you make the amount stated in the recipe book? It's always been enough for a packed house of guests as well as extras to leave in the break room for the housekeepers and landscape crew."

Now she's accusing me of lazy baking? I wave her red binder. "Four dozen, just like *your* recipe calls for."

"Interesting," Cate says. "I did see Mr. Howell from room six with three on his plate." Then to Polly. "We're also low on coffee."

A curt nod from Polly before she swoops up two fresh pots then swishes out the door.

I glance briefly at Orion, who's been leaning against the counter, cross-armed and cheeky-smiled, enjoying the latest edition of the Polly-Lila standoff. Better than any of Mami's telenovelas. I tell Cate, "Polly's had me on the morning sweet selection for the past few days. Should I be making more?"

She moves to the kitchen door, garden shears and canvas bag in hand. "You should, yes. I thought it was a fluke, but there've been no leftovers since last week."

Orion thumbs through Polly's book. "What are you putting in your sweets, Lila?"

I make sure we're alone. "It's more what I'm not putting in them. Polly insists I bake her family recipes and not my own. But the proportions are sometimes off. So, I've been tweaking them." I stack bowls on the open racks.

"But those recipes are British classics and decades old from her family."

I whip around. "Have you ever had one of Polly's Chelsea buns?"

"Many times. She often sends them when I bring tea."

I grab a small plate near the fridge. "This one of mine came out slightly misshapen so I didn't put it out. Go on."

His mouth twists before he samples a large piece. Then another.

I put away washed spoons and measuring cups. "I mean, the guests are *clearly* taking extra helpings out of pity and little old me has totally ruined the—"

"Lila."

"And tampered with—"

"Lila."

"What?" I whisk off Abuela's apron.

"This is the most rich and mind-numbingly delicious Chelsea bun I've ever had."

I look at him like this is old news.

"And," he continues, "it's still somehow so like the ones I've eaten since I was in nappies, but also worlds better. Did *you* get to eat any of your baking today?"

"Only a chef's taste."

Orion rips off half the remaining bun and holds it out. "Tell me why it's better."

Between bites of sticky goodness I say, "A smidge less sugar in the dough. A pinch of cardamom along with the cinnamon, and lemon peel infused into the glaze." Just like Abuela would have done.

He licks his fingers. "I'll never doubt you again."

I lick my fingers. "You'd better not if you want to work out with me. Also, I'm a really good runner."

"I'll manage. But I should've asked first. Either you're going to tell me running is something you do alone to think, which is fine. Or you're going to let me show you some new routes. Most locals tell visitors to run the loop into town across the college foot path, by the river."

"That's the only route I've taken," I say. "The only one I know." I hadn't even considered changing something that works just fine.

"Well, then." His face ticks into something between a smirk and a smile. "I can show you what you've been missing."

11

Orion runs beside me, possibly disguising some seriously out-of-shape lung burn with staggered breaths and silence. I don't tell him I'm not pushing my usual pace. I'm really not that bitchy. Usually. But the view is worth our slowness.

He pants, dolling out, "What is that. Glowing, circular orb. Just making an appearance?"

I laugh, but no need to look skyward. We stride from pavement to hidden path. I don't even try to hide my gasp as Orion leads me into a living kaleidoscope. Trees sag low with the weight of star-shaped leaves, while spindly armed bushes reach up and over, ends touching. Sunlight filters through, shifting lacy patterns over hard-packed dirt. It stripes Orion like a tabby cat.

"Scene's worth the unexpected company?" he asks.

"So much. Amazing." But the path tugs at more than my muscles because this is just the kind of place I'd choose to come alone and cry. To miss people. I would sit like I do in the wooded

Oleta River State Park off Biscayne Bay. Waiting for the bright to blacken, matching the shadowed pieces inside me.

But I'm not sitting now. I'm running with purpose, slower than usual, but still pushing all of myself through. Forward—I'd forgotten what that feels like. Will it last? No se. But this airy tunnel doesn't trap me like a British Airways cabin or the one-way ticket that brought me here.

We keep our pace until the trail opens, closer to the city center than I thought. The four-cornered spire marking Winchester Cathedral pokes up in the distance. Commerce and cars reveal another type of life.

Orion nudges me. "I've brought you through sort of a half circle, probably three miles worth."

"Are you saying we should stop?" But that's actually a worthy start for someone who hasn't run in a while.

"Maybe walk a bit? It's not far to Maxwell's and I need to fill a quick order and run it just a couple streets down. And you can sample some tea."

"Tea sampling. Is that part of my Winchester initiation?" I slow to a walk, rolling my neck.

He doesn't answer. He's bent at the waist, gulping in air like he's storing it for later. It's more than a little . . . *cute.*

I circle back. Playfully jab his shoulder. "Is it alive?"

"Ha bloody ha," he says and unfolds himself. "You're a good runner, Lila from Miami. But I'll work up to you yet. Let's move. We can walk around by the cathedral."

I follow him through a footpath near Winchester College, the mid-morning air cool against my heated skin. I know this section well, but Orion stops again by a low brick retaining wall that marks the end of the path.

I immediately see why. Just like the secondhand clothing store last week, the wall has been tagged with black spray paint. "Again?"

"Same crew, too." He points at the twisted graffiti shape. "What does that remind you of?"

"Kind of like those linked construction paper chains we used to make in school where you rip one off every day in December until Christmas. Only shorter."

Nodding, he says, "I think they're infinity symbols. But unlike the single one I cleaned at Come Around Again, this is supposed to represent a few linked together." He traces his finger along one of the shapes and he's right. A chain of three infinity symbols.

"Who's doing this and why?"

"No one local. I'd bet the shop on it. See, there's a London indie band—actually, a front man and his bass player and drummer, as well as their entourage. They spend a lot of time in Winchester. Too much time, as far as anyone's concerned. They're always trying to score something rare and interesting at Farley's. And more often, creating a ruckus in the pubs, getting into brawls and disturbances most everywhere they go. They're our age, give or take, and complete wankers."

My brow arches. "But the graffiti?"

Orion motions us into an easy stroll. "My fellow shop owners and I have no concrete proof it's them. But more than enough reason to suspect. The graffiti's been happening now for about a year.

Each time, they tag a symbol straight out of their song lyrics. Not from titles, that's too obvious. But one of their jams has the line, 'throw me into infinity.' We've also seen arrows, crowns . . . all key images found in their songs. Again, we can't do anything because no one's been able to catch them in the act."

I feel my forehead crease. "You'd think a gigging band would have better things to do with their time than pester Winchester."

"Our little Hampshire city has one thing the front man, Roth Evans, wants very much. More than rare vinyl at Farley's." He looks right at me. "Jules."

"Remy must have a few or ten things to say about that."

Orion gestures aimlessly. "Oh, he does, but not like you think. I told you Jules was talented, but that's an understatement. Not only a brilliant songwriter; Jules is an extraordinary vocalist. Like future record deal, name in lights good."

"Wow." I'm smiling, inside and out. I already liked Jules. "So, this Roth wants Jules to join his group?"

"Obsessively so. He's been trying to woo her away from Goldline, her band." We move through a greenbelt park; illustrated signs point the way to the cathedral. "Especially since he edged his way into singing with her once. I'm afraid that's Flora's doing."

I almost trip over my own feet. "Flora?"

He sighs. "Last year, Roth's whole posse was shopping at Farley's. Flora got into it with them about some stupid music trivia matter. A bet was made, for actual money, of which Flora has little."

I shake my head. "She lost the bet."

"She did at that. And Roth stepped right into a goldmine, rather a Gold*line*. He told Flora they'd be settled up if she could convince Jules to sing one song with him at Win-Fest." When my face scrunches, he adds, "We have a huge street festival here every October. Roth was performing and he wanted Jules for the other half of a duet. You should've seen the crowd."

"So this actually happened?"

"Yeah, because Jules loves Flora enough to perform with Goldline's biggest rival to save her arse. Jules reluctantly agreed and it's still a source of drama within Goldline." He nods slowly. "Roth and Jules did an unplugged version of 'Blackbird.' My God, I hate admitting it was absolutely stunning."

My heart clenches—Stefanie is a huge Paul McCartney fan. Whenever I drove us around Miami, she'd insist on playing his Spotify station.

Orion brings up a web browser on his phone. "This is Roth, short for Maximillian Evans Rothschild III. No one who values their limbs calls him that to his face."

My insides flinch for another reason. "Wait, let me see that again." I take the phone. "I was at Farley's the other day and saw this guy with Flora. It looked like a heated conversation, but they left together."

Orion swears under his breath. "You'd think she'd learn to ignore this lot, but my sister's impressionable. And Roth's bass player, Fitz, has a brother who does tech and promo for them. He's into Flora. So far he's just nosing around, but if it comes to more

I'm going to have issues with that. After what Jules sacrificed for her, it's just shit. Plus, he's nineteen and she's barely fifteen. I don't like it one bit."

I look Orion over, his face weighted and weary from more than running. "You want to watch her every second, huh?"

"More like enough seconds to matter. But it's like trying to keep track of a bumblebee," he says wryly, and I think of Pilar trying to manage me all these years. Protecting, guiding, giving me hell when I stepped out of line. More often than not, it was me returning all that hell, doubled, and keeping her in line right back. Miami floods my mind and heart. I miss my sister.

Orion does a quick shoulder stretch. "Now you know the story of our graffiti problem. Roth and his crew are just trying to manipulate. You know, bully and taunt because they can't get their way. And one day we're going to catch them." He scrubs his face and takes a cleansing breath. "But now you and I are going to have a quick look around a little church before heading into town."

Little church? Hardly. The stab of homesickness lifts as we approach Winchester Cathedral. I'd passed the massive gothic structure from afar, but this is the first time I've stood right in front of the towering facade with its arched stained-glass window bay. The cathedral is so ornate. I don't know what to throw my vision at first.

"Impressive, right?" And when I can only nod, he adds, "Eleventh century. One of the largest cathedrals in the U.K."

We wind around the side to the sprawling nave, anchored like a long rib cage set with hundreds of stained-glass windows. The

middle section juts out slightly on both sides—cross-like—just like Notre Dame in Paris. But I've only seen that cathedral in pictures.

Orion clucks his tongue, a glint lifting off his eye—also cute—and I know what's coming. "A Russian superstition says if you take an old coin, walk 'round a church with it three times, then go home and put the coin in a spot where you keep valuables, you'll get rich."

"Oh, is that all it takes? And here I was planning on making my millions by feeding Miami Cuban pastries."

We exit the cathedral grounds through a narrow access street. More quaint houses and shops, more *old*. "About those Cuban pastries, then?" he asks.

"You mean about you eating them?" I spurt out a laugh. "I'm just getting started here, but after one visit to the supermarket, I might have some trouble. No guava paste on any shelves, and that's a must. My mother's sending some. All I found was fig paste. I mean, *fig*!"

"Wait." He actually stops. "Lesson one from your tour guide. Never knock the fig around here. One look in Polly's book must've shown you figgy pudding and fig tarts and fig rolls."

"Me cago en diez," I say from one corner of my mouth. "Never mention that red book monstrosity around *me*."

"Look at that." He tightens his shoelaces. "I pissed you off right into Spanish. Bet that was a curse. I'll need to learn those."

He gets my best side-eye. "Keep mentioning Polly."

I'm checking out the flavor brochure and price list inside Maxwell's Tea Shop. I've already met Teddy and Marjorie, local college

students who double as clerks. They deftly handle customers while Orion slips into the back.

This shop holds more surprises for me than gourmet teas, though. I didn't expect it to look so much like the storefront at Panadería La Paloma. Same blond wood flooring and clean white counters. Similar industrial pendant lights and fresh cream paint.

Orion appears infuriatingly scrubbed and fresh in a new long-sleeved tee (does he have a closet here?). He jerks his thumb toward the arched opening behind the counter. "We have a washroom in back if you want."

Oh, my damp forehead and sweat stains want very much. "Thanks." The passage leads through a small commercial kitchen space, but it's a culinary ghost town of covered equipment and counters doubling as storage. No one cooks in here. I can't help but feel sorry for this space, or any space that's so obviously missing its own chef. Silly. I roll my eyes at myself and welcome the washroom's gardenia soap and hot water.

When I return, Orion's packing up a wholesale order. Weighing and filling little foil sacks with loose teas, he could easily be an apothecary who's been shot forward in time to a modern, light-filled space and running clothes. Dozens of metal canisters line the wall behind him. His own variety of herbs and potions.

"All set. I'll run this by the bistro on my way home to clean up." He waves me to the small tasting bar that caps off one end of the counter.

I drop into a stool. "Are you officially working today?"

"Later, when Teddy heads to class. First I'm gonna go and see

Mum." The small word flickers between us. We hold it for a few beats before Orion exhales through a resigned smile. "Now, how much do you know about tea?"

"About as much as you know about Cuban coffee. Other than that, Miami's more about iced tea at outdoor cafés."

Orion grimaces, the tiny cleft in his chin creasing slightly. "Oh God, that's sacrilege. I have my work cut out for me." He moves to the huge selection on the wall. "Where to start? Hmmm, let's try something simple and classic. English breakfast."

I observe his motions at a little service area, where he boils water in an electric kettle, then warms a small porcelain pot with a quick rinse. He waggles his brows and reaches for one of the canisters. Measures. Places two teacups on a tray with mini containers of milk and sugar.

Watching him calms me. My breathing slows. "That's quite the ritual."

Orion swipes a tea towel along the counter. "If you appreciate rituals, just wait until I make you some of the Asian green teas. Or oolong." He places the fixed tray in front of me then drops into another stool.

Him doing all this for me is more than cute. It's kind. Smiling, I reach for the pot, but he stops me with a palm. His fingers are long and slim. "One minute more. Timing is everything. Can't be rushed."

Timing. For the next three months, my family has taken over mine, from clock to calendar. I haven't been able to get an early plane ticket or rush them, either.

"Lila?"

"I . . . thank you." Orion pours deep brown, fragrant tea into our cups. "Customers can buy loose tea, but they can't order a cup to drink here? Maybe with a pastry or scone?"

"Not at the moment. We inherited the back kitchen with the property, but we're not set up for food service."

I meet his eyes, nodding before looping my fingers into the handle. I know taste. But English breakfast tea coats my tongue with flavors I can't name. "It's really nice. Bold and full."

Orion smiles. "I'll take that. Now, do you want to be really British and add a splash of milk?"

I find I do, in this small, insignificant way. Maybe it's just the way he asked, his smooth, syrupy accent spiced with a pinch of cheekiness. I pour the milk and watch the tea lighten to pale mocha.

Orion adds a bit to his cup, too. "Say, with all that talk earlier about Jules and Goldline, I forgot to invite you to their show next weekend."

I sip again. Remembering Orion gushing about her voice and stage game earlier has me nodding an easy yes.

"Great! It's a . . ." He blushes a shade of red our run had nothing to do with. "It's you and your Winchester city guide making sure your dance card's booked for Saturday night."

"Can't wait," I say, and find it's true.

"So, Lila from Miami." He points to my cup. "Most locals have a tea they consider theirs. You know, their signature favorite. For instance, Victoria from the secondhand shop loves this Ceylon black we offer. She chooses it before all others. We have to find your go-to. I know you need to try more varieties, but is English breakfast in the running?"

I've almost finished my cup. "Not sure. I mean, I like it a lot. I might not know tea, but I know quality and this is *that*. I just don't know if it's mine."

"No matter. I guess I have nearly three months to figure it out." This he says like that's both plenty and not nearly enough time.

12

Today is my warmest day yet in Winchester. I've gotten by with a little dress, trolling the farmers market for passable Cuban cooking ingredients. A thin, lemony glaze of sunlight clings to late afternoon, enough for me to toss on a denim jacket and find a lounge chair on the inn grounds. I'll FaceTime Pilar from here. Across the lawn, Spencer and Cate are picking veggies from the kitchen garden.

I catch his sweet peck on her forehead and can't help but lose myself inside another garden—my great-uncle's in the Little Havana neighborhood of Miami. It was the first place Andrés ever kissed me.

That small plot of land holds all our family roots. Four years after Abuela left Cuba, my great-uncle followed her path across the ocean. He brought his meager possessions and a cloth bag filled with dried corn kernels from the family farm. The corn in Miami, the corn in all the United States, would not do. He still plants the crop every year. We grind it for masa. We eat from what was born of Cuban soil, more than fifty years ago.

Tío's house is also the site of most of our big family dinners. For years, Stefanie came along to feast on roast pork and black beans and Abuela's flan. The summer after I turned fifteen, I invited Andrés, too. Stefanie had one job after that dinner: distract Abuela and mis tías and their ever-curious eyes while I snuck Andrés out back. I had a plan.

I led him on a purely innocent tour through beds of calabazas y lechuga y cebollas. We wound around avocado and lime trees. Then the corn plot—the garden's jewel. Bold as the Caribbean, I grabbed Andrés's hand and pulled him into a hidden spot between the stalks.

The corn swallowed us whole. Spit us out into a secret.

When he kissed me there, tingles fizzed through my limbs, sparking inside my belly. He tasted of flan and the Coke and lime Papi had placed into his hands. The silent language of my father's acceptance.

Todo está bien—all is well.

Thousands of miles away, in this English garden, I wonder just how well Andrés really is. Is he still single? The words have been sitting inside of me, gathering weight, ever since I saw his Instagram. I finally release them over FaceTime after Pilar gets through her Miami update.

Pili sputters over her soda, bubbles shooting up her nose. "Lila." She coughs again then glares at me over her glass.

"Just tell me. I swear I haven't looked at his Instagram for days, but the last time I did I saw him at—"

"South Beach." Of course she saw the picture. And that's Pilar. She'll tell me a hundred times to move on and ignore this boy who broke my heart. But as sure as sisterhood, she'll be right there adding up tips and clues, her checks and balances. It's what *she* does.

"Well?" I press. "Do you know who he was with? Anything?"

She exhales heavily. "Okay. Annalise is now taking ballet barre with Christopher's girlfriend Jacqui and—"

"Just get to it." I know how information travels.

"That day at the beach. Andrés was there with Chris and Jacqui . . . and Alexa."

Alexa Gijon. She grew up with Andrés in Coral Gables, and even hung out with us in groups a bunch of times. I'm suddenly witness to a slideshow of every interaction I saw between them.

"Hermana," Pilar stresses, "I swear I don't know if it means anything." I believe her. We might embellish stories, but Pilar and I do not lie to each other. It's one of the reasons we're destined to succeed together as partners.

"It's fine." Andrés probably went to South Beach with her as friends. It could be totally innocent. Or, maybe he *was* on a double date. All I want to do is run from this thought, along any Winchester path I can find.

"Don't take this too far, okay?" she says. "Stick to what we know for—"

"Pili, I need to go. We'll talk later. Besitos." I end the call before she responds, needing some space from her revelation. While my sister is faithfully present with her proof and fact gathering, Stefanie was always different. News like Andrés and the beach would have her pacing with rage and purpose around these beautiful English grounds. Forget trying to solve anything, Stef would simply indulge me in being overly dramatic. We'd bitch and complain, sometimes planning grand revenge schemes in our minds worthy of any tele-novela. Often, we'd end up laughing as much as crying.

I miss that part of us. And be it drama or telenovela plotline or real, honest life, I am simply out of excuses for not contacting her. I've been putting it off. I've been putting *her* off. I cue up my e-mail, and after typing and erasing at least ten different lines, I settle on nine little words:

Dear Stef,
Hey. I think we should talk.
Lila

Tomorrow is now up to her. I press *Send* and stow my phone in my jacket pocket, catching Spencer helping his wife up from the garden beds. They move toward me instead of through the kitchen side door.

"Good haul?" I ask as the couple drops into the two remaining chairs.

"The garden's coming up nicely. Good enough for decent salads this week." Cate shakes her basket before setting it on the grass. "In other news around here, Polly gave her two weeks' notice for leave today."

I'm zero percent surprised by my quick flash of joy, even sweeter after my call with Pili.

"She's not quitting," Spencer corrects. "It's only temporary. Polly's mother has a heart condition. Her caregiver is scheduled for knee surgery and taking leave until sometime in August. Her mother refuses to allow a stand-in nurse. Stubborn. Polly has no choice but to step in herself. We'll have a look around for help in the meantime. Since you've been working with her, we wanted you to know."

The beautiful Crow kitchen snaps into my mind. An empty space with no red binder and no hovering Polly cramping my style? "You don't need to look for more help. I can take over all the baking, no problem. And Polly doesn't even have to finish out the two weeks."

Spence cocks his head. "Well, then. You're certainly capable enough."

"Capable, yes, but the full load might be more than you want to take on," Cate adds. "You're not here as Cinderella. Forced to work all day without any time for fun."

I stare at my hands, noting the careless burn marks and persistent dry spots from just that much flour all the time. But to me, it's beauty. The kitchen is all the fairy-tale castle I need. "Please. I want to."

Cate silently consults with Spencer. Nods. "All right, but on one condition. You prepare the breakfast and teatime offerings, but I'll set up and serve the afternoon tea like Polly does. And you find time to get out."

"Deal," I say, then finally give words to a wish. "I know this is a traditional British inn, but would it be okay if I started adding in some Cuban breads and pastries to the menu?"

Spencer says, "We're game for you to float a bit of variety. How about we see how it goes over?"

They leave me with more than a new job. Thoughts of Andrés and Alexa together on South Beach sand sprout again, growing as well as anything in Tío's garden. I can't hack them away this time. Maybe I smudged the truth to Pili, at least a little bit. It's not fine. And I want to know—was Alexa watching us in groups for years? Watching Andrés's mouth on mine, his hand sliding up my bare thigh while we all lounged on his pool deck? Has she been waiting all this time, and is she now the one with skin beneath his hands, oiling on Sun Bum, his finger playfully snapping the bikini top band between her shoulder blades?

Stefanie always used to talk about emotional hooks, small points of trauma and memory that snag you every time.

Is Andrés still single? This one's mine.

13

Orion's supposed to be here in fifteen minutes for Jules's show and I'm in a wicked staring match with my closet. So far I'm winning. Which doesn't mean I'm actually dressed. Besides my general procrastinating, it's hard to concentrate on picking an outfit when my mind is acting like a sort of wardrobe of its own. My thoughts are hung with recent images—old friends and news about ex-boyfriends and beaches and unanswered questions.

Recipe for a Breakup
From the Kitchen of Lila Reyes

Ingredients: One Cuban girl. One Cuban boy. One champagne-colored prom dress. One pair of gold strappy sandals. One gold clutch bag. One best friend. One sister. Flour. Water. Yeast. Sugar. Salt. Lard.

Preparation: Listen—stunned—as your boyfriend of

three years tells you he's not leaving you because he doesn't love you. He just can't be with you anymore and needs his space. Run to your best friend's house and cry for hours as she plans his demise in endless creative ways. On prom night, while classmates dance, bake a dozen loaves of bread.

*Leave out all the prom finery. Your sister will clear it from your closet before you have to see it.

Cooking temp: 450 degrees Fahrenheit, the perfect temperature for pan Cubano.

I'm startled from my virtual closet by three strong raps on my bedroom door. "Lila? My ride's out front, so I'm off!" Gordon yells. "Ri's never late. Just a word to the wise."

I'm certainly not about to admit my lagging ways and meandering thoughts to Gordon. "All good here, thanks!" I call. "See you at the club."

"Right!"

Bundle up, Orion warned this morning during our jog along the River Itchen. And one last time when he dropped me at the Crow before work. After a brush-through of smoothing hair serum, I try on a few more clothing options in my head.

My phone dings from the writing desk.

Orion: Out front

Me: So early!

Gordon wasn't kidding.

Me: Down in five

Orion: Yeah, I'll just freeze out here

That gets no reply.

Back at the closet and out of time, I give up and settle for one of Pilar's black merino sweaters. I rip off the tag and pair it with dark skinny jeans. And as long as I'm going for *What Not to Wear, Miami in Late June edition*, I slip on thin socks and my sister's black ankle boots. Orion's accent rings between my ears, so I toss on the thick gray and black animal print scarf. One swipe of MAC lipstick in Impassioned colors my lips like ruby-red grapefruit.

I race down and rip open the Crow's front door. I'm more winded than any decent runner should be. Well. Orion looks perfectly toasty in his brown leather bomber jacket and navy tartan wool scarf knotted around his neck. "Freezing out here, my ass," I say. "Also, is being early a British thing?"

He steps back and I secure the door behind us. "It's called being prompt, and the way you ask makes me wonder if being late is a Lila thing."

"Not *always*." A crack in my bright pink pout. "And never when it comes to kitchens."

His smile is the warmest thing he wears. "You look nice. You heeded my warning. Sort of," he adds sheepishly.

I sling my purse across my body. "What do you mean, 'sort of'?"

This whole weekend, the parking strip in front of the Crow is blocked off for minor road work. We walk around the corner and I halt abruptly. "Hold up. That's our ride?" I'm no chicken. But I've never been on a motorcycle, which ranks at number five thousand on my top-ten list of must-dos.

"That," Orion says, pointing to the black, two-wheeled early death machine with tan leather seat, "is a 1982 Triumph Bonneville. Fully restored, even if she is a bit loud."

I recall the rumble invading the Crow kitchen the first time I met him. "Um. But."

He chuckles, shaking his head. "Come closer, Lila. Her bark is definitely bigger than her bite."

No moving, no closer. "Her?"

"Why, yes. She's called Millie and she was my granddad's. Now she's my best girl. They don't make these anymore. Millie's a classic."

A tremor pings through my body. "Maybe there's a valid reason they don't make them anymore. Maybe because they're metal speed sticks of bodily destruction."

"Look, she's harmless." He takes my bent elbow. Leads me up to Millie. "I shined her up earlier and everything. You're not scared, are you?"

¡Carajo! "Of course not. It's just really dangerous out . . . there."

Orion plants himself as mediator between me and the bike. "I've been handling this motorbike since I was a kid, way before it was legal. Hundreds of hours with no incident, and I can navigate the route to the music hall with my eyes shut. Of course, I can't promise nothing will *ever* happen to us. Can you make that claim when you step off any given pavement in town?"

Make a claim against something, or three things, upending my world? Never. I shake my head.

"Right. But I don't get off on inviting people." He arches a chased me down with replays of sun-dripped, tropical breeze and cruising Collins Avenue. But Orion's motorcycle has something to say about my memory. Louder than the old words in my head, the engine and her skilled driver fight to win. Fresh pine and grass wrap around the wind, shooting up my nose like a street drug.

The dashing speed presses me into Orion's back. Partway in, I squeeze harder and rest my cheek on battered leather. I'm warm in his sweater, my arms full of his solid frame. I close my eyes and just *feel* until the bike slows and Orion turns into a packed parking lot. "Already?"

Did I just say that?

Apparently I did because Orion's laughing as he parks. He helps me off the bike. My body still thinks we're in the middle of turns and dizzying bends, the growling throttle echoing in my ears.

"Got you here in one piece and you even managed to enjoy it."

"I . . . yeah," I say as my legs recall how to work.

"Then you might want to release a guy's poor, innocent jacket before we head inside?"

I look down; my hand had instinctively clamped like a vise around his forearm. "Oh—sorry. I didn't even realize."

"Millie does have that effect." Another laugh, his features both warm and smug. "You did like it, then."

brow. "Especially my tour guided plus-ones, for activities I know will likely hurt them."

No, he doesn't—he couldn't. Not this boy who's suffered enough hurt to pave every street in Winchester. My body loosens. "Okay, fine." I grab the hair tie around my wrist, securing my flat-ironed locks into a ponytail. "I'd better run back for a jacket."

"No need. Plus, we've got to get moving or we'll miss Gold-line." He opens a knapsack and pulls out familiar gray wool. "After what you said about your Winchester packing, I wasn't sure of your outerwear situation."

I layer his cardigan over my merino crew neck. Orion's sweater is softer than the trench hanging in my closet. I could get lost inside it. I adjust my scarf so the ends trail down my chest. "This is becoming a habit."

"I know of worse ones," he says then hops onto the bike. "Your turn."

I straddle the remaining patch of leather seat behind him, resting my boots where he shows me.

Orion bends around. "Grab my middle and don't let go. And lean with me into the turns." He revs up Millie. The engine vibrates under my thighs. "Hold on, Miami!"

Orion starts off slowly as we ride through St. Cross. Then ignores my motorcycle virginity when the frontage road widens. I've jogged this road. We've jogged this road. But on his bike, all my senses are bit by night and speed.

For the first hesitant minutes, I couldn't help but think of Andrés's silver convertible. Even at full throttle, our Miami days

14

My legs manage to adjust from post-motorbike to normal by the time we reach the white, pitched roof building with black trim. The sign over the entrance reads *Heaven's Gate*, but locals just call this club the Gate.

Inside the venue, filtered light casts a ghostly hue. Sweat, hoppy beer, and a bouquet of a hundred perfumes follow our elbow-pushing through the crowd. Orion plants his palm on my back and guides us dead center. Remy and crew have been saving us seats, and good thing—there aren't any left.

Our group has snagged two bistro tables and pushed them together. I spy Flora with a couple of girls and guys at the far end. We squeeze into our chairs.

Gordon waves, and Remy salutes from my left, saying, "You survived Millie, then? You've got guts behind your apron, Lila. Ri's a beast on that thing. Usually ends up swiping his Dad's ride when he's toting companions."

Orion juts forward. "Enough out of you."

I turn, slanting my gaze at my chauffeur. "A car? You have access to a car and—"

"Goldline's up next." Orion's left eyeball strays my way. His mouth purses infuriatingly.

"We are not done discussing this," I say.

"Time for music, Lila."

The truth saves him and the crowd cheers Goldline onto the stage. Remy takes roll call for me. Leah, the drummer appears first, then Tristan and Jack—one on keyboard, the other on bass. Lastly, Carly, a petite brunette with an acoustic guitar steps up to a boom mic. She introduces Jules. The lead singer appears in a burgundy maxi dress topped with a black leather biker jacket, hair blown straight and tinted like pink lemonade.

Gone is the goofy girl who belches over hard cider and can't sit right in a chair. Mic in her hand and a capable band at her back, she's a professional temptress of smooth and polish. Jules eats the stage.

After a few songs, I learn their particular brand of music. Pilar would describe it better, but even I know Goldline borrows its eclectic vibe from many sounds and decades of musical references. Part alternative, part folk, they sprinkle in enough edge to keep the polyphonic array of synth and guitar from being too precious.

Orion catches my sidelong glance. "You like?" he asks, as low and misty as the light, and I know he means the music. A breath still trips across my tongue.

"She's made for songs." Her airy but controlled voice snares my heart on a fishhook.

Orion shifts, leather brushing against my arm. "She writes most of the music. That purple book she always has." He dashes a long arm toward the stage. "This is why we indulge her."

I lose time between an acoustic ballad and a dark, alternative jam. My eyes blink me back to the present when the house lights raise for a quick band break. Five songs felt like nothing.

Remy strains his neck to scan the venue before leaning toward Orion and me. "Christ. Jason Briggs is here. Six o'clock."

Orion points out a tall redhead with a two-week scruff. "He's a production assistant with Four Points Records. Jules has Remy stalking London scouts' and managers' Twitter feeds to see what shows they're hitting up. Always a chance of this happening."

"You think he's here for Jules?" I ask, which perks Gordon's ears.

"More bands on later, but we hope," Remy says. "I don't know when he got here." He swivels, side to side. "He bloody needs to hear her, but there are no more seats, and management won't let anyone loiter on the side for long."

Musical Chairs happens after less than ten seconds of deliberation between us. Gordon flags Briggs into his now-empty seat next to Flora, then slides into Remy's chair. Remy slips into my chair. And me? I end up in the most logical place: Orion Maxwell's lap. I don't make a habit of sitting on guys' laps, especially after knowing them less than two weeks, but Jules is worth the awkwardness. The lap owner is full of smiles, too, motioning me closer like it's really not a big deal.

Still . . . "Is this? Are you sure? I'm not too heavy or *anything*?" I stress the *anything* with everything beating through me with moth wings.

"No anythings to worry about." Orion shifts me sideways, my legs draping over his right thigh.

Houselights drop and the crowd calls the band back to the stage. Jason Briggs settles into Gordon's former chair, texting, but we'll take it. I'm more concerned with trying to balance myself on Orion's lap without completely invading his personal space. Jules sings the first bars of a haunting unplugged cover of Aerosmith's "Dream On" and I'm twitching with drunk Cuban ants in my pants.

Not helping: Orion's thick sigh, warm against my neck. He closes his arms around me, pulling me against his chest. "Relax," he says as Jules launches her death leap soprano into the chorus. "It's just like us on the motorbike."

He's right. It stills me. We ride out the rest of the set together, leaning into phrases and turns, shifting into melodic bends. I lose myself to feel and sound again, but it's more than just one thrilling motorcycle ride and a set of brilliant songs. It's everything new around me and it's happening more and more. Happening right now—a Miami girl in an English club listening to an English band, sitting on an English boy's lap, his sweater warm around me. And I can't help but enjoy it for real. My pulse and breathing score a steady rhythm, playing against chewy brown leather and the minty-citrus scent of Orion's soap.

*

Backstage feels like being stuck in the middle of a Mardi Gras parade. Orion and I stick together but lose the others. I almost get trampled by a girl group wearing sequined leather miniskirts and ice-pick-heeled patent boots. Jules finally appears, scooting ahead of the crew rushing through the narrow hall with cables and tuned guitars.

After Orion and I barrel into a gush fest over her set, Jules grabs my shoulders. "Tell me Remy wasn't jiving and it's real. Jason Briggs was actually at your table? I couldn't make out shit the way the lighting was up there."

I clear my throat and decide to leave out the part about our seating situation. "True. And he saw the second half of your set for sure. He was still there when we left."

"Naturally, that means I have to Twitter stalk him now. He always does a weekend wrap-up and teases what he likes," Jules tells me then casts her gaze to the rafters. "Why do I torture myself?" She points to the band lineup printed on the wall. "You didn't want to stay? GLYTTR's on in a few."

GLYTTR? Wow. But I think back to stilettos and sequins in the hall. Fitting.

Orion says, "We were here for you. Besides I've heard them before and their sound is like this cosmic mash-up of EDM, Adderall-infused K-pop, and a circus act."

Cringing, I'm about to comment, but Gordon sneaks up between us. "You guys seen Flora? She was with us when Remy and I went to fetch drinks then . . . vanished. Everyone wants to bail, but we don't want to leave her. She's not answering texts."

Orion shifts from relaxed concertgoer to protective guardian in less than a half second. He frowns at Gordon. "We'll find her. Get the others and wait by the ticket window."

I follow in step as we make a couple of passes across the main floor, finding our previous seats snapped up and Jason Briggs still watching. But no Flora. "Is it like her to disappear and ignore her phone?" I ask.

"No . . . yes. Yes, it's bloody like her." Orion shoves his hands into his jacket pockets. "Six months ago, you'd have gotten a different answer."

We split up. I check the ladies' room while Orion pokes around the service entrance. On my way back, Flora-less, I find concert-goers coming and going from a narrow staircase in the lobby. The stairs lead me to a mezzanine where people can mingle, but thick support pillars obstruct most of the stage.

I can't find guava paste in Winchester, but I find Orion's sister ten seconds after I weave through the mezzanine crowd. Flora's flat against the back wall, a guy wearing a beanie and a flannel shirt hovering in front of her. I send a quick text while GLYTTR jams below. Orion's review of the band was spot-on; their sound is the bad kind of strange.

Orion appears, stepping around me and calling out to Flora. Her face shifts from dream to nightmare at the sight of her brother. "You didn't answer your phone," he says. No Pink or other endearing nicknames tonight.

"It's loud up here," she retorts.

Orion plants himself strong, crossing his arms. "Your friends are waiting by the booth to leave. *With* you."

The boy pulls back, but only a step. "I'll see Flora home. Safe and sound."

"Another time, William," Orion says.

Flora huffs, checking her watch. "But we were going to—"

"Another *time*, then. You're with Gordon and your friends tonight. And they're heading out for some grub."

Surrendering, William holds up both palms at Orion. He turns dark, narrowed eyes on Flora. "Ring when you can."

He gets Flora's lone smile before she whisks past us without another word. William lifts his chin at Orion before heading back to the mezzanine rail.

"So," I say as we descend. "You two have met."

"That's Will. Remember I said one of Roth Evan's tech guys has been sniffing around Flora?"

Instinctively, I glance back up. "That didn't look good. Definite, um, sniffing."

He guides me outside. "It could look even worse. If Will's around, chances are the rest of Roth's posse is or was here as well."

"So Jason Briggs wasn't the only one here to check up on Goldline."

We cross to the lot, weaving through double-parked cars. "Exactly. Jules debuted three new songs tonight, including the one about trains you liked." He motions toward a silver Land Rover. "There. That's Roth's. I knew it. They didn't come all the way from London tonight to watch GLYTTR. A hundred great female artists in London, but Roth wants Jules and her particular sound, and I can't really blame him. But he won't quit." Orion stops cold about five feet from his motorcycle, exhaling. His sourness loosens into a half smile. "After Flora and all that, I could use a walk. There's a cool spot nearby that's already on your Winchester to-do list. You game, or you have to get up early?"

I already told Orion about my Owl and Crow baking gig. But I also front-loaded all of today's plus Sunday's baking this morning (chocolate scones, morning buns, Abuela's pound cake, and sugar cookies), the only habit of Polly's I'm keeping. "Sleeping in tomorrow, so I'm good. And there's a to-do list?"

"I'd be a poor excuse for a tour guide without one."

Orion's sweater keeps me the perfect amount of warm as we stroll into the little section of town near the Gate. The River Itchen cuts through the city center at this spot. We pass over ancient bridges, the water rushing beneath us. And Orion's a history book.

"This old mill has been here since 1086. It was used for laundry during World War I.

"Our River Itchen is twenty-eight miles long.

"Winchester has been inhabited since prehistoric times, but a fire destroyed much of our city in 1104. The archbishop had much of it rebuilt."

I listen contentedly but the scenery and streets begin to look familiar. Too familiar. I dredge up a little history of my own. "Wait. If The Broadway's right there, then we could have ridden straight up here on St. Cross Road in minutes. But we took this super-long rural route around the edge of town and came in the back way?"

He rises up and down on his weathered boots. "And?"

"And? *And* Remy said you can use your dad's car."

"I often do." His stomach growls and we both huff out a laugh. "Snacks, then? We can pop into Tesco. My supper earlier was kind of . . . not."

We head toward the supermarket down the block. "Are you trying to distract me from your motorcycle shadiness by telling an obsessive cook you're eating like crap?"

"Only stating facts. I just rummaged up an apple and a cheese sandwich."

It works. "Pitiful. Now that the Crow kitchen is mine, I'm going to start making all the Cuban food I can with English ingredients." My voice thins. "I miss it."

"I imagine you do. There are a couple of places in London, but I don't think I've had Cuban food. You'll be sharing, then?"

Shady Brits with unnecessary motorbikes shouldn't get smiles, but Orion Maxwell's empty stomach, boyish eagerness, and wagging brows are stronger than my scowl. "No tour guide of mine is going to survive on tea and cheese sandwiches." We reach Tesco. "You're on snacks and I'm going hunting for new face mask." My skin is missing the Florida humidity.

Exiting the supermarket, we leave the city center behind. Orion won't give me any hints on our final destination as he leads me up a steadily rising grade through a high-end district with grand homes.

The neighborhood feeds us into a trail marked with wrought-iron railing and wide steps. "The lighting's questionable and it's a bit steep, but we both have sturdy boots. And what's waiting at the end is worth it." He pulls his phone, taps the flashlight icon, and urges me to do the same. "Trust me?"

I trust three things without question: Abuela's recipes and her signature variations, my family's business—the way it works, and the city it works in. But so far this boy has kept a reluctant Miami transplant taught, mapped, entertained, and warm in soft gray wool. Right now, I trust him, too. Maybe even more than I know him. "Lead on."

15

The path and steps are steep but no match for my runner's lungs. The secret trail ends with a fenced platform and a view that swallows all my words. Like Stef and I as kids at Disney World, I rush toward the city-sized night-light of color below us. Winchester spreads out like an upside-down galaxy of golden embers. We're so high. Trees glow and buildings gleam against a blue-black sky. Railway tracks wind through like comet tails. In the center, the massive cathedral is dipped into spotlight yellow.

"St. Giles Hill." Orion gestures to the sprawling hillside park at our left. "Come. I just hope the grass isn't too soggy."

It is—well, not exactly soggy—but damp enough, because this is England. Orion finds too much joy in my scrunched face and the hesitant settling of my jeans into the layer of dew.

"Since you find my wet ass so hilarious, I'm waiting for you to spout some random cultural myth about grass," I say.

"Now you're requesting superstitions? And here I thought all my facts and Winchester history was gonna bore you straight back to Miami."

The word *ambush*, just that quick, and I'm unarmed and weak with scenery and motorcycles and music. *Estoy aqui—I'm still here*, Miami says. Like I could forget. But this time Miami only grazes my skin because I've let this sparkling city view change mine. I can wholly belong to one place, but I'm going to sit on a hill and enjoy this one right now. Maybe even love it.

"Lila. I didn't mean to—"

"Show me what's in that bag," I say.

"Yes. But I know you want—"

"I want your groaning stomach to shut the hell up."

He breathes out, whether out of relief or humor, I don't know. But he jiggles the brown bag. "Some classic British snack foods for your initiation."

"Hey, my life is not a hundred percent devoid of British 'things.'" I fish out my phone and show him a photo of my turquoise Mini Cooper.

"No kidding." He looks up, smiling. "Suits you. The color is very Miami and it's lively."

"And fast. I miss driving it."

"Won't be long. Before you know it, you'll be reunited." He delivers this like an oath. "Three months, and waning."

And waning like the moon. I find that, too; it peeks through a tree bordering the hill, plump and round. Then I turn to Orion, and maybe gazing on one beautiful thing lets me appreciate another. Orion Maxwell is an attractive creature. More like *really* attractive.

The worn parts of him—battered leather, scarred boots, the hair that always flirts with curl—are *interesting* against a city-lit face of honed edges and blue eyes straight from a painter's palette. My next words come out like they've been stuck inside imagination, full of clouds. "What kind of food service provider am I? I distracted you right out of your junk bag."

"Right." With a flourish, Orion arranges our little snack food picnic. "Walkers bacon crisps, which you call chips. Erroneously. And for a sugar rush, Aero and Dairy Milk bars." Lastly, he presents a familiar-looking jumbo-sized bottle. "Yeah, Oldfields again. Was in a hurry, so I went for the safe bet."

He pours hard cider into two clear plastic cups. "The clerk at Tesco threw these in when he saw our stash and I mentioned the hill. So we wouldn't have to drink from the bottle." He clinks his cup against mine. "Like heathens."

I snuggle into Orion's sweater and drink cider and sample the foods. The bacon chips—crisps—are a fast favorite. So is the view. Another thing I could get lost inside, even with a tour guide like him—and maybe even a new friend—showing me all the ways around.

Orion catches me with my gaze to the sky. "Checking out the stars?" he asks.

I lean back along the slant, my hair in the damp grass, but I don't care. "I was looking for you. Your constellation."

He smiles. "That was my dad's doing and why Mum got to name Flora. Orion is a mythological Greek hunter. Dad has always hunted faraway places. Combine that with a love of astronomy and you get a name kids tease you for in school."

"It's the best name. Unique and strong," I find myself saying.

"Thanks, I like it now. Had to grow into it. But you won't find me in these skies tonight."

"Why not?"

"Orion is visible at night in the Northern Hemisphere in the winter months. It comes back again here around early August, but only at dawn." He bumps my side. "Orion keeps bakers' hours."

"I'll still be in Winchester in August and up with the bread dough. I'll have to go out and look, if I can even find it between all the fog and city lights. I've never been to a good stargazing spot. Too much city in our travels and in Miami, too." My bright, beautiful home is never dark enough.

"You're kidding." Even in the dim, I catch the mock horror on his face. "Your tourist to-do list grows by the minute. There's a stargazer's dream spot, dark as sin, a bit of a drive, but still not too far on Millie."

"I'd like that." A thick breath, in and out. "It's only in the last few weeks that I've even been able to look up at the stars without breaking down. After my abuela's funeral, I couldn't." I swivel my head, and find him still and waiting. "They call me Estrellita in Miami, around my neighborhood. Little star. Like I'm lighting up the night sky—and the kitchen—while everyone else sleeps."

"You do," Orion says. "It shows in your food."

"Thanks. I need that drive for what I'm going to do when I get home."

"For your family's business? I know about those."

I nod. "My mom doesn't bake, but she's a skilled cake decorator. When Pilar graduates next May, my parents want to open a small custom cake shop in another part of Miami. And Pilar and I will take over La Paloma—it means dove. I'm going to supervise the kitchen staff and all the food. And Pilar's gonna handle the books and business stuff."

"A winning team." He reaches out with one finger but doesn't touch me. "That explains this charm. If all that's waiting for you at home, I see why it's hard to be away."

I sit up, feel for the golden dove. The way my scarf folds, the little bird hangs just below the cheetah-patterned wool. "Being away is like being away from my heart. But it's my fault. I kind of pulled a Flora times a thousand."

He hinges up too, munching his Cadbury bar. "I figured they didn't send you away for three months because you snuck off and ignored your text messages."

"No, but one day the loss won and I got reckless. I missed Andrés, and Abuela's death was eating me up. Then Stefanie left. Everything I knew was slipping away and I felt like I had to reclaim my whole city to make it better, grounding myself."

"And how does one claim a city, then?"

"I ran as much of Miami as I could, for hours. I didn't answer any messages. Pilar ended up tracking my phone, and found me nearly twenty miles from home. I was lying in some random park on the grass, dehydrated and cried out into nothing. Basically, a mess."

"Christ, I see why they were so worried. Someone could have robbed you . . . or worse."

"Yeah," I whisper. This is the first time I've talked about that night. It feels better than I thought to loosen some of the images I still think about when my hands work into dough. The panic of burning lungs and not having quite enough air, my throat parched into more desert than Florida could ever imagine. And Pilar gently combing out my washed hair before she heated up soup.

I find myself wanting to continue. "See, sending loved ones away is not what my family does unless it's a last resort, so I guess that's what you'd call my ticket here. Abuela coming to America as a teen was more of a special opportunity my great-grandparents couldn't pass up—a foreign exchange program through their church. But after a few years, most of my relatives followed, cramming into houses until they found work and could afford their own. We stick close and that family unit is everything." My eyes cloud. "So much of mine is . . ."

"So much of yours *is* Miami," he says.

"Exactly. It's where we started, in a way."

Orion's phone dings. "Go on. It might be Flora," I say.

He tips his chin at me before reading the text. "Not Flora. It's Remy. Remember Jules and her producer Twitter stalking?" When I nod he says, "Jason Briggs tweeted about some Saturday highlights from the small town of Winchester. But not a word about Goldline."

I straighten my spine. "That's ridiculous. Jules is one of the best singers I've ever heard."

"Yeah and sometimes a text won't do. We should ring her." He does and when Jules answers, Orion puts her on speaker. "So that's just bloody fucking shit," he says.

"Now, those are some fitting lyrics, Ri," Jules says over the line, deadpan. "Briggs even gave a nod to GLYTTR—*GLYTTR!*"

"Jules, it's Lila. You and your band were way better than anyone else on that stage tonight. I heard some of that GLYTTR group and they're a zero. I'm really sorry."

"Thanks, love."

I go on, "So Briggs's studio is in London? I could always bake him something you know, special, with an extra ingredient to keep him stuck in the loo for long, painful hours."

A harmony of laughter fills the quiet hill.

"She's sinister, that one. I like it." That comes from Remy.

"Me too, and tempting, but I think not," Jules says. "This is how it goes. The entire industry is subjective and all about catching someone's fancy at the right time. I'll just put on my big girl pants and roll out my new songs right over that Jason Briggs. And from now on, I don't want to hear another word about my purple book from the lot of you."

We agree and tell her so. Then we hang up and Orion catches me, again, with my face in the clear, black sky. "You trolling for other guys with constellation names?"

"Ha bloody ha," I say, mimicking him, which earns an amused snicker. "I thought I saw a shooting star, but it was only an airplane. And I was also thinking of Jules and how she's not waiting and hoping for her big break to just drop onto her stage. She's working so hard for it."

"She's not hanging her future on any wishing stars, that's for sure. She's gonna make herself the star."

I look up and out again. "But it's still fun to wish. If that little falling light wasn't an airplane, what would you wish for?"

"Trying your Cuban food."

I slant my gaze at him. "That's a given."

"Is it really?" He swivels, resting on one elbow. "You *say* these things but I've yet—"

"You will. I'm starting you off with something called the Cubano sandwich. No hints except it requires braising a couple pork shoulders and baking a ham. So, days, Maxwell. No need to waste a wishing star. Now, what's your real wish?"

His happy grin cinches closed. He dashes his hand toward the muted stars. "I've stopped wishing on those long ago. I mean, I still have hopes and dreams. And it certainly doesn't mean I sit around waiting for things to happen. But I've made this deal with the universe. I've learned not to ask more of it than what I'm given, both good and bad."

"Since . . . your mom?"

"Since that, yes. I've grown to find peace and acceptance in not fighting what I can't control. I don't come to God or the universe as a beggar anymore. It's helped me." His mouth wobbles slightly. "And see, sometimes the universe gives me really fun nights showing visiting Cuban bakers around my friend's music, and motorbikes, and our native snack foods. So you might want to be home.

I get that and all the reasons why. But right now you're here and I can't find myself thinking that's all that bad, Lila."

"No. It's not bad at all." The words rush out of me, outrunning countless Miami echoes and Cuban roots, and everything I packed in my bag for this cold, foreign place. It's entirely true. I'm wearing his sweater and it's okay and a new kind of good that I'm starting to wear his city, too.

A night wind comes through, blowing through all the heaviness and swirling our empty plastic cups down the hill. So we share the rest of the cider, passing the bottle back and forth. Like heathens. And it doesn't matter that his namesake constellation is only visible in Australia or New Zealand in June. I'm here, in his hemisphere. I find Orion anyway.

16

It's because of Spencer that my mid-morning run starts and ends with the Crow kitchen. All Spence had to tell Orion when he ran into him by the rose arbor gate was four words: Cuban pastries, Cuban bread.

Winded, I wash up then toss my running partner a water bottle. "I think that's the fastest we've done that loop. Your pace wouldn't have anything to do with pastelitos, would it?"

He swipes the cold plastic across his forehead and hits the sink. "I'd completely forgotten about those."

"Liar." I turn my back on his snort and grab his secret stash. The kitchen gleams, newly organized and arranged to match my setup at La Paloma. With Polly gone, it's finally my kitchen. At least until the end of summer. Earlier I repurposed one of Orion's tea delivery boxes as a bakery box. I lift the lid to reveal a half-dozen pastelitos. The rectangular turnovers are scored at the top to reveal sweet fillings.

"Oh God. Now I see why you made me wait until after our run. No way I'd stop at one bite and it would drag me down to nothing good." He inhales butter and flaky pastry dough.

I point out the two kinds, coco y guayaba. "Coconut and guava. My mom sent guava paste, but I'm using that for friends, not guests. And no, they aren't all for you." I shake my head at his pout. "Two other people live in your house."

He bites into the guava pastel then makes a loopy, half-drugged face. "Should be illegal. Can't remember the last time I had anything this good in my mouth."

My eyes lock onto his, faster than a finger snap. Ready, set, blush. I can't stop it. Please let him think it's only my post-run face flush.

His laugh rumbles inside his chest. Fail. "What gutter did you drag that one into? I was strictly talking about the pastry dough—so light. You made that, too?"

¡Tranquila! Chill, Lila. I clear my throat and shoot off a look that says, *do you even know me?* "I spent all day yesterday making a freezer full of dough sheets for the next couple of weeks."

While he munches, I bring over a large oval bread loaf, perfectly golden with a split top running down the center, still warm from the oven. "Pan Cubano. Cuban bread. Many cultures have a native bread and this is ours. It's similar to French bread but uses lard. We love our pork products."

"I approve of the pork." He raises one brow when I slide the loaf forward. "The whole thing is for me?"

"For you and your *family*. I'm glad I hid it back here. Cate says she only had a half loaf and six pastelitos left for the service crew to share. I need to up my quantities again." I grab a serrated bread knife and slice off a hunk, then slather it with one of my new favorite things—the grass-fed Irish butter I keep nearby in a small crock.

He tucks into the carbs and fat and makes another expression of ecstasy. "So perfect. This will make a brilliant cheese toastie, too."

"I knew you'd say that. My mom owes me a coffee shipment, so I can make you some café Cubano." Mami actually forgot it in my last care package but was sure to include one extra sweater and a new pack of underwear. *Por Dios.* "Anyway, we dunk the bread in the coffee and it's the best thing ever."

Already mostly finished with his slice, he says, "You make it, I'll try it."

I waggle my brows. "Next you're trying Cuban sandwiches. That's tomorrow since the meat will take all day to roast. Come around seven if you can. And you can learn how to make them."

"Oh, I can." He hooks one hand on his chin. "I'm beginning to wonder if all this running is about to be negated somehow."

I sample my own cooking, nibbling the warm buttered bread, a corner of the pastelito de guayaba Orion hands over. It tastes like home. "Most Cuban cooks are on a mission to feed you until you can't walk, breathe, hold normal conversations, or any combination of the three." My shoulder springs up. "What you do with your body is your business. Sorry, not sorry."

"Like that, is it?"

Our eyes meet for another sparring match. I lose—the first to break, giggling. He does too before he returns to his pastelito. His tongue darts out to nab bits of guava filling at the crease of his mouth. A fine mouth, really. Full and the perfect amount of wide. It's not like I haven't noticed before. Now, noticing stretches into wondering. I can't see how my wondering could mean or be anything more right now. But hot, red blood still pumps from broken hearts like mine.

Spencer and Gordon trample through my musings, trudging through the back door with grocery bags bursting with farmers market finds. Spence tips his head at Orion and tells me, "Success. Not only did they have your figs, they were on bulk special."

Gordon dumps the figs into a mixing bowl and plunks it on the butcher block island.

"Bulk is right. Thanks guys," I say before Spence takes his purchases out into the service hall.

Gordon has already found the guava pastelitos I'd put aside for the loft kitchen. Hand on the plate rim, doe eyes on me.

I concede with a huff. "*One* more. Save some for your parents."

Gordon wastes no time in taking a bite. "My favorite of all the foods I tried in Miami. Plus, I paid my dues to the elliptical machine." He tugs his sweaty workout shirt.

"Huh. All the while I thought these fancy new gym clothes were just for show," Orion says.

Gordon gets up close and shoves a huge chunk of the pastry into his mouth. "Piss off, Ri," he says, muffled but comprehendible enough. We snicker as he leaves.

I remember the figs and step up to the bowl, eying the stash from many angles. Warily.

"Lila," Orion says, "they're harmless fruits, not tiny monster egg pods about to hatch and attack."

"That's what you think." I look up at him, sighing. "But I have to make friends with the fig because of my guava rationing. Only so many fruits work well as filling for pastelitos." I pick one up of the purple-black figs; the size and texture are similar enough to my beloved guavas. "My deal with the Wallaces was to integrate Cuban and British baked goods. But I'm going to try actually combining ingredients and technique sometimes, instead of just serving them side by side."

Orion nods. "So, fig pastelitos? A sort of British-Cuban mashup?"

My mouth twitches at the word, pastelitos, all wrong but completely adorable in Orion's warm British lilt. "Yeah, my abuela would have done the same. She loved changing her recipes as much as cooking dishes the traditional way." I cut into one of the figs, revealing two purply-reddish bellies I can scoop out to cook down with sugar, oil, and pectin.

My phone dings from the pocket of my running tights. It's Mami—early for her to be up—but a busy cake day will do that.

> Luisa came in last night. Stef will be traveling to a place where wifi is better. She's going to contact you soon. There's more, after I do a few orders. Besitos

Luisa Lopez, Stefanie's mother. I'm still not used to my new normal where Stef and I have to go through others to have a simple conversation.

I read the text again then out loud to Orion, translating. "No one from Stefanie's family has set foot into La Paloma since she left for Africa. They've been shopping at our rival bakery. Until last night."

"No way that other joint is as good as yours."

I cringe, shaking my head. "So that tells you how awkward things have been. Everyone knows." I show Orion the e-mail I sent Stef the other day. Still no response.

Orion leans in, forearms plunked onto the butcher block, eyes never leaving mine as he bites into his bread. Swallows. "Maybe she's afraid and going through her mum was easier for now. What do you think the *more* is from your mum's text?"

"Not sure, but I'll find out, from either Mami or Pilar. But . . ."

"But what?"

"I . . ." Words I've never told anyone make it all the way to the edge of my tongue. But they stop short. It feels too far to jump.

"Right," he mutters and hunts around, reaching for a small wooden bowl of sea salt. "Way back in the way back," he starts with a spark in his eye, "salt represented friendship. One of the first superstitions I learned. Salt was a prized commodity, and spilling it was not only costly and considered unlucky, it was thought to signal the impending loss of a friend." He pushes the little bowl toward me. "To prevent that, you throw a pinch of salt over your left shoulder."

Mami uses salt to draw oil stains to the surface and make them cleanable. But it's not only the salt that makes it feel safe to bring out some of my hidden truths. It's Orion, eating my food and feeding me back something of himself. Even though it's only a superstition, it tells me he's not just curious or making small talk. He cares.

Just as I'm about to say more, he steps close. "I do have to get on to work, but come by the shop later?" Even though we're both flushed post-run, he invites me in for a hug I didn't know I needed, more than the tastes of home. "You'll straighten it out, Lila. Old friendships are valuable, way more than old salt. But so are new ones."

My head finds a home on his shoulder. He smells like soap and clean sweat. Around the time I'd usually pull back, I find I don't want to. I fit my cheek right above his collarbone. Sensing the shift, he shortens his grip, his palm planted firmly in the center of my back. As moments come and go, my pulse lulls from a vigorous salsa to a spring formal slow dance. The whole kitchen just breathes. Finally, I lift up and he smiles, tucking a stray hair behind my ear.

When Orion leaves, a stab of fear nicks through all my settled parts. Minutes ago, I felt more than just okay and maybe a little bit happy that I was in Winchester. For thirty real seconds, I wanted to be inside Orion's hug with his superstitions and listening ears more than I wanted to be on a British Airways flight home.

Way back in the way back, salt represented friendship.

I grab the wooden bowl and toss a pinch of salt over my left shoulder, just like Orion said. It's silly and ridiculous, but I do it anyway. But I don't do it for my friendship with Stefanie. I don't want to lose Miami. My oldest friend of all.

＊

I'm riding a bicycle. I'm riding a green bicycle on Jewry Street. I'm riding a green bicycle on Jewry Street with six pounds of pork shoulder and a five-pound ham in my basket.

Also, I'm not a sweat-sicle like I would be riding a bike in West Dade. I'm beginning to know Winchester. Now I can pedal off from the Crow and vary my route, watching brick homes and flower arches and monuments without worrying about getting lost.

I stow the bike in an empty space across the street from Maxwell's. Two bags full of roasts, gourmet pickles, and yellow mustard come along. As I wait to cross, tapping thumps from the window behind me. I pivot and find Jules at a table, motioning me inside an organic juice bar.

A dinging bell welcomes me into the tiny shop that smells of cut grass and oranges. I slide into her spare chair and set down my groceries. "You caught me!"

"Just in time," Jules says brightly. It's the most casual I've seen her—marbled gray sweatshirt and boyfriend jeans, hair coiled into a topknot. "Carly from my band just left. We had an exam study session, and now my brain is totally fried. Keep me company until my mum comes?"

I grin; I like her style. Her confidence.

"Want to order a drink?" she asks. "There's nothing quite as jolting as the wheatgrass shot."

I believe her but shake my head. "Next time. That much green goodness might revolt against all the carbs and fat I ate earlier."

"Too right," Jules says before she starts telling me about her upcoming summer gigs. I share about my work at the inn, and some tidbits about Florida. Soon the rate and volume of our chatting balloons inside the small shop. We learn we're both unapologetic food snobs. And her parents are just as addicted to British soaps as Mami is to telenovelas. I don't even have to explain how this can spill out into the rest of our homes, even when the TV is off. She gets it, and more.

Jules understands how it feels to have a protective older sister (hers attends uni in Scotland). And all about the sad and confusing parts left behind when we lose someone close. Her favorite uncle passed away from cancer last year. He was her biggest supporter, music mentor, and the first person she told about liking girls as well as guys. It was Uncle Albert who urged and inspired her to write her first song.

Like a familiar refrain, her revelation is still turning inside my head when my phone dings. I look up from Mami's messages and Jules asks, "News from home?"

I'd normally brush this off. But in twenty minutes, I've learned Jules isn't just a cool girl with stellar talent. Besides similar views on family and eating dessert first, we seem to get each other. There's no way she's lived sixteen years without having at least one row, as Orion would call it, with a friend. So I decide to share more about *my* friend, and all about Mami's update.

"Stefanie—I didn't think she'd last there," I add after a short pause.

"In Africa?" Jules asks, scooting closer.

"Yeah. It's one of the reasons I didn't want to leave Miami. I thought after a couple weeks she'd show up back on my porch and realize all we'd planned was bigger than fieldwork. She'd realize maybe Africa wasn't for her. I mean, the Stef I knew was a picky eater and couldn't go two days without her hair dryer."

Jules crinkles her nose and slowly raises one hand. "I may or may not know someone similar."

It's like a shot of life itself to laugh—better than wheatgrass.

"Most of all," I continue, "we had our Miami plan. I wanted to keep that close. Before coming here, I ran and shopped at our regular places, and sat at the same plot of South Beach we always went to."

"Like it would bring her back somehow?"

"Thinking us, the university nursing program, what we'd been since we were kids would bring her back. But she's not coming home anytime soon. I tried, though. I stayed inside those Miami places for both of us."

"I get that." Jules leans in like her next words are a secret. "Do you know why she left like she did?"

I've dragged this question everywhere, even across continents. "I was too upset to stick around long enough for a real answer. And I can't come up with anything that makes sense." I trace the grain along the wood tabletop, stained the color of beach sand. "I guess people aren't always who you think they are. What Stef did to me hurt. But I know it wasn't all her. And I hated the way we left things."

"Right—broken, like you said," she muses. She wears the same kind of concentration I've seen on her face while writing a song.

"Thing is, when you put something back together it's never exactly the same as it was before. What if she wants to fix things, but it means everything's different from how you used to get on? Can you do that?"

If there's anything the last couple of months have shown, it's that I don't do well with "different." Still, I answer, "I hope so. But I don't know what that would even look like. I only know what our old friendship looks like."

"Well, she needs to contact you first, and it sounds like she will. And her mum did tell yours that she's happy." Her brows narrow. "Question is, are you happy for her?"

"Always. No matter what went down." My voice comes out small.

Jules offers a warm smile. "Then it sounds like you two will be just fine."

She waves through the window at the black BMW pulling up to the curb.

"So, that's me," she says, and gathers her things. "Look, you know what it's like here. Small city, tight community. I know I'll keep some of my mates forever." Her blue eyes meet mine—thoughtful but vibrant, just like her music. "But there are others that I don't see much anymore, and I've realized that's okay." She smiles pensively. "Sometimes I put them into songs, and that's where I keep them. Plus, there's always room for new friends."

My heart swells, testing the space between my ribs. Orion had said almost the same thing. Lingering on the rewind of him, I miss Jules rising and walking toward the door.

"Hey, Jules . . . thanks."

"Yeah," she says over a smile, letting the outside in. "See you, Lila!"

A few moments later, I cross over to Maxwell's. After Jules, my steps are lighter than they've been all day. Orion's at the counter helping an older man in a raincoat (although it's actually sunny outside), rows of foil tea bags lined up in front of him. A busy Orion greets me with his eyebrows.

I entertain myself by checking out a few corners of the shop I missed the last time. Built-in shelves display delicate porcelain tea ware, and small Asian teapots in deep russet and iron black metal. A lone table offers books about tea preparation, as well as stacks of linen towels and tea cozies.

I glance around at Orion's thick sigh. Besides a navy checked button-down, he's wearing a strangled *help me* face; the customer is being overly inquisitive or some other kind of annoying. Of course, I make it worse. Cubans can play cheeky as well as certain Brits.

Behind the oblivious man, I grab one of the wrapped pork roasts and pretend it's a long-lost love. I pantomime sweet nothings and bat my long lashes, gazing dreamily into its "eyes." One corner of Orion's mouth jiggles, but he keeps his cool as he grabs another tin—Earl Grey this time. Oh, he's good, but I'm better.

I twirl and sashay, silently dancing like I'm Clara and the pork is my super special Christmas nutcracker. I win. My target's neck blazes pink and he's forced to hide his crack-up with an obviously fake coughing burst. When the customer finally finishes and moves to the cash register, Orion takes the chance to shoot me a glare full of warning and toy knives.

"You are a dangerous human, Lila Reyes," he says, meeting me at the tasting bar.

I sit and lift the sleeve of my Pilar-pick striped top. "My warning label must've rubbed off."

"Ha bloody ha." He sets his jaw like he's trying to keep his face straight. Fails. "You hardly deserve a cuppa after those antics but I'm a sucker and just can't help myself. Plus, we still need to find your signature tea."

Intrigued, I watch him grab a tin and follow the same steps as last time. After a few minutes he pours the tea. This one fills our white cups with deep burgundy. "What is it?"

"Assam," he says. "A single-variety black tea grown in India. Give it a try."

I do and tell him, "It's full and . . . malty. That's the best word I can find."

"Exactly. It's robust, and that's why it's used primarily in Irish breakfast blends, which are some of the strongest out there." He pushes the milk toward me. I add a generous glop.

I sip again, the tea warming my tongue with comfort and flavor. I get why Brits look forward to this ritual every afternoon. "I swear you can taste the land it came from, all the plants around it. But I don't think it's a contender for my favorite. Good, but maybe a little too smoky?"

"Ahh, I'll keep at it, then." He peeks into both of my shopping bags. "This might sound off, but that's a hell of a lot of meat you have there."

I laugh. "Mr. Robinson, the butcher, hooked me up. I'm making a hell of a lot of Cubanos tomorrow. You'll probably eat at least one and a half, if not two."

"At least," he says.

Our chatting and drinking makes the space between us light and easy, the way the milk settles the strong Assam in our cups.

A man enters the shop floor from the back and no introduction is needed to tell me he's Orion's dad. Orion plus thirty years equals the tall blond in a thin black sweater and chinos. He spots me and Orion, smiles, and approaches.

"Phillip Maxwell," Orion says to me. "Dad, this is Lila."

Mr. Maxwell shakes my hand. "So you're the brilliant baker who made the delicious pastries on my kitchen counter."

"I'm glad you liked them."

Orion hooks a thumb toward me. "If I put on a stone and my trousers don't fit, it's her fault. And watch out, Dad, she's sending Cuban food home for you and Flora, too."

His eyes are kind, the mirror of his son's. "That's so generous. You might find me jogging behind you soon." His smile wanes as he pulls out his phone. "Elliot just sent this along to a load of shop owners. Have a look. Definitely not in the running for any gallery space."

We both lean in and, there it is again—black graffiti on a large whitewashed brick wall.

"Elliot owns a tool shop near Farley's. This is his back wall, at the alleyway," Orion tells me, and pegs me with a knowing look.

I study another close-up shot; the same infinity symbol is there, plus some other wonky symbols or designs I can't make out. "Sounds like Roth and his crew, from what you said."

"But they always manage to keep this rubbish up without being caught. Ri, Elliot wants to know what you used to clean Victoria's shop. Get back to him?" Mr. Maxwell yawns as he eases away. "Sorry, jet lag. And also invoice time. It was lovely to meet you, Lila."

"You too," I say then tell Orion, "If your dad loves his shop half as much as I love mine, it must be hard for him to leave it, even if he's really into travel."

"Leaving Mum's the worst of it for him. As for Maxwell's, it's partly mine now. And him leaving gives me the chance to manage everything on my own." He glances left, then right. "Anyway, enough of my shop when we can talk about yours. I looked up your bakery. You get rave reviews! And clearly we have similar tastes in interior design."

"Thanks. Pilar runs the website, of course. And yeah, a few years ago, my parents remodeled the showroom, all modern industrial. Even though the bones are the same ones my grandparents started with."

"Old and new together," Orion muses. "A mash-up, kind of like modern Winchester."

"And fig pastelitos."

And maybe an old friendship between two West Dade girls that can only survive with new rules. If it's going to survive at all.

17

"You do realize I'm a useless dolt in the kitchen," Orion says a few seconds after stepping into mine at the Crow. He turns, eyes widening at the Cubano sandwich assembly line I arranged on the butcher-block island.

"Useless, huh?" I sweep my hand inches above the flat top grill on the range. Almost hot enough. "Can you make a sandwich, or do you need a tutorial on cheese slicing and mustard spreading?"

He goes for side-eye but ruins it with a sputtering laugh. "Christ, it smells fantastic in here. I followed it like a rat up the walkway."

"The Cuban siren song. I lure my prey with pork fat."

"I'm a goner, then." Orion washes his hands. Winks. "But worth it if I get to eat that before my demise."

He's at my side. I drag over two of my Cuban bread rolls and hand Orion a spreader. "No Remy and Jules?"

"Remy's doing late shift at Bridge Street Tavern—that's his

family's pub—and Jules has practice with Goldline. But I mentioned pork and homemade bread and I think actual tears were shed in group text."

"Bueno. No one cries over me not feeding them. I'll make them a care package."

Gordon whips through like our personal hurricane. "Don't mind me. Not staying," he says, shielding himself from us with raised arms like he's interrupting. "Thought I'd ride one of the guest bikes to the gym for a bit of extra."

He's gone before we can tease him, so we settle for slanted gazes. "He ate two Cubanos with the Wallaces. Which explains," I gesture to the back door, "that."

"Does it, though?" Orion peers into the pan containing the roasts I slow-cooked for six hours. I tear off a hunk. He chews. Swallows. "I was right before. You're dangerous."

I aim for full-blown assassination, leading Orion through the steps of Cuban sandwich making. A mayo-mustard hybrid goes first, then Swiss cheese, thinly sliced pickles, pork, ham, and another layer of cheese. His first effort is worthy; we brush softened butter on the outside of the rolls and I tote them to the stove.

Orion follows. "Oh, it's hot?"

"And melty. At home, we use a big sandwich press, like a panini maker. But here I have to improvise." I grab a potholder and the big cast iron pan I've been heating. Our sandwiches sizzle on the flat top; I press down on the tops with the pan. "With this method we have to flip them, but it works in a pinch."

I griddle both sides of our Cubanos to a perfect crisp, cheese oozing over all the meat. Two counter stools and white plates later, I watch Orion take his first bite. He loses all words, a British drama school demonstration of a classic swoon. His free hand drops over his heart.

I laugh and dig into mine. We eat in food-drunk silence for a bit. Miami fills my senses, feeding all the rest of me.

"I call Cubanos the Miami fourth meal. People used to eat these after dancing at salsa clubs. Still do, actually. They're also one of our most popular catering items for parties. Graduations, birthdays . . ."

"When's yours?" Orion asks, then adds, "Your birthday. I meant to ask earlier then forgot, and now I'm bloody shocked I can remember my own after your food."

I tip my head at the compliment. "August tenth. The big eighteen."

"You'll still be here."

"Now you know how serious my parents were about sending me away. How . . . I guess the word is desperate. How desperate they were, knowing they'd miss my birthday, and buying a ticket anyway."

Our eyes meet over bread. "I imagine it will be hard for your sister. Wanting to celebrate with you."

"The truth?" His eyes widen and I rise and grab a handful of sliced rolls for Orion's family and friends and slather them with the mustard spread. "I was supposed to go to Disney World for my eighteenth with Andrés. We had it planned for months." I stack sliced meat and cheese on eight slabs of bread. "Pilar jumped in and said we'd go instead with Stefanie and one of her friends. Girls' trip."

I set my finished sandwiches on a tray for heating. "Then Stef bailed and I didn't want to think about it. So I didn't leave any epic plans behind, if that's your next question."

"That wasn't my next question." He plunks one elbow on the butcher block. "Which is something I won't ask because I'm meddling and wretched."

"I'll answer that question and any others you have." Santo cielo, the words just fall out. I pull square parchment sheets to wrap the Cubanos for takeout. The last ten seconds replay and I realize Orion Maxwell is a wretched genius and a better interrogator than any one of my relatives. I know their ways. But Orion—challenging me? Making the hairs rise on my arms, curious and dared? It's a tantalizing food I can't resist. "Go on."

Blue eyes like smooth marbles. "Andrés. Do you still love him?"

My lungs deflate. Heat fills me, a hundred degrees above the smoke and sear rolling off the flat-top grill. I loved Andrés for years. And I tried to keep my feelings the same, binding them against me until he came back, just like Stefanie. But in all my missing and wanting him, I never thought to check in with my heart to see if all my trying was really working. Tonight, hidden inside my cooking and the peaceful quiet of his town, Orion asks me. Any girl trapped in a love holding pattern should say yes, sure and quick. *Yes! I still love Andrés.* Shouldn't these words just fall out too?

But they don't. "Andrés is still there. The feelings are there but different, like they've changed shape." *This* comes quicker than a blink. "I know what it feels like to fall in love. But I'm not sure what falling out of love feels like." Abuela never taught me this part. And she left my world before I could have asked.

The way his mouth curls, he's biting the inside of his cheek. He takes one of the sandwich parchment squares. Starts to fold and crease. "I told a girl I loved her, but that's long done. And when it ended—her idea," he nods into the words, "it was rubbish. But I noticed I was eventually able to think and do things without my mind always running into her first. She was there, like you said, for a while. Then not as much and now, next to never."

After one last crease, he produces an Origami tulip bud made from kitchen paper. "So when your mind stops running into Andrés so much, you'll know." He places it into my hands.

I sit and ponder the little craft. "Maybe I will, and this is adorable, and where did you learn paper folding?"

Orion takes a second wrapper. "You aren't the only one who picked up a few tricks from an amazing woman."

I search him for sadness too, head to toe, but I can't find it. He works with childlike animation, shaping and turning and making me another tulip.

"Did your mother show you that so you'd have something to do with dinner napkins to, let's say, impress a date one day?" I ask because I am also desgraciada. Wretched.

He doesn't even look at me. "Did your abuela teach *you* to make incredible sandwiches so you could make a guy's stomach do backflips?"

"No," I say through a laugh. "Not necessarily for that. But if my food inspires spontaneous tumbling, I'll take it."

"There's your answer, then." He places a second tulip into my hands and my smile blooms like a pink bouquet.

I'm tuned differently after a little more than a month. On my West Dade street, blaring voices ghosting through walls wouldn't even make me look up from a book. Here I *get* up and peer out the side window. I know these people now, their shapes and silhouettes. Jules and Flora are in front of the churchyard with three guys who are definitely not Orion, Gordon, or Remy. I reach for the window crank but remember it screeches louder than a trumpet high note. I go for the other window.

I cross over, open, and listen. I can't see them from here, but I know it's Jules who says, "How long were you guys waiting, then? Minutes, hours?"

"If you'd unblock our numbers, I wouldn't have to—"

"Wouldn't have to what, Evans?" It's Jules again and . . . *oh!* Roth and his cohorts.

"Will you bloody listen?"

"They're not saying your Goldline stuff isn't stellar." This from Flora. "It is, but—"

"Not now, Flora. And I am not the reason you guys haven't signed with North Fork yet," Jules says.

"The hell you aren't! They heard 'Blackbird.' You, me. It's the sound they want." Roth's voice sharpens even more. "I'm not about to let your playtime gig mates ruin my chance."

Whoa. No me gusta—I don't like it. Before I think about whether I should, I *do*. A running jacket zips over my oversized tee and the yoga pants I'd thrown on for FaceTime with Pilar. Only now, my sister will have to wait.

I slide into flip-flops and creep downstairs. Between the Wallaces' flat and the foyer, I plot my strategy for jamming up a sticky situation without making it worse. My plan naturally takes me to the kitchen. Always my war room.

Lightning quick, I grab the leftovers I made for Jules and Remy and box an assortment of the fruit-filled butter cookies I baked while pork was roasting all day. I still have racks full, more than enough for two teatime servings, even after Orion inhaled a handful before he left.

I use the side door; dozens of tragic outcomes pass behind my eyes. But I keep walking. Spine straight and armed with live baked-good ammunition, I reach the group and ignore five puzzled faces. Conversation halts. I hold the paper bag up to Jules. "Had these ready for you then heard you out here. Cuban sandwiches, as promised." I check my watch. "Remy should be off by now? I mean, these are better off in your refrigerator than mine."

"Um, yeah. Thanks. He, err, is." Jules reaches for my sandwiches in steady slow-mo. Her face is an original song. A timid melody of confusion arranged with *I see what you're doing* harmonies.

A quick look at Flora reveals a mouse-like gaze and posture, smaller than I anticipated. I open the box of Abuela's favorite cookies—so buttery, the scent clouds over afternoon rain and honeysuckle. The guys instinctively step forward. Ha! The Cuban siren song strikes again. "I'm the new baker at Owl and Crow and I've been experimenting with fillings. I tried fig, strawberry, and lemon." Now to turn up the temp. "I mean, I'm new around here and can hardly predict which ones the guests will like best, you know? Maybe some locals can weigh in?"

Will/William/Whatever, Heaven's Gate concertgoer and the reason Flora's probably breaking curfew, gives a *What the hell? Biscuits!* shrug. He plucks out a lemon variety from my box. Flora immediately chooses strawberry.

My smile's laced with more sugar than I add to any recipe. I point the box to Roth and the other flannel shirt guy, who looks enough like Will for me to peg him as his brother. Both dig in, then Jules takes a fig and strawberry.

There's no tense talking now, no accusations. Only chewing and pleasant reaction noises carrying down the pavement.

"What are we all eating?" Gordon shuffles up in joggers and a denim jacket. He yawns. Rakes his hand through his hair, creating a red tempest cloud. "Heard a scuffle out here."

"No scuffles. Just some taste-testing and voting." I offer Gordon the box. One of each flavor for him.

He bites then consumes the other two in less than thirty seconds. "They're all brilliant. Also, do you ever stop baking? What is it, half-past ten?"

"Something like that," I say then shoot Flora an innocent but knowing look. Orion's gonna blow his top. Past her curfew *and* running around with this lot—I throw it all on my face and cock my hip.

Flora answers with a messy sigh. "I would maybe eat the strawberry one again. I'd better get on."

No way am I giving Will and Flora any "FaceTime" at her door. I turn to Gordon. "Hey, can you walk—"

"I'll see you home," he tells Flora, right at her heels. "Less chance of hellfire if your dad peeks from his window and sees little old me leaving." He pivots toward me and swipes a hair band from his wrist, cinching back the frizzy mass. "And my vote goes to lemon." A silly, courtly bow and bent arm make Flora crack a reluctant smile. "Milady?"

Bien hecho, Gordon. But seeing his goofy grin, now I'm wondering if it's more than just a random "nice touch." The other three guys are actually voting on cookie flavors. Strawberry and lemon are the clear winners. I plant myself next to Jules, a united front, and I'm not leaving. If Roth and his buddies want to pester her, they'll have to go through a bag of sandwiches and me.

Silence.

Roth scratches his temple—the one without the crow wing flop of hair dangling over it. He looks his buddies over. "Okay. Yes. We'd better get on as well, then. Jules, we'll be seeing you."

"Don't bother," she says.

When the band leaves, Jules flicks my cookie box. "Bloody biscuits. I can't believe you came out here and fed those wankers biscuits and turned them to kittens."

"It's just my way."

"I was about to use *my* ways before you turned up."

Wait. Is she pissed at me? Did I go too far? Stick my spoons and spatulas where they didn't belong?

Jules slants her body against the courtyard wall, closing chunky wool tightly around her. Her long cabled cardigan reminds me of another gray sweater. "Your tricks are all well and good," she says. "But I'm used to digging myself out of my own shit piles."

"I . . . I'm sorry," I say and mean it. Unlike my new British friends, I dole out apologies like they're rare and costly ingredients. I don't part with them easily and add them sparingly. "I heard you guys and saw Flora. Orion told me the whole backstory and I just wanted to help." It's what I do, sometimes without even thinking. I take over. "I should have let you handle it."

"Well." Jules waves a hand. "There will always be a next time for me to handle if I know that lot."

I slant too; the wall is cool against my back. "Also sorry about that."

"Flora." Jules makes a rough noise of frustration. "As much as I love that little sprite, I could wring her neck right now. She let it slip to Will that we'd be jamming in Tristan's garage. We have a set-up there." She gestures with her head. "It's just 'round the corner. They were waiting, just casually 'hanging out' between Tristan's joint and my flat. Followed us this way with that bloody shit you probably heard."

"Subtle. Doesn't Flora get that you're not interested?"

"Here's the thing. Flora has a tough road and two men who love her very much. And I don't mean that arse, Will. I try and I've known her since I was a girl. But she just won't settle. She goes with the wind and forgets . . . she forgets that what she does in one, small moment can affect tomorrow."

The words nudge softly, like Abuela waking me at dawn to start bread dough. "That sounds like a song lyric. Where's your book?"

"Ha. Perhaps you're onto something." Jules pulls the purple notebook from her messenger bag, waves it proudly. "My mum and dad still ask sometimes why I don't just join up with Evans. I mean, he's got a trust fund bank roll, the latest and greatest equipment."

"Why don't you?"

"Easy. I don't trust *him*. He hit on a girl I was seeing for a bit, before Remy. Her dad owns one of the local clubs. Then he totally denied it."

I give her a sympathetic wince.

"And professionally, he's a great singer, but he wants to run the whole of it. In Goldline, we collaborate. Listen to one another and make sure everyone's heard. Roth swears I'd have a lot of creative say. Says we'd do my songs and all that. But . . ." Her eyes complete the thought.

"It sounds like he'll say anything to get you to sign. Then you'd end up following his lead all the time."

"Yeah and I'm no follower. I think my music would get lost," she notes with an audible breath. Her gaze breaks away as she studies the bag of Cubanos at her feet. She pulls one out. "Almost forgot about these. Orion texted right before I ran into Roth. Said you killed him good and dead with whatever's in this package. And now I'm thinking what the hell does it matter that it's nearly eleven and I'm knackered?" She unwraps the parchment.

"There's actually a version of that sandwich called the media-noche, with softer egg bread. They got their name because they were usually eaten late at night, after clubbing." I urge her to dig in. "So I figure, salsa dancing, band rehearsal. Close enough, right?"

Jules grins and takes a hearty bite. "This is aces, my friend."

She's accepted my sorry; we're good and we lean against moss-painted stone that was built eons before either of us was ever imagined. A friend, eating my food after late-night music. Miami, Winchester—like salsa dancing and band rehearsal, they're different but also kind of the same.

patches. Three hundred steps, Orion tells me. We take them slowly, not wanting to workout, just to talk. Halfway up, we trade info about Jules and Roth and Flora. Unfortunately, my magic fruit-filled distraction biscuits failed to keep his dad from finding out about Flora's little late-night jaunt, leaving Mr. Maxwell somewhere between annoyed and pissed.

"You planning on eating flies for lunch?" Orion asks.

We've reached the summit and my mouth wants to hang wide open. To the north, the city lies below, a daytime version of my view from St. Giles Hill. But southward ... qué bonito. The southern expanse opens to endless downs. Green, greener, greenest, farther than I can see.

My eyes are too small for this England summer day. "I could eat this whole place for lunch. But I brought Cuban food."

Orion bops against my side, eyes hooded. "I knew you would." He takes my cue for our landing spot; I want to look southward for about twenty-seven hours, at least. "I'm prepared, this time," he says and unrolls a thick tartan wool blanket from the backpack. "When I say I'm thinking of your arse, you'll have no reason to slap me."

"Plenty of other reasons." My laugh runs free as I sit. He's eyeing my cooler bag with predatory attention. I take my time. "Leftover Cubanos, freshly heated."

Orion pantomimes a knife into his heart.

"Lemon pound cake I made for teatime." I reveal a little sack with two slices and forks.

"Holy." He breathes out the word.

18

Today is too bloody summer to run, Orion declares. He has other plans, plus a suspicious knapsack tossed onto Millie's caramel leather seat. I had one job: pack lunch. This time I fit onto the bike and around Orion easily. I wear his backpack and balance Cate's insulated tote on one shoulder.

We're in thin layers for rising temps, open chambray and checked cotton shirts flapping over tees, jeans, and almost matching Chucks. I breathe in the sun-wind-freshness of it all. Can I bottle some to take home?

We ride to the edge of town, parking Millie off a tree-stamped road. A grassy hill rises high and proud. "Today your tour stops at St. Catherine's Hill." Orion uses his radio announcer voice. "The site of an iron age fort and now a prime picnic spot." He gestures to a small wooded grove crowning the top.

Too steep to climb without help, the hill's man-made steps resemble a line of railroad tracks carved into grass and wildflower

That's all—holy. Perfect. "And finally, these are from breakfast service. Today the Crow guests got to try empanadas." I show him the miniature dough semicircles. Sugar dusted egg wash gleams on top and the edges are fork-pressed. "Cuba meets England, again. These are strawberry and cream cheese."

He bites into an empanada and makes a noise straight out of a steamy love scene. I call him on it. "You're wicked and crude, Lila Reyes. But so am I and this pastry's damn good."

We eat in companionable silence until I remember food wasn't the only thing I dragged up this hill. "I want to float something by you," I tell him.

"Yeah?" He's the lazy one now, body stretched long and lean on the blanket, arms butterflied behind his head. His tee rides up and his jeans hang low. So, Orion Maxwell wears red boxers and has been hiding plank-flat abs? "You could float *me* like a buoy. I'm bloody stuffed."

"Lila?" he says louder, crashing into my mental detour over the ridged sinews of skin above his waistband. How many crunches does he do?

"Um." I busy my hands by adjusting my top and detangling my hair. "I mean, I had an idea. Pilar runs our books but there's enough business inside me to say this and maybe not be wrong." After a cleansing breath I press *play*. "I think your business needs something from mine."

"A Cuban sugar witch?" Wry. His whole damn face. "I'm just jiving, Lila. Winchester is only borrowing you." *And so am I.* Unsaid, it's deafening on this hill.

I can't think around it. But dissecting all the reasons why is going to take more time than I have between sentences, so I cling to what's at the front part of my mind. "You already have the web store, but your brick and mortar shop can offer one more thing, besides personal connection. How do you feel when you eat one of my pastries?"

"Like I want more."

I ignore the flip-flutter-drop of my stomach. *Business, Lila.* My smile wobbles. "Right. What if you sold brewed teas and a small assortment of pastries? And they were so good, customers would line up early for tea, and take a treat home before they're sold out, or stay to eat them? And word of mouth—"

"Yeah, I get it. Contracting with a baker or two."

"If you did, I predict your business would grow even bigger. At La Paloma, we have café tables where friends can meet and chat over a coffee and a treat. They sometimes sit there all morning and order more food. Or decide they want rolls plus bread. We keep them there and end up selling more. And keep them coming back more often."

His expression sours. "Yeah, but I told you we're not set up for that."

"Maybe just think about it? With some small tweaks, you could be set up."

"Small? I don't think so. We don't have tables or display cases like your joint, for one. Then there's food handling and more man power to brew drinks. So even if you're right, if I run your idea by Dad, don't be put off if he doesn't see it the way you do, yeah?"

Enough bristle peppers his words, mine naturally sharpen. "Well, sometimes we don't see new things because we're so used to seeing things the way they were." New places. New people.

I straighten my spine, drawing in my knees and caging my hands over my face. Thinking how narrow my life back home actually was. The spaces I've lived and cooked in seem so small against all this green—and countries and continents more—beyond the base of this hill.

Fingertips press against my arm. I ignore them.

"Lila." A whisper so close, hot breath puffs over my ear.

I turn my head and Orion's lifted himself up, his face inches from mine. "Sorry if I got cross. It's just been a lot."

I search for his hand, squeezing. "I know. I'm the last person who needs an explanation."

He nods and squeezes back. "Speaking of new things, you do seem happier here lately. You smile a lot. Especially when I take you to see wide-open landscapes you probably can't find in Miami. Except the ocean, I suppose. The Atlantic goes farther than your eyes work too," he muses softly. "Are those smiles for real?"

"Realest. Even though I miss that ocean and it's colder here. But there are sweaters for that and why are we whispering?"

"Because we're ridiculous fools. And yes, lots of jumpers and wooly sheep to make them."

This would not happen in Miami. A woodland boy talking about sheep, our sides fused together, faces tipped to catch every ounce of blue raining down from a cloudless sky. We've been touching more lately—and not in any way that feels deliberate.

Even with Andrés's face still in the back of my head, my body always seems to drift close to Orion's. And his drifts right back. More than sometimes, his fingers thread into mine or his palm spans the curve of my back. We hug for the perfect amount of too long, but never talk about it. We need to talk about it.

Guy friends have never touched me this way. Sure, Orion *is* my friend, but he's also something else. Whatever that something is sits unknown on my palate, a taste I can't describe. He's not my boyfriend or trying to become the one I so recently lost. He's also not acting like a guy who's hours or days away from a hookup. Eight thousand miles—there and back, what I've left, and what I'm returning to—tells me that. It doesn't whisper, either.

I'm going to do it. I'm going to ask. But just when I think I've found enough words to start, the FaceTime icon flashes on my phone and straight through my nerve.

"Want to meet Pilar?" is my only question for now.

"I do want to meet Pilar."

We flip around, bellies down on the blanket, heads pressed close with the phone between us. The intros are quick and pleasant: accounting queen, meet tea expert. Most important person in my life, meet . . . Orion.

"So Pilar, your sister is trying to bury me in pastries and Cuban dishes," Orion says.

"She can't be stopped and also, Lila, his voice is like natilla. Can you record him for about two days straight?" She gives me *The Look*. I'll be getting another call later in which I will have to explain this guy and I will not be able to explain this guy.

I push it out in a long breath, watch it roll down, down, down this fairy hill. "He never stops talking, so I got you, hermana."

Orion mock-glares as Pili asks, "Where are you guys? It looks like Mami's terrarium behind you."

Orion does the honors, taking Pilar on a panoramic tour of St. Catherine's Hill.

"Oh . . . Lila." And that's all she needs to say. In our secret sister language with our secret sister faces, I'm healthy and okay, my cracked heart cushioned in all this soft green. And she's okay too.

My hand domes over the phone to cut the glare. I notice the vast array of foliage behind Pilar on our dining room table. "Speaking of plants, um?"

"Dios mío. Ashley's wedding. It was Sunday." She turns the view and *wow*.

All is clear, now. My neighbor's daughter's wedding, which I would have attended if I'd been home. "Okay, Mami's rule is usually one centerpiece per person and that," I point, "is way more than a couple."

Pilar smacks her hand on her forehead. "Mami did her thing and we got two. Fine, okay, I can deal. But then Isabella had some of her kids take them. Only, she forgot their Italy trip. The flowers would just die. So last night, little Grace shows up toting four centerpieces in her wagon. Mami was thrilled of course."

Orion is laughing and he doesn't even know the full story yet.

"Are those *carnations*?" I ask.

"It was awful. So tacky. Only Mami's wedding cake was on point." Pilar plucks out a pitiful flower. "They dyed them ombre blue to match los vestidos de las bridesmaids."

Ombre carnations—gasp.

Orion sits up after I vow to call Pili later and stow my phone. "So what's the deal with all those flowers?"

"Ready to hear the Cuban-American centerpiece episode of *Mission: Impossible*?"

"More than ready."

"Every self-respecting celebration—wedding, baby shower, and so on—requires centerpieces on each table. Super important. And it's the mission of many Cuban mothers and aunts to take home as many of these centerpieces as socially possible. All posh party gloves come off, let me tell you."

Orion barks out a laugh. "Like a competition?"

"Of the highest order. Stefanie's mother and mine have been in this unspoken centerpiece rivalry for years, but Mami is the undisputed champion. Since forever, her wedding strategy goes like this: near the end of the party, she sends Pilar and me to 'mingle' with friends at other tables. We then slowly inch their centerpiece toward us while trapping tablemates in conversation. Then when it's last call at the bar or the final dance, we grab the flowers, air-kiss our goodbyes, and bolt."

"That. Is. Incredible." He's grinning over one last empanada.

"I don't know if it's incredible, but it's *us*." My family, my Miami.

"Why centerpieces, though? Besides your dining room smelling like a garden?"

I do some nibbling of my own. My lemon pound cake is moist with Abuela's citrus peel sugar syrup poured on top, fresh from the oven. "Celebrations are a crucial part of our culture. We're gener-

ally a social bunch. Sharing our joy with loved ones is also important. Like, it's not uncommon for Cuban fathers to start saving for
their daughters' weddings years in advance, if they can. Just my
opinion, but I think it's about wanting to bring home a piece of
the party and make it last. It's a token of a happy event that keeps
blooming for a few days."

He smiles over the image. "I quite like that notion. You don't
want the celebration to end. The sharing and memories. It's more
ritual than superstition."

"Oh, you want Cuban superstitions? I can think of a few."

He levels a mock glare. "I've known you for weeks and you're
only bringing this up now?"

"Hey, I've been busy trying to make other fruits act like guava
and feeding guests." One finger pokes his stomach. "Feeding *you*."

Orion snatches my finger and slides his hand to capture mine.
He rises, using a firm grip to pull me up. "Let's go check out that
wooded patch and you can school me."

As we hike up to the small cluster topping the hill, I tell him
first about the mal de ojo. Evil eye.

"I know about evil eyes but say those words again?"

"Mal de ojo. Why?"

"I like hearing you speak Spanish."

Instant blush—I angle away slightly as if that will erase the
pink. "Well, one hour with me and Pilar and some smuggled rum
and you'd beg us to stop." We enter the hilltop grove, our sneakers
crunching damp clods of soil, rocks, and dead leaf mulch. Trees
huddle closely, trapping us in dappled shade. "My family's not big

on the mal de ojo, but the curse stems from jealousy and is usually brought on when people pass by and gaze at newborn babies or young kids. They're most susceptible."

Orion spots a felled tree trunk; we sit under a leafy umbrella. "There must be a charm to ward off the curse?" he asks.

"Typically a black eye charm or tiny carved piece of black jet, or azabache." Again, we're close, thighs together and arms brushing. "Then there's the one about never going out at night with wet hair, and the three-hour rule about swimming after eating. These are both crucial. Not obeying them will surely bring on a stroke or a cough or maybe you'll need a heart transplant."

His laughter comes wildly, dimples on display. He settles and my head is already tipped against his shoulder before my mind realizes.

"My mum was adamant about the no swimming after eating, although her rule only required an hour," Orion says.

I want to joke that he got off easy, but I smack the words back and down.

"See, we're not so different after all," he adds.

No, not on the inside. But our outsides are as opposite as our coasts—my Cuban, tanned and brunette. His British, light and blond. Beach sand and cobblestones, spaghetti straps and sweaters. But I remember we are both stars. Estrellita and Orion, a fierce little star and a warrior constellation. We sit close on this tree a bit longer, golden warm but silent, like one sun in the cooling shade.

19

No tacky centerpieces top our table at Bridge Street Tavern, but this party doesn't need them. With school exams well over, a summer holiday for Winchester youth plus Gordon nabbing a coveted part-time job at an architectural firm is plenty cause for celebration. Last night, we all went to the cinema, but this Saturday evening is all about food.

Everyone is here. And by everyone, I mean not only Orion's friends, but parents and siblings, too. Even Flora doesn't look miserable from her seat down the table. Remy's mom plants our massive party at one end of the pub, then passes off her usual hostess duties to join us. All the parents huddle together at an adjacent table and pay us no mind. It's a tight fit; Orion's smooshed into the corner and I'm fairly smooshed next to him by Jules to my left.

A waitress drops off my lemon water and places two pints in front of Orion, one pale amber and the other golden brown.

"Thanks, Bridget," he says.

"Extra thirsty then, Orion?" Bridget doesn't wait for an answer before serving drinks to the rest of our crew.

I cock one brow. "This is what happens when I visit the loo? *Two* beers?"

"Oh, I'll likely drink two but not together. You've still got a few weeks before you can order one yourself. So technically, I wanted a light pale ale." He points to the first. "As well as a darker, but slightly sweet nut-brown ale. Try both and you can have your favorite."

I wink at his slyness and smile as his thoughtfulness before yet another taste test. "The nut-brown," I decide. It's richer and bites back just a little.

Remy bends around Jules and says, "I see what you're on to, mate."

"Where do you think I learned it?" Orion motions toward sixteen-year-old Jules and the similar pint of golden amber sitting closer to her place setting than eighteen-year-old Remy's.

I sip my beer. "Have you picked what I'm eating?" Bridge Street doesn't believe in menus. A big chalkboard on the central wall lists specials and I decided it's Orion's turn to feed me. Spencer usually cooks and I've had only a couple of pub meals out with the Wallace family. I appeal to my local guide.

Gordon leans forward. "Best make it black pudding, Ri. Lila needs an initiation."

"If he does, he'll be wearing it." I picture the round sausages. No. Nunca. "Lila does not need anything made with sheep's blood or weird meats."

Orion holds up both palms. "My clothes are safe. I already ordered while you were in the loo and I aced it."

Truth. When our meals arrive, I learn how close shepherd's pie is to our Cuban papas rellenas. Spiced ground beef sits under a carb lover's dream of mashed potatoes, baked until the top is golden crisp. I eat heartily while also sneaking fried potato wedges from Orion's fish and chips plate.

"Hey." He pretends to swat my hand away but also passes me the curry dipping sauce Remy's mom makes from scratch.

I will ask for this recipe, I decide, then pause from stuffing my face to take in the scene.

A wily beehive of voices. Clanging glasses and crude jokes. Remy kissing Jules on the temple while arguing with Gordon over the pros and cons of two new gaming systems.

If I could twist people and places, this could be any one of my extended family's big dinners. At Bridge Street Tavern, I sit inside another kind of family. They welcome me in—all of me: my lost and prodigal parts, too. But I'm not any precious thing here. They tease and give me hell like their own, deeming me the middle child and squishing me into an extra chair.

After another moment, my mind clicks back into now. My beer's down to a third and Orion's already ordered himself another. And Gordon's telling his friends about his upcoming job.

"I'll likely be on coffee-stirring and menial shit, but at least I can get a feel for how it all works." Gordon bites off a hunk of sausage and mostly swallows before saying, "They saw photos of my house drawings on Instagram. Got me the spot over another bloke."

I picture the little Miami house framed in my room. The peachy-pink tones and palm trees. "So all that work skipping between songs at your drafting table paid off. What are you going to draw next?"

He tips his Coke at me. "Maybe a few more structures typical of Winchester housing."

"But Winchester's so boring compared to London," Flora says. "Take Notting Hill, for one—all the colors. Here it's the same red brick after gray stone. Blah, blah, blah. We need a few wonky joints. Like a bright purple house with triple mismatched stories and black trimming."

Jules swoops in. "Yeah or one painted in zebra stripes with a rainbow of flowers all messy in front."

"You want bright and colorful, come visit me in Miami," I say, snagging Orion's eye over the words. Gray, dim, shade—those are the colors on his face before he thumbs his chin and half-smiles for me. Blue eyes twinkle. Which face is closer to truth?

Tonight my truth is still this: eighty-five days, and no longer quietly waning. Lately the hours turn like seconds. We lock gazes and Orion raises another curry-dipped potato between us, the twinkle now a burst of playful fireworks. I snatch it before I miss my chance.

"Look, Henry's here," he says while I munch. "I know you'll like this." Orion gestures to a portly, older white man, hair a disorganized clop of gray and black, with a straggly beard to match. Henry drags a pear-bellied stringed instrument to an appointed stool and mic. This local crowd must know him. They cheer then settle, hushing. Lights dim and everyone across from us turns their chairs to watch.

"He's a lute master," Jules tells me. "Traditional British folk music is dying off and it's a real shame. London's all about new sound and rave. But Remy's parents want to keep our history alive."

The first honeyed strums and lute trills drain the tension from my shoulders. Relaxed and loose, I listen, thinking of Miami youth regularly hitting up Little Havana salsa clubs or teaching younger cousins to play dominoes while snacking on plantain fritters. My culture also has too much wanting to die out in the new. We work to keep it growing strong, as tall as Cuban corn stalks in my great-uncle's garden.

After a couple of tunes, the crowd chants Jules's name. Henry spots her and waves her over. I love how they know and recognize her. Jules-never-Juliana *is* one of Winchester's gems.

"Go on, love. Show Lila what else you got going on with those vocal cords," Remy says.

Jules waves it off. "Just a bit of fun," she tells me then snakes out behind seats to consult with Henry.

My mind catches up to the music. "Was I hearing things, or did parts of a couple of Goldline's songs seem inspired by Henry's tunes or the chords?"

Orion nods. "That's what Jules does. She's the mash-up queen in her songwriting. She loves to reference old themes in her modern music. That train song you loved is a nod to old English lullabies."

We turn back when Henry plays a new intro. Jules sings less than two lines into this wood-paneled pub and my mouth falls open. She demos what must be years of training, her classically fierce soprano commanding a timeworn folk ballad.

"This one's from the sixteenth century," Orion whispers, leaning in. "'Flow my Tears.'"

The tune floods over me. Haunting melody, bittersweet lyrics, and that *voice*. By verse two, I can't stop a few of my own tears flowing down my cheek. Orion lays a hand on my shoulder, inviting me under his bent arm. I go without question, the way I fall into my bed. The way my hands curve into a ball of dough. Safe against the cotton of his black pullover, I meld into him.

I peek up at his gentle face, finding I'm not the only one with misty eyes. I'd bet my bakery he's thinking of his mum, who'd probably love to eat fish and chips and hear Jules sing tonight. I squeeze his side. *I know. I get it.*

Orion's lips sweep across the crown of my head as he shifts. Friends do not usually sit like this. Lately, I always seem to be touching Orion Maxwell. It doesn't matter that my days are few here. He seems to always be touching me back, every single one of those days. With who I am, and where I've been, and where we live, what could it ever mean? What does it mean right now?

After more music and "pudding" and goodbyes, Orion and I are halfway to Millie before he halts. "It's nice out, yeah? Want to walk back and Dad can ride the bike home?"

I nod. "He rides Millie too?"

He leads us down the little side lane pocket off High Street. "She was Dad's when he was my age."

Pero.

And there it is. One syllable in his language, two in mine.

"But, indeed," he says, back to me. "See this is where I'm terribly stuck." He reaches out to touch my forearm, elbow to wrist. "If this were normal or usual . . ."

We're not completing sentences, yet I comprehend pages full. "Right. Only it's not. Normal."

His hand drops into mine. "Not at all. I understand what you've been through and all you lost. I also get your ticket was never one-way."

Miami. The third heart on this pavement, trying to love me harder.

"But you and me," I say. "I really like us and I'm having fun—"

He braces my shoulders. "*I* like us, and I'm having loads of fun. Way too much to walk away now."

"Don't?" *Don't leave me too.*

"No, Lila." He hugs me to seal it and stays to say, "So let's do this. Let's create a new category for our kind of us. We don't have to define it. We'll leave it blank and take things day by day."

"Is this what you meant by not asking too much of God or the universe or life itself?"

I feel his nod. "Exactly what I meant."

"I've never done that. I've always demanded what I want from anyone who'll listen. Even when they don't listen I make it known, and that caught up with me. It brought me here." I pull back so he sees me say, "But it also brought me *here*."

He exhales and slants his arm around me, leading us forward

I smile at the image, but my insides still scatter with questio
From corner table to concrete pavement, he hasn't let go. H
elbow hooks into mine, our heads tipped so closely we can easi
chat over the whirl of traffic and commerce. But Winchester i
perfectly small. It's not long before we merge into St. Cross with
only the noises of trees.

And I can't stand it anymore. I've forgotten to remember I'm
bold. I command kitchens! Can't I take command of a question?
Bold, that's who I am. I'm not a helpless wonderer. "Orion."

"Lila." A rumble against my side as we step and step and step.

"What are we doing?"

"We're walking home, love."

One adorable word and my bold splinters. "No. You and me.
What . . . is this?"

Orion stops, swinging around to face me. But he is still so close
because that's all we are lately. A jester dances across his face; ugh,
he knew exactly what I was onto before. Cheeky-ass *ass!*

"Okay maybe we do need to hash out a few things," he says.

I nod.

"First and always, you are my friend."

"You're mine."

"Good, that's good." He smiles. "But how we are, the *way*
we . . ."

"Yeah, all that. I mean friends don't . . ."

"No, they don't. So that means *we're* . . ." He says this to the sky,
stars paled by yellow streetlight.

"But."

again. "Miami is waiting—lucky-arse city. And so are your family and your business," he muses.

"Yes." The golden dove charm knocks against my chest.

"And when it's right, you can find someone again." He tightens his grip. "But I have a few requirements for any future bloke. Hypothetically speaking, of course."

My laugh spurts out. I sniffle. "What requirements?"

His look, like I'm dense. "Obviously, he has to have a motorbike. Now, I'm okay with him not naming it."

"How generous."

"I am that, if anything." He shakes a warning finger. "And he must be able to make a decent cuppa. Because you need your afternoon tea now. And he'll have to take you to just sit and look at this beautiful world, because you tend to work too hard."

"Deal." My voice is a ghost. "Anything more?"

"So much more, Lila."

She'll need to make him sandwiches. I jog through St. Cross, and not normal jogging—the kind where I run like a wildfire and hope the running leaves me hollow and sweated clean out like a tamal husk.

Cate made me promise never to run at night, but I had to. When Orion left me at the Crow, we were resigned and cool with not defining tomorrow and overthinking ourselves. My head knows it's best, but un-planning feels new for me. Un-plans are new for a girl who's had her nameplate written in indelible ink for years: *Lila Reyes, Head Baker*. New for a girl whose life has been lovingly mapped, Cuban Lila, daughter and sister and niece, Miami born and destined.

My heart didn't have a clue how to work out Orion's notion of day by day. I had to drag this onto the streets.

I strike the pavement hard. Mist skirts around me and the settling fog tempers all the heat that rises onto my skin when I am extra bold with questions.

She'll have to bake him treats and pastries. My mind drifts here, onto this requirement. Muy importante. He loves lemon. They don't have to be Cuban pastries, but they need to be decent. She'll totally use too much sugar, this girl who will win Orion's heart.

But my mind shifts again as I change course down another fork. How many plans did I recently make that ended up exploding? An apartment with Stef and a carefully orchestrated trip to Disney for my eighteenth birthday? *Poof.* The future I carved into our kitchen, cooking next to Abuela and watching her go all-the-way gray? *Shatter.* Her headstone date is a monster.

Orion and I are not going to plan or define. Maybe that will give it a real chance of working.

Or, the opposite is true and, in a few weeks, time will be another monster.

She'll have to run with him. Around mile three, he will probably start slowing and definitely start whining. She'll need to push his ass to get through mile four. He'll make it, though. Then she'll have to let him make her tea, this lucky, lucky girl.

This lucky girl that I maybe even hate? Just for being her, for being here when my goals mean I'm always going to end up . . .

there? Emotion burns my throat. No puedo. Tonight, there's not enough pavement for me to work this all out, so I decide to try my best at Orion's un-planning method. It feels like trying a new recipe.

I work my body instead.

Now it's so late the trees are specters in the fog. I run inside an eerie night cloud that makes my spine tingle. I'm safe, though. For miles, all I've heard is the wraith-like breathing of leaves, my sneakers slapping, the metallic *clink, clink, clink* of my jacket zipper pull. But when I reach another fork, the one that leads either to town or onto a highway frontage road, a foreign sound carries around the next bend. *Shhh shhh shhh, hiss.* Then again.

I slow to a walk and pull out my phone, just in case. I flank the retaining wall that curves around the corner. Turning, I see the outline of a figure in a hoodie. Then, streaks of black spray paint on a small section of brick—an infinity symbol. I've got them! I've caught Roth or one of his buddies in their graffiti game, something Orion has been trying to do forever.

The figure turns, sucking in a noisy, startled breath.

I see the face clearly. But . . . "You?"

20

Flora.

"It's you," I repeat unnecessarily. For months, Flora Maxwell's had her brother and half the town merchants on a useless chase. Roth and his gang and their bullying, my ass. The town vandal and graffiti artist, if you could call it that, has been eating the same breakfast cereal as Orion the whole time.

I swear I can hear Flora's heart drum. Her gaze fidgets left to right, like a rabbit about to bolt. But then she sighs, her shoulders drooping in defeat. I'm a fast runner with a working cell phone camera. I've got her.

"Why?" I ask.

She flinches. "You're always right there, aren't you?"

"Excuse me?"

Flora drops the spray paint can, shoves her hands into her kangaroo pocket. "Every time I turn around lately, you're there like a bloody shadow. At the club with Will. By the inn."

Is she actually trying to deflect? "Don't put this on me. Now, I asked you a question." Will I wait until tomorrow or should I drag her back home myself? "You hurt your town. Real people with businesses like yours. Orion was out there scrubbing walls and—"

"Oh, God, please don't tell him," she begs and steps toward me. "Please, Lila."

Whoa. Okay. Was there a shift in some time-space continuum? Orion would know about those. I only recognize the look of Winchester-cold fear.

"Please. I'll stop. Just don't tell Orion." She trembles, her blue eyes wide and wolf-like in the filtered dark. "You don't understand what it's like. There's so much. *So* much they're dealing with already." So much she's dealing with.

"I actually do know what it's like. You have no idea what I'm coming from." I exhale in slow motion and point to the obscure shape on the shoulder-high wall. "Can you just tell me why?"

She stares at the ground, telling her shoelaces, "My dad and brother mean well, but they are always *on* me. Way more than my friends' families." She frees a hand, dashing it aimlessly. "All my steps, checked so carefully. Because of Mum."

The ice in my veins cracks.

"I feel like a little kid sometimes. Like my wishes get lost and forgotten."

"So this is you outsmarting them?" I gesture at the wall. "Showing them they can't control everything?"

She shrugs. "It's like . . . on the train into London, you can see all these stately buildings. But pass one that's been tagged, and that's the first thing your eye goes to, right? You see the building, but you really *see* the paint. The letters or symbols. I found the can in the tea shop storeroom and I remembered that . . . the being seen and known." She approaches the wall and rubs. Still wet, the paint smears black on her fingertips. "Not forgotten."

Dios, the dementia. I reach for the thought of Orion, peacefully accepting all that life gives and not disturbing the universe, demanding more. Flora, with the same root of pain, lives the opposite. Her disturbance is the streak of paint over walls. Controlling it, changing it. *See me.* She fights a universe that denies her—one that brings a disease so cruel it makes her own mother forget her. *I'm still here,* the paint says.

But Flora is still hurting herself, and others. I know this because I've done the same. I understand what it means to be on the grass, dehydrated, filthy, and tear-spent. I ran so far and hard into the loss that had run me over, because I could.

Oh. I look over Flora and for the first time, I see Pilar looking over me at the park. My belly heaves with it, nausea swirling fast. I see myself through my sister's eyes. I'd run so far. How much further and deeper would I go, hurting myself trying to outsmart my own universe of loss? Pilar had no answer that night, only fear. But she and Mami and Papi had England, a chance at a new place for me with a new purpose. Flora needs one too.

"Please. Please don't tell Orion."

He is not a person I want to keep anything from. But I study the weak and strong and resolute and destroyed face of a girl, begging me. *Flora*. Sneaking out, aching to be seen and remembered, marking walls and fences.

I study a memory, nudging me. *Lila*. A girl sprawled out on Miami grass, miles from home.

Would I lie for that girl?

My family did worse in their eyes than lie. Something far over the edge of painful. They put me on an airplane, away from my everything. Away from them.

With a sigh that makes me sound just like my father, I cross my arms at my chest. "I won't tell Orion on two conditions."

"Yes. Okay."

"Promise right now you'll stop tagging."

She nods rapidly. "I promise, Lila. I won't tag again."

"Good. The other thing—three days a week, you will work with me in the Owl and Crow kitchen. I start at six in the morning."

Flora takes a deliberate step back. "I can't cook or bake."

"I'll teach you. Easy stuff at first."

"But I'm already working at Maxwell's most afternoons." She pokes her jaw out. "So now my mornings, too? Who wakes up that early during the holidays? That's not . . ."

Here she goes. Flora's about to say my idea's not fair and, *no*. Sympathetic circumstances or not, she still vandalized. "Three days a week. You'll survive." I tip my hand to her. "Up to you."

She stares at me until the look goes stale. "Whatever."

Sí, claro, that's a yes. This is another language I know well. "Good. Monday, then. See you."

Flora picks up the paint can. "Don't freak, I'm gonna throw it out."

"Do I look like I'm freaking?" I check my watch. "I'll see you home, though."

"It's close. I can see myself home."

I should make sure she gets to her porch. But when she said she felt smothered, I listened. Flora can make it four blocks home. I need to give her this. "Yeah. You can."

I let her flee then walk to the Crow on a close, parallel street, knowing Flora is doing the same. I'd hear anything out of place. Planner that I am, I should probably decide what to say to Orion when he mentions the tagging and Flora's new training experiment. Even the thought of keeping something from him rots in my stomach like spoiled food.

When I reach the rose arbor, a few second-story lights show proof of life from guest rooms. The third-floor flat is dark, though.

I'm familiar enough with the upper staircase to ascend while checking my phone. Late for me is the perfect time to call or FaceTime Pilar. I've had the sound off; I switch it back and notice the message bubble on my home screen. Busy with Flora (an understatement), I must've missed her text. I nearly trip over the next step. The name under the message doesn't read Pilar Reyes.

It says Andrés Millan.

Minutes later, my phone vibrates, but not from any setting. It's me on my bed, shaking, reading Andrés's text again and again.

Andrés: Hey you. I know this is sudden but I wanted to check in

Another message comes through.

Andrés: Are you busy?

My mind spins. I should block his number. I should hurl the entire device out the window. I do neither of these things. Even though feelings have rearranged and shifted, the shadow of Andrés is still there, dark and heavy with sweet memory. And I still fall for the hook.

Me: I'm here

Not even five seconds before he replies.

Andrés: FaceTime?

Me: Call

He does. I answer with one, dusty old word dragged out of a dusty old trunk.

"Hello to you too, Lila," Andrés says in the voice I heard against my lips, and in the shell of my ear, and finally in a terrible goodbye.

"I know this is weird. Out of the blue," he says.

I open my mouth, but the words don't work.

"So, England, huh?" He must've been checking my Instagram too. "How, um, is it there?"

"Cold." But there are sweaters for that—one sweater, and it's soft and warm and gray.

"Right," he says.

"Why?" Because my bold decides to show up now. "Why today?"

I hear his thick sigh. "I was just thinking about you. Wondering if you were okay. I know it was shitty—me. Us. Prom. Abuela. And I found out about Stefanie. That really sucks. So, I wanted to check in."

"I'm okay. I really am." My answer is not a lie.

"Good. I'm glad. You know, you can always call."

My eyes fill. Haven't I been waiting? Haven't I been wanting this for months? But it doesn't fall soft or even fit the same way inside me, as dependably warm and secure as the city he's calling from. Instead, it slicks my throat with bile. "'Kay."

"Can I call you again too?"

Wicked. Wretched. Weak. "Yeah."

21

The side door closes behind him; it's a rainy Sunday morning and Orion finds me easily. It's my day off, but I need the kitchen after last night's new anxiety trifecta:

1. Orion and our un-plan
2. Flora's the vandal
3. Andrés and a three-minute phone call

I return his greeting, ogling a few treats from Mami's second care package—she doesn't know how timely it was. These small items, I *need* them. Yesterday before the pub, I got the brown shipping box that smelled of my West Dade house when I opened the flaps.

Orion shrugs out of a damp windbreaker and I'm all opposites. The sight of him in jeans and an untucked blue polo makes my body settle, drawing near to him like it's homeward. But seeing him in the aftermath of Flora and Andrés ties my stomach into complicated knots. Impossibly, both are true.

"Ahh, more gifts from your mum?" Orion says and rubs my shoulder.

I show him the stack of guava paste containers and the plastic bag filled with three miniature tins of golden yellow Bijol seasoning. I dance the bag in the air. "Consider me way too excited about spices. Now I can make you arroz con pollo."

"Well, I've got this one sorted: chicken and rice." His brows drop. "That sounds rather simple, though."

"After one bite, if you think my arroz con pollo is anything resembling simple chicken and rice, I will hang up my apron before your next mouthful."

"Nah." He's a blink away. "Pointless of me to even doubt you. A lesson I should've learned earlier."

A flash of smile before I feel it fade. Orion does have reasons to doubt me, though. It rumbles now, even more with him beside me.

I show him the last Cuban coffee treasure—a can of Café Bustelo. "You probably had enough caffeine over breakfast."

"Brew away. If I'm a wired fool later I can blame you and that's always fun."

I move to swat him, but he's quicker. *¡Basta!* The new trifecta has me limp and slow. Orion snatches my hand and squeezes. "Speaking of brekkie, Flora joined Dad and me this morning at the café. She usually doesn't. I'm a bit surprised by this new development too. Sacrificing her precious sleep, popping in here to help and learn a few things?" His mouth pulls sideways and his gaze hones quizzically onto mine. I can't help but sense there's more than curiosity behind his raised brows.

What aren't you telling me, Lila?

I don't want to lie to this boy. "Sorry I didn't text. I bumped into her super late." Tagging a wall. Begging my silence.

"She said she was on her way home from Katy's and you were running." He wrinkles his nose. "Alone. You know, I could've gone with you. Not that you need an escort."

So much information. First, I realize what Flora's alibi for sneaking out has been all along. Then there's the part that makes me look directly into Orion's face, staring at a sweet sun. Staring at a precarious black hole. Both are true. *I couldn't run with you. I was running because of you.*

I need to put my hands on anything but Orion. Easing away, I jiggle the coffee can. "We, um, decided on three mornings a week." I pull out the metal stove-top espresso pot I use for coffee-infused pastry fillings. "I thought it was a good idea. I can show her around the kitchen. That's always cool, right? Basic skills?" I measure coffee then set the flame high.

"Err, right. But I think there's an ulterior motive behind her shadowing you."

I suck in an anxious breath, whipping around to face him. "What? I mean, how did she bring it up?" How did she spin it?

"Like you said. She's off for holiday and you make such delicious things for us. She figured it's time she learned a couple useful tricks. While you're . . . here."

Barely voiced, the word sounds miles away.

He adds, "I suspect there's more to it, like she's trying to find ways to prove herself. All her sneaking around with Will. And remember the other night when Gordon brought her home past curfew? I think she's trying to show she's taking initiative. Gaining focus and trustworthiness."

Blessedly, it's not much longer before the coffee's ready. I rummage for two demitasse cups and a small glass pitcher. Like Orion's tea preparation, I demo the steps for perfect café Cubano. "We make an espuma, or crema, by whisking a bit of the coffee with sugar."

He grins. "Always the sugar with you."

"But never too much," I muse to the work between my hands. I pour the rest of the brewed coffee over the crema and dollop a little bit of the foam into both our cups. Finally, I pour coffee into the cups, careful to not disturb the foam.

We move stools to the island. "You already had brunch, but you know me."

"If I said I'd lied about brunch and I'm on an empty stomach, would that get me closer to whatever you're offering?"

I drag over a fresh loaf of pan Cubano and cut two thick slices. Irish butter clouds on top. I slide his plate across wood.

He licks his lips before he drinks.

My eyes go there, then up. "You don't lie." But I do now. Please let it matter. And then there's the *matter* of Andrés. The other night I spoke so freely about him to Orion; I should be able to spill about the surprise call. I can't, even though my silence feels wrong. I need some time alone with it—time to tell myself what Andrés's reappearance means before I can tell a boy I can tell anything to.

Almost anything.

"I knew I'd find you in here," Cate says, the push door swinging behind her. "And you, Orion, are never far from her baked goods. Is that Café Bustelo?"

"I'm getting an initiation. It packs a worthy punch," Orion offers.

"I can make you one?" I tell Cate.

She sniffs over my cup. "Mmm, next time. I spoke with tu mamá last night and now this. Oh Miami, te extraño tanto." She smacks one hand over her heart, missing her childhood city. "Anyway, I was just chatting with one of our guests. I told her all about La Paloma. She was so taken with your baking and wanted to meet you before checkout."

"Sure, of course."

Within minutes, Cate has ushered a petite redhead, likely in her twenties, into the Owl and Crow kitchen. She introduces herself as Lauren, and we introduce ourselves as Lila, who made her breakfast, and Orion, who sells the English breakfast tea she drank with it.

"The tea was superb," Lauren says. "I'll have to pop into Maxwell's on the way to the train." Then to me, "But, Lila is it?" On my nod, she says, "I was here for a wedding all weekend and got to sample many of your offerings. I must say, the flavor balance and texture were noteworthy. Those flaky pastries and adding cinnamon to those fig rolls—clever." She points to the cooling oven. "And your breads were extraordinary."

"She is that," Orion says.

I pout-smile at him then tell Lauren, "Thank you. It's always nice to hear my cooking made someone happy."

"I agree," Lauren says. "I'm in culinary arts school, myself. Le Cordon Bleu in London."

I've heard of Le Cordon Bleu in Paris. Any cook worth her kitchen clogs knows about the most prestigious school of French cuisine in the world. But . . . "There's a London campus?"

"Yes, it's fantastic. I'm part of the Diplôme de Cuisine program but there are a few courses of study. We have the Diplôme de Pâtisserie coursework too. Pastry and baking. Have you had any formal training?"

"Just my grandmother."

"She taught you well. But check out the school, if it fancies you. Goodness, you're so close to London."

She says this like I'm from here. Like I belong in this little medieval town that happens to be so close to London. I don't correct Lauren before Cate leads her to check out.

Orion's buttering another slice of pan Cubano when I shuffle back to my stool, phone out. After a few moments he asks, "You're looking it up, aren't you? Le Cordon Bleu?"

"Just curious." I shift my phone so we both can see the grand website, fit for a grand institution. We scroll through, finding the details of the extensive program and full-color food photos. "Look! The desserts and cakes. I can make good pastries, but these are on another level." Intricate details and delicate shapes, almost too beautiful to eat. Works of art.

"Have you even thought about culinary school before?" Orion asks.

I shake my head. "Abuela taught me everything I need for La Paloma." I scroll through and find the three successive levels of classes. Nine months of study in exquisite French pastry, learning new techniques that I could apply to my own baking, setting it apart even more. London. Another city elbows in: Miami and all it's ever been and still is. "This is, I mean, it's kind of impossible."

"But you keep looking at it." Orion sips his coffee. "Let me see the school's address." I show him then he dashes his hand. "It's in Bloomsbury. Right in the heart of London, near Covent Garden. One of my favorite areas." He looks horrified at my blank expression. "As I'm saying all this, I realize I'm a shit tour guide for not taking you to London in all these weeks."

"I've been caught up here, but I would love to go. And the school, it wouldn't hurt to just pop by. See where it is and all that."

"Sure. Dad and I are off to visit Mum later, so today's out. Besides, we should take a full day." He frowns. "Next weekend it's my turn to manage the shop."

"Two weeks, then. I mean, it will fly," I say, gesturing with my lifted cup. Overgesturing, apparently, since coffee sloshes over the butcher block island.

Orion clucks his tongue, eyes twinkling with mischief. "Oh, *this* is interesting. Now you've done it."

I towel up the mess. "I sense a superstition coming my way."

"Maybe a lot more is coming your way," he tells me. "Traditionally, if you spill coffee, it means a lover is thinking of you."

All it *really* means, I don't find out until after supper. So ironic, I think the state of Florida itself is playing sick jokes on me.

Only hours after Orion equates my spilled coffee with thoughts from a lover, Andrés's name flashes on my phone screen. Instant emotional rewind to last night. Even so, Andrés Millan is no longer mi amado.

The FaceTime notification pings, on and on. I am interested in the way I reach out to click the familiar green *answer* icon. I am interested in how the sight of him goes down like my first sip of hard liquor, how my entire body ingests it.

"Lila." His face and voice, the tilt of his jaw, even his long, dark eyelashes that I'd deemed grossly unfair—they all look the same. Not even three months have passed, I remind myself.

"You found me," I say. *I lost you.*

"I know I called only yesterday but . . ." He scrubs his face. "God, you look good. You look really good."

I can't help a few stray tears. My head shakes.

"Lila, please don't cry. I didn't call to make you cry again."

What does he expect? Don't feel? Don't remember? Doesn't he realize he's a huge part of the reason I'm even here? "Why are you doing this?"

"I'm . . ." At length he says, "Trying to figure that out as I go."

And he could easily figure out he was right the first time, leaving me last spring. So easily. My head throbs; I swipe hair off my face. "You've been keeping busy, no?"

"This and that, yeah."

"I'm sure you've been at the beach a lot. Your favorite." My laugh carries a tinge of hysteria. "I miss South Beach. Even more since I saw it on your Instagram. You still never go alone, right?"

His face wilts, and this little hint of confirmation strikes me back. Now he knows I know about Alexa Gijon. Pilar's Center for Cuban Sleuthing wins again. "Lila."

"How long?"

He inhales sharply. "It meant nothing. A mistake."

Tears flow freely now, hearing him say it for real. I breathe the knowledge in, hold it there. The burn.

"It was like two weeks, Lila. It's done."

"Two weeks is more than a mistake." He moves to speak, but I say, "I only want to know one thing." He tips his chin. "Spare me the 'it's not you, it's me' shit. What. Did. I. Do?"

"We had almost three years," he says. "That's like three forevers in high school dating years."

Silence.

He shrugs. "We grew up together. You've always been bright and intense and powerful. I fell in love with that. But toward the end . . ." My expression presses him; he tucks his lips inward. "I was losing myself."

"What do you mean?"

"You always moved us at full force, planning everything so far out. Pushing me—what classes I should take or telling me to stay in Miami for school. You were directing me like you order around the junior bakers at La Paloma. I just needed space, and to move myself for a while. Think for myself."

The burned-out star, just like Abuela said. I'd brushed off her warnings then, dismissing them under our thinnest pastry dough. But here they are; he shines them back in my face. He shines them on Stefanie.

I should've listened to her when we ran every week.

"Why do we do this again?" Stefanie had said last winter, panting the words as we passed the next mile marker along the Key Biscayne Bridge.

I dragged my gaze from the turquoise bay. "It's Saturday."

"No, I mean. Why do we. Torture ourselves. Running?" Her blond ponytail bounced in time with her feet.

"More room for pastelitos? Besides, you love it."

Stefanie said, "*You* love it."

But she had never loved it. And I had never really heard her. I can't apologize to her now, but I can to Andrés.

"I'm sorry," I whisper. "For all the planning." Inhale, exhale.

His mouth snaps wide, then small again. "The thing is, I think I moved myself too far away. From you."

Oh.

Two months and even two weeks ago, I would've been my burning star self and run back across countries and the entire Atlantic, just for this.

Now, I'm the one not moving. I'm still. I tell him to give me some time and not call for a while. After the session goes black, I stretch out along the quiet of my antique bed in this old, old inn. I stop and stargaze, but my telescope is backward. I turn my search inward.

Maybe Orion's earlier superstition was spot-on. Maybe he nailed it. But as the sky dips into dusk, the lover who is thinking of me after I spill my coffee is an unexpected one.

Myself.

22

My kitchen. Not Flora's kitchen. My sanity. "More dishtowels in the next drawer," I tell my reluctant protégé, who's been relegated to clean-up duty. This, she can do unsupervised. Maybe.

"We only made three things. How can three bloody items require so much equipment?" Flora grumbles, suds foaming up to her elbows.

I unmold strawberry tea cakes for later, ready for a six-hour nap and a new head to replace the one that wants to pound free of my skull right now. *Brilliant, Lila.* What have I done? Maybe I'll just have Flora work in here for one week. It would make a statement. It would keep me from going Full-Force Reyes on a fifteen-year-old.

I'm baking sweets, but I'm all salt, thanks to a night of tossing and flip-flopping over a gut-rip FaceTime session.

The back door whines. I turn and catch Orion's smile before he finds his sister.

"Look at you, Pink." He approaches the sink. "How was your first go?"

My heart clenches—his encouraging smile, the note of curiosity, bright in his eyes—masked by the deceit I can't all-the-way shake.

"I did fine." She shrugs, and I swear I detect the exact moment Flora Maxwell remembers to sell herself. She shoots her brother a lopsided smile. "I made the simple syrup for a cake. And we mixed bread dough, weighing and measuring and all that. We also did a fruit platter with a vanilla cream dipping sauce."

I purposely kept today's offerings simple. No labor-intensive cinnamon rolls or temperamental French or Cuban bread. "Your pre-running snack." I point to the plate we set aside for him.

Sparkles flash from his eyes as he dips sliced melon into vanilla cream. "Delicious," he tells Flora. "I'm really chuffed you're doing this. Dad is too."

An ounce of Flora's smile might be real.

I exhale over the last of my work. "Flora, you can bail. I'll finish up the dishes."

She towels off her hands. Loosening ties, she hands me her apron. Our eyes meet over two truths. She does not want to be here. I possess information she's decided is worth her being here anyway. I keep my third truth inside but hope there's enough mixed with the weariness on my face. *I won't give up on you.*

"You did really well," I say. "I'll see you Wednesday?"

Her shoulder springs up. "Wednesday."

"And I'll see you later at the shop," Orion says.

Alone, Orion munches more fruit and cream as I drag myself to the sink. "How'd she really do?" he asks.

I want to explain that she has zero skills. But guilt will slice him end to end. "Learning the kitchen takes practice. She'll get it."

My hands have replaced Flora's under the soap and hot water. Scrub and sponge. Lather, rinse, repeat. All this cleaning can't scour FaceTime plus the sight of a graffitied St. Cross wall from my mind.

"Lila. What's wrong?"

I can't tell him yet, and my self-imposed silence hurts as much as the details. Again, I stick to what's true. "I'm beat. I had a rough night."

"Well, I can't make pastries, but I'm good at hugs?"

I nod and he drags me into him, sudsy hands and all. I dissolve into Orion Maxwell like sugar into butter, eggs, and vanilla. "You're the *bestest*-best at hugs." I breathe inside the soft whirr of his chuckle and his smell. Rain and apples and his natural soapy spice.

If possible, I burrow further into him. The calm strength of him shrouds all my dying things—the secrets I'm keeping—and the one I've been keeping from myself. My secret truth becomes a question: Does this really have to stop? Foolish. Ridiculous. Impossible for a girl who belongs to Miami.

"I'll help you sort out these dishes before we ditch your terrible night for Winchester's jogging trails. Then I'll take you to the shop and make you some tea before you hit the farmers' market." Orion pulls back, fixes my hair under the headband.

Fixes more.

✳

It's not any of the greens. My signature favorite tea, that is. Running done, Orion and I camp at Maxwell's tasting bar with a trio of miniature Asian teacups.

"Still no?" he asks over a cup of what he calls silver needle green. A delicacy—sharp and grassy.

"I like these, especially the jasmine-infused one. But I dunno, naming it my favorite is a big commitment. But I know you'll find it."

His smile shifts to his dad as he trails customers through the front door. Teddy handles the orders while Mr. Maxwell stops by the bar.

"Lila." We exchange greetings. "Thank you for what you're doing with Flora. With her help, your tasks likely take double the time, but I appreciate the effort."

That effort is starting to feel better and better.

Mr. Maxwell tells Orion, "I'll handle things here later. Take the rest of the day, then?"

A heaviness settles between father and son. I know the latter well enough to detect it clearly. There's something up.

"I will. Thanks, Dad."

When we're alone with tea again, I ask, "Everything okay?"

Orion stares at the rim of a cup of Dragonwell, the strongest of the three greens on the bar. "Well, before I get on to that, I approached Dad with your business idea. You know, get ourselves set up for some food service. Maybe arrange some bistro tables so people can order a tea and sit and eat an artisan pastry with it."

"He didn't go for it?"

Orion shakes his head.

As one fourth of a business owner, I don't get it. The answer's so easy, so clear in my head. Do this one thing and your business will grow. Do more than stay at the same level.

"He would like to, and he sees the value. But I can't push him into anything past the minimum now. Life's taking an enormous toll on all of us."

"Okay." I exhale my no-fail ideas, my *way*. I could hammer them all day into the white walls and I would be right. But Maxwell's is their business, not mine.

Orion adds, "We went to see Mum together yesterday. It strikes in waves, this disease. She'll plateau for a good while, then dip again." He ducks his head.

Oh. My hand over his. "She dipped again?"

"You could definitely say that. It was sort of the next thing we were anticipating, and well, it's happened. She's stopped walking altogether. She hasn't been all that mobile for a while, but this week, it was like her brain just said, 'We've had enough of this now.'" Winter-cold blue eyes lock onto mine, and before I can think of any words good enough, or right enough, he says, "I want to ask you something. And you know I make it a point to never ask impossible things. But lately I've been feeling my request isn't so impossible."

Anything. This word leaps from my mind. I repeat it out loud.

He links our fingers. "Will you come with me one time? Soon? Come meet my mum even though she can't meet you back?"

The trust overwhelms me. "Yes."

"Good. Then one more question. Since I'm gonna listen to Dad and take the rest of the day, take it with me? We can get out of town or something?"

Always another yes.

After my farmers' market stop and a shower, Orion swoops me up onto Millie. We wear helmets for our longest trek yet into the Hampshire countryside. He promises three things: something disgustingly pretty, an older-than-old surprise, and fish and chips.

We ride far into an uneven checkerboard of grays, greens, and browns. Livestock grazes along snaking roads and the sun blinks through clouds as we stop at the edge of a small town. Stowing Millie along a side lane, he swears my black trench will be safe folded into the saddlebag. I choose to kick the afternoon chill with Orion's sweater, and I wasn't even surprised when it showed up along with my helmet as "gear."

We walk an access road until it descends sharply, depositing us near a whitewashed brick tunnel bridge. This one for small boats.

"Is this the disgustingly pretty thing?"

"Just ahead." Orion grabs my hand, leading me down the steep final steps. Greenery, more than I can take in, riots around the smell of moss and decaying leaves. We're on a graveled towpath that stretches along a narrow canal of water the color of deep jade. "It's downright hideous. Gross, even," he says as we begin a lazy stroll. He tells me we're at the Basingstoke Canal—hundreds of years old—that links this region with the River Thames in London.

I digest most of this, as well as the sprinkling of historical facts about the Hart region of Hampshire. Mostly, I'm just stunned that, except for a few stray tourists and bikers, we're alone with the lull of water and disorganized foliage. Rows of trees bow before me, their canopies dipping into the canal surface. I remember I'm in a country with a monarchy. Why not pretend I'm a Latina princess in a court of prostrating trees? This, I admit to Orion, making him swear to never tell another soul.

As if this watery trail didn't already seem straight out of a fairy tale, Orion spots a pair of swans floating along a half second before I do. "Look at those guys! But don't get too close. They're deceptively fierce buggers."

"I like them already," I say, pulling him to a stop. I just want to watch them circle around and fluff their feathers and swivel their curvy necks.

I watch for so long, Orion pokes at me. "You surely have swans in Miami?"

"Yeah but not these swans in this place." And not him watching them with me in a life-worn leather jacket, so at home here it's like he was born between the tree stumps. Spiced and woody and strong.

"True. But what awaits us here is better than swans. For those who are brave enough to press on through hours of, err, rough terrain."

I fix him with an unwavering side-eye until I break and then we're both laughing. After a heavy morning it tastes better than loaves of pan Cubano drenched in butter.

We start off around the next bend, but Orion suddenly jumps one pace ahead and urges me onto his back. "Milady, your chariot awaits." A piggyback ride no one would refuse. "Just a little farther is your special surprise that's older than old can be."

He stoops lower and I grab onto his shoulders. He hooks the bends of my legs and hoists me up. I hold on as we move, but Orion starts to zigzag along the path like the British boy's version of Mr. Toad's Wild Ride. He ignores my mock distress and only slows when I start beating one fist on his back.

"Okay, okay, I'll behave. We're nearly there, anyway. You see, every Latina princess needs her castle. I'm afraid Odiham Castle has seen better days and won't meet your specs. But it's still very special."

At the end of another winding curve, he sets me down and my mouth drops. Just ahead, a castle ruin rises up and out of the green along the path. "This is an honest-to-God real castle? Right here?"

He urges me toward a little footpath. "Honest to God and built by King John as a hunting lodge in the year twelve hundred and seven. Here, we're halfway between Winchester and Windsor, so it was a practical location."

A family of tourists passes as we ascend the narrow path. A wide, circular donut of grass surrounds the scraggly fort, and a tall arc of trees keeps watch from behind. Older than old is right. All that's left of the structure are thick exterior walls, worn to resemble dark gray masses of sea coral, laid out in the shape of a letter *C*. It could be a sandcastle; no hard edges remain. We can walk straight through to the center, stopping and spinning a slow circle inside the ancient mass. Posted signs describe castle life and detail the way the building used to look, hundreds of years ago, with artist renderings and cross sections.

After the history lesson, I'm not quite ready to walk, not ready for the best fish and chips, just a few minutes' ride away. We plunk down onto the grass next to Odiham. No one is here but us and small sounds—the wind through canal water, the lyrical gossip between birds.

But I hear more. If there are ghosts hanging around the battered castle walls, they speak things into my mind. Or maybe it's just me who's been hearing the same whispers for days, and it's finally time to listen. "I've been keeping a secret."

He's toying with a blade of grass. "That it's not really you making me all those delicious Cuban foods?"

"Ha—never. But here's the backstory. Today at the farmers' market, one of the merchants personally helped me pick the best peppers and onions and tomatoes. He said he knows how picky I am. And while there, I bumped into Mr. Robinson, the butcher. He told me he's getting some particularly fine free-range chickens in this week and would I like him to save me a couple of the best ones."

Orion shrugs. "That's Winchester. How we are."

"And I have dozens more examples. People have welcomed me. And everywhere I look it's a storybook. Castles and cobblestones, old things mixed with new things. The countryside—there's so much space. Then I just found out about Le Cordon Bleu, too, and I keep thinking about the pastry program. And thinking some more."

I'm tinkering with the soft grass too. "I didn't even want to come here."

"I know."

"But now, I'm in love with England." Right behind it, there's a star-named boy. My heart goes on beating when he's not with me, but the *missing him* pumps as much as blood. "That's my secret."

"It's more than just a tourist having a favorite travel spot," I add. *"Love,* love. Real love."

His smile gleams. But if he has words or answers or even more questions, he leaves them with the castle ghosts. It's okay, though. It's all okay. Today, I just want his smile. I want mine.

So I don't tell him the other part, that it feels like I'm cheating on my own city, loving another place the way I do. I acknowledge this exactly one time, being extra precise like I'm measuring out cake ingredients. Then I prove to myself I *can* be good at forgetting.

"Your secret's safe with me, Lila Reyes," he finally says, more to the castle walls than my face.

I know, *I know* what I should and shouldn't feel. Like vegetables and vitamins, I know what's good for me. But today I am going to love something just because I do. I'm going to love a place so magical, even I could believe in the spells and potions of it—the air, thickly sweet like butterscotch. I'll focus on Orion's promise to take me to dinner at a cute pub, and mine to steal chips off his plate. And the promise an England summertime night will make when we ride back on a vintage motorbike, bodies open to the road through shaved-ice wind.

I love England. I just do. And if there's one thing I know, it's what it feels like to fall in love.

23

Wednesday calls for fruit empanadas. Flora assembles them on the other side of the island. Her task is simple: fill the dough circles, seal and fork-press the edges, then brush them with egg wash.

We prepared two sugary filling choices, but my mind is focused on the bittersweet. Monday was swans, a haunting castle, and delicious fish and chips—and the boy who showed me all of it. I shared a secret. England has turned from place I wanted to hate, to a place I can't leave without ripping myself away. At the castle I refused to think about this part and just enjoyed all the others. But two days later, that ripping away part is back, hidden behind my heart.

The timer dings into my memories. I dart from sink to oven to transfer four loaves of honey oat bread to a cooling rack. Now, empanada time. "Can you grab the pans of strawberry filled?"

"Yeah." Flora brings the unbaked pastries from our prep rack.

I look them over before letting the oven do its magic. "Nice. I always make extra. They're a guest favorite." The mini half-moons are uniformly shaped—perfect. Earlier, I taught Flora the way Abuela taught me: I do a few, then we do a few, then you do a few.

On tiptoes, I try to gauge the progress at her workstation. "Do you have the blueberry ones ready?"

She nods on a flat smile. "Just one more pan to go."

Flora did so well on the first two dozen, I let her take over the blueberry batch while I cooked and chilled a pot of Cuban vanilla cinnamon pudding. I wipe my hands, then wind around to the prep rack where she's been stacking her empanadas. "Let's see your mini masterpieces," I say and pull out one pan of twelve. And stare in disbelief. Stomach tying into knots, I hastily pull out the other pan. "Flora, what happened?"

Two dozen of the empanadas aren't close to being sealed evenly. The top folds don't even reach the bottom edges in half of them, and filling is overflowing onto parchment tray liners. Some are over-filled, some barely have enough. And then the egg wash! So uneven, and she tossed on sugar in icky clumps. I can't serve these.

"I don't understand. I watched you do the strawberry ones myself." And besides that, I got up early to start honey oat bread on my own, setting the dough to rise before she arrived. That way, I had extra time to teach her some basic kitchen skills. We worked on measuring wet and dry ingredients consistently and using different kinds of knives. I thought she was starting to care.

Flora unties the bottom half of her apron. "I told you I'm no good at this. Working here. I'm only going to drag you down." She peeks into the oven; the little strawberry pastries are coming to life. "At least you can put these and the last pan of blueberry out. I mean, that should be quite enough."

Espérate. This kitchen is starting to smell like fish. I remember Jules's words about Flora from the other night:

She forgets that what she does in one small moment can affect tomorrow.

Flora did this on purpose so I'd cancel our deal. She saw an easy moment of escape but didn't think of me or the entire inn. It'd be so easy to just take her apron and show her the door, but again, I see myself in this act. It's probably something I would have done—no, not with food—but this scheme hails straight out of the *Lila Reyes Handbook of Situation Manipulation.*

I'm tempted to actually slow clap her on it—bien hecho, Flora. Well done. Yet, because I know this game so well, I don't have to look far for what should come next. The only problem is the cost: my reputation.

Before I think it through from end to end, I'm doing it. "Um, no we won't have enough. All the guest rooms are filled, and many with families. The guests have been wanting more than one pastry each." I exhale a resigned sigh. "I don't have time to make more empanada dough, so we'll just have to serve the ones you made."

"You're really going to put those out?" She looks at the tray, her mouth parting. Does she only now realize how awful they look?

"I have no choice." I gesture to her. "Now tie up your apron because we need to make butter biscuits to go with the pudding for later."

"You mean, you don't want me to leave?"

I try to paint my face with the color blasé, pretending it's part of MAC's new summer collection. "Leave? Of course not. Every cook screws up once in a while. And you're just starting out. Don't beat yourself up."

Thirty minutes later, the pastries from hell are in the parlor. I'm washing my hands of it, literally and for real, while Flora scrapes the morning off the wooden butcher block, head bent.

Cate enters. "Lila, a quick word?"

I nod, my mind just ahead of what I think is coming.

"Are you feeling all right?" Cate tilts her head then ogles me curiously.

"Yeah, just tired. I've been having trouble falling asleep." Which is true. The tangles around my mind and heart have reached the rest of me, wanting to keep me up past any baker's normal bedtime.

"Ahh. I was only wondering because of today's breakfast pastries." Her brows drop. "They're so unlike what we're used to seeing from you. Your usual impeccable quality and consistency."

Ouch. I steal a glance at Flora. She's frozen, her hand clenched tightly around her scrub brush. I could shift the blame where its due, but Orion's words elbow in—Flora's drifting, more flighty than ever. Whether or not this small thing I'm about to do will matter, Orion's family is worth me taking the hit. But only once. *This* is not happening in here again. I exhale a quick puff of air. "You're right. Sorry about the blueberry ones. It's my fault. I was a little distracted."

Cate rubs my shoulder. "I see, Lilita. It's only that our occupancy has never been this solid for months. We're booked until September! Yesterday, I overheard the gentleman from room six raving about your food. He'd convinced his brother's family to stay here instead of a place closer to town just because of it. And our rating on that TripTell travel site has never been higher. The comments about the afternoon tea alone! What you do here matters—don't forget that."

"I won't forget."

"Good." She cranes her neck. "And Flora, I'm so pleased Lila has gotten herself some help in here."

Eyes like saucers, Flora only nods.

At the swing door, Cate says, "Tonight I'll have Spence brew you some of his turmeric tea with coconut milk. Will knock you out cold."

I'm back at the sink, then Flora's at my side, her lips tightly curled together. "You can go. I'll finish up," I say.

"I . . . you took the fall for me. Why?" she says to the floor.

I transfer a glass mixing bowl to the drying rack. "What happens in this kitchen is my responsibility."

"But—"

"Orion will be here soon to run." I return to my washing. "I saved him one of the strawberry empanadas we made together. They're one of his favorites and he's going to love it." One final direct glance at Flora. "So. Friday, then?"

"Um, okay. Friday."

"What do you mean you told Andrés Christian Millan to chill and not contact you for a while? And how long is a while?"

"Ugh. Shit. *Ugh.*" I'm sure Pili can still see me just fine through her laptop FaceTime window as I plunge, face-first onto my bed. "I don't know," I say into the duvet. "I don't know anything right now."

"Lila."

I drag my head sideways, still belly-down.

"But it's Andrés," she says. "The guy you cried over in the walk-in freezer! And now he's having second thoughts?"

Yeah, it's Andrés and the *us* that's been such a mainstay of my life for years. Put our faces on a flag, wave it high over West Dade. Andrés Millan and Lila Reyes forever. But the second I find out Andrés might want to get back together or at least talk about it, I tell him not to call?

"You look different," Pilar says softly. A wistful smile graces her face.

"Different how?" I drag out my forearm, pronate it. "Paler?" I grab a chunk of the hair we share. "Mira, no summer highlights like at home."

"The sister I know would've called, texted, FaceTimed, hired sky writers to get Mami and Papi to get you the hell home early over this."

"Yeah, so what else would she do? The Lila you know?" How has Pili really seen me all these years, not as family so much, but simply as a someone?

Pilar snickers a bit. "Let's see, you'd probably speed over to the Gables. Kiss Andrés senseless. Make him call you his again."

Make him. And she's so right, about the girl she left at the airport. I stare at my sister, this part of me I love so very much. "Pili," I say with a hitch, "it's getting warmer here. But I've been wearing all the clothes you sent. I miss you."

"I miss you more. I miss us."

Her blade slips by all the knife skills I know, getting me good. She pulls me in, she pulls me home. Las Reyes, Lila and Pilar. Our plan of world pastry domination is as bright and alive as ever in my eyes, my heart. So easily, so effortlessly, this is my future as it's always been.

"I can't just run back to Andrés so quickly," I say. My own heart matters too much. "I can't rush this time. You don't understand how broken I was."

"Don't I?" Four thousand miles of knowing shadows her face.

"Thank you." My hand tips, conceding. "For making me come here."

Pilar lets out a long, slow breath. "I was right. Different."

24

I'm cooking big time. The work centers me. The chopping, and the simmer of onions with butter, milk, and flour for a béchamel sauce. I'm using nothing from cans today, peeling and steaming my own farmers' market tomatoes for sauce, boiling bones and herbs for chicken stock.

My phone vibrates from my apron pocket. Not a text, an e-mail. The header makes my heart clench. Stefanie.

Dear Lila,

Yes. We should talk. I'll call soon, promise.

Stef

Well, it's something. But as steps forward go, it's a tiptoe. Will our first face-to-face feel like walking on shards of glass or sitting in the middle of a burning-down room? Dozens of clichés flood but I have to remember: we can do this. We can find ourselves again, even if we have to start by leaning on all we used to be for years.

The backdoor creaks open then smacks shut. While it's usually Orion, this afternoon, Jules and Flora slide into my kitchen, mid-conversation.

"Yeah, yeah, Nicks is worthy. Legendary." Flora shakes a finger at Jules. "But Benatar. Trained classically at Juilliard and all! It bloody well shows in her range."

"I hear you," Jules answers. "Nicks, though? Come on. She practically wrote the manual for eighties rock."

I give the broth a stir. "Um, hi?"

"Sorry, love," Jules says. "Okay, maybe you can settle our squabble. Undisputed queen of eighties rock, Stevie Nicks or Pat Benatar?"

"You're better off having that conversation with my sister," I say. "She speaks vinyl."

Jules points her nose here and everywhere. "Christ, Lila, if this isn't what Heaven smells like."

"Angelic is always the goal. But didn't Orion tell you guys seven? You're about four hours early."

"That's on me," Flora says. "We're headed into town, and I think I left my sunnies here this morning?"

I remove the finished stock from the heat, pointing my wooden spoon at the opposite counter. "Out of tomato splatter range."

While Flora retrieves her sunglasses, Jules peers over my shoulder. All burners are occupied with prep sauces, stocks, and fillings. "We're so chuffed about tonight. Remy, too. Usually when we get invited for tea it's pizza or maybe takeout from the local chippie."

I pantomime a fatal wound.

Jules laughs. "I don't do much cooking myself either. My mum does a worthy job, and then Rems and I are always scrounging pub food."

"You cook songs, Jules."

"Too right. But it would be cool to learn a few tricks."

Kitchen tricks are *my* music. I rest my spoon. "You could stay and cook with me?"

"Lessons from the boss?" Jules beams, then turns to Flora. "What do you say? We can grab lattes and scrounge around Victoria's shop any old day. Lila is only here so long."

The melancholy words poke gently, but I'm already full of them. *I know, I know.*

Flora shoves a plate of leftover lemon biscuits Jules's way. I always have them close to feed a certain tea merchant. "Try one. I helped bake them."

Jules bites into one of the crisp wafers, then makes a big show out of trying to pocket the entire batch.

"Yeah," Flora says. "We'll stay and help."

Tasks explained and divided, I get my sous chefs washed, aproned, and set up on the island. We turn up eighties rock while Flora peels potatoes and Jules handles vegetable chopping like a pro.

Cate waltzes in. "Lila you said arroz con pollo, not half of a Cuban cookbook."

I wave her over. She pokes her nose into the bubbling pot of rice pudding. "Arroz con leche, too?"

"And papas rellenas and croquetas de jamón."

Cate drags over a stool. She observes quietly, but I can almost see the thoughts zooming behind her eyes. "Before you were born—way before I met Spencer—your abuela and abuelo had me over for dinners like this. All the time. Your mother knew plenty, but Miami Cuban food was Abuela. Her old kitchen was like a shoebox, but she used every little corner. The smell, Lila—just like this. I followed it in here. The guests are going to wonder when supper is served."

The Cuban siren song.

"If I close my eyes, I'm in Miami again," Cate continues, "and the air conditioner is broken and we're all dripping sweat with portable fans blowing loud behind us and the music playing louder." Her hands on her heart. "Your abuela Lydia could have been in the most high-end kitchen in her mind. And more than me, she fed everyone. When times were tough for her neighbors, she brought pots of caldo de pollo and pan Cubano."

I lift my gaze through the molasses drag of memory. Flora and Jules have stopped chopping, just listening. *This* is my Miami, my history. This is me. "Stay," I tell Cate. "You can cook with us."

She reaches into the stack of aprons, grinning.

My Cuban relatives came from a small farm near Cienfuegos— one hundred fires. The inn kitchen steams and smokes with nearly that much heat now. I show the girls how to cut up chickens, then work with Flora to brown the pieces in cast iron for arroz con pollo. Cate and Jules tuck spiced ground beef picadillo filling inside a coating of the mashed potatoes Jules boiled and seasoned. The pair watches me, then takes over forming the mixture into balls. Next, they roll ham croqueta filling into breadcrumbs. We'll fry them up at the last minute.

"Keep the veggies moving so they don't burn," I tell Flora.

Flora dutifully turns and stirs. Then I let her add the dry white rice and stock and finally, the Bijol spice. "It's supposed to turn yellow, then?" she asks.

"Arroz con pollo must be this color. Like saffron. And this spice adds flavor, too." I give the mixture a final stir. "Watch for a rapid boil. It will bubble up, but when it gets fast, that's how you know it's time to lower the heat to simmer and put on that cover. I need to check our rice pudding, so you're in charge."

Flora gives me a thumbs-up.

With trays of potato meatballs and ham croquettes ready for frying, Cate hauls over four Cokes. I shoot her a knowing smile when she cuts a lime and hooks a wedge onto the rim of each glass.

"Lime with Coke?" Jules questions.

"A Miami regular. Try it," Cate says.

"Oh, that's quite good. Zingy." Jules moves her shoulders to her own rhythm, sipping again. "I'm feeling so South Florida."

"Well, if you really want to feel Miami, you need to hear it," I tell her. "Let's ditch the eighties and get our salsa jams on."

"So much dancing, so many nights," Cate says. "The clubs with Mami and our friends."

I sync my phone to my portable speakers and fire up the music of my culture. With our supper covered and ready for a long simmer, Flora steps away from the stove with her drink. Her neck and face are flushed from the flaming pans. But she smiles.

"This music!" Jules says, eyes bright with wonder. "The polyphony and drum work and rhythm are fantastic. It sounds like a tropical resort and a colorful street lined with merchants and . . ."

"What?"

"I know it's weird, but it sounds like this food smells. Spiced and sexy."

I elbow the inn co-owner, less Cate Wallace from Winchester than I've seen her in weeks. "Catalina, we need to show them the dance."

"Yes please," Jules says, grabbing Flora by the elbow. "Teach us."

We do, and we look like a couple of fools but manage to show them salsa dance basics. "That's it, chicas," I call out. "Pause on beats four and eight. Drag the foot, don't place it." We demo where to put hip and shoulder. How to sharpen each movement, locking it up. Flora holds her own, but Jules takes her salsa instruction to another level. Why am I surprised?

Jules can't help but dive her gorgeous voice right into the songs. With a trained ear, she picks up the Spanish phrases and creates her own harmonies with the singers. She's beautiful, my friend.

My eyes flick to the doorway. The boys have materialized, all three of them snapping shots or videoing and way too pleased with themselves. How long have they been standing there?

"No clue what the hell is going on," Remy says. "But one day when Jules is famous, this video will show up online and it will be amazing."

Jules is already beaming over to him, making a play for his phone.

Gordon's face carries a dose of horrified shock. Trouble processing a new side of his mother and her formidable hip sway? "I have no words."

"For once." Cate fluffs his hair. "I'm going up now. Bring your dad and me our portions when Lila serves it?"

"Yeah, Mum."

Cate traps my stare at the hallway push door. She presses fingers to her lips then her heart before she leaves.

I find Orion peeking at the arroz con pollo and eyeing the finger foods. When I approach he draws me in for a brief hug. After hours of frantic fun, my breathing lulls.

"Now I'm all guilt. You worked so hard and all we brought were a couple of bottles of plonk and some ale." He points to Remy, who's setting red wine and beer bottles on the counter.

"There must be a few last-minute tasks we can do to pitch in?"

"More than a few." I playfully scratch the sleeve of his faded band tee. "And no guilt allowed. This is what I do. What I love to do."

He smiles then rubs a gentle finger across my face. "You've flour on your nose."

"I probably have a lot more all over the rest of me." I glance down at the skinny jeans and black tank under my apron. "I must look like a wreck."

"Nah." He lifts my chin with his thumb, a lazy smile across his face. "You're always lovely."

Oh. He's never said that before. Many times, I've felt it hiding behind his gaze. Only the words are new and my heart is no longer lulling. We're back to frantic. "Pour me some of that plonk you brought?"

The evening starts with his first pour of wine then stretches long, loud, and delicious. Remy's a pro at the fryer from working at the pub. Ham croquettes and potato balls come out golden crisp and the fillings ooze in greasy wonder. Orion helps serve the arroz con pollo. The crowd *oohs* and *ahhs* over the steaming platter of chicken over yellow rice with peas, peppers, and onions, dripping with reduced stock and the flavor of bones.

We all lean over the wooden surface, bellies filling with food and ears with stories. Orion accepts a second ale from Gordon and offers me one, but I stick to the house red Remy lifted from the pub.

"Lila, tell me you've seen Ri sloshed?" Gordon asks. "Like well and truly pissed?"

I grin over the thought, and at Orion's glare at his buddy. "Hmm, I know I've witnessed buzzed. But I can't say I've had the pleasure of his fully sloshed presence."

Remy chimes in. "Well, that's gonna require more than two beers. But speaking from those who know, it's *gorgeous*."

Orion swallows his last bite of his millionth potato ball. "Bugger off, Rem."

"I don't think so." Remy only spurs himself on more. "Orion's a sleepy drunk. The last time I saw it, he was at my place."

"Oh God, I remember this," Jules adds with a snicker.

"Yeah," Remy tips his bottle. "Crashed on my sofa and before he went clean out, he was mumbling all this random shit. Some coherent, some not. We weren't sure if he was awake or dreaming."

"Wanker," Orion says, annoyance ghosting over a wry laugh.

"Doesn't make it untrue," Gordon says. "Next time, we're recording."

The teasing and jibes on my England tour guide give way to eating. My guests are the good kind of quiet, pausing to throw out accolades and begging for seconds. When it's "pudding" time, I have Flora fetch chilled ramekins of arroz con leche.

"I must compliment my worthy, salsa-dancing helpers, Jules and Flora," I say, my words jostled by the effects of three glasses of wine.

The girls bow over the boys' applause, then we all dig into the rice pudding, one of Cuba's sweetest comfort foods. Afterward, everyone helps with dishes, and before I know it I'm alone with Orion and the final seal of plastic ware. I place leftover rice into the fridge and spin around. Maybe too quickly.

Orion was near enough, but he's lightning-quick, steadying me. "Easy, there. Sloshed, you're not. But you left tipsy back with your second glass."

Warm. Yummy warm. My cheeks and his arms and the rush through my head. As if to prove him right, I let out a noisy yawn.

"Right. I was going to suggest we watch a film, but you're dead on your feet and have an early wake-up, too. We have plenty more nights for films."

Do we?

His smile changes with ticking seconds—dimple-big, then lopsided, then small. "It was *not* simple chicken and rice and might be the best meal I've ever eaten. And seeing Flora here, with you . . ." He doesn't go on. Doesn't need to.

"I know."

"Sleep now. But be sure to exit the bed on the same side you enter to avoid the worst of the worst kind of luck."

"Can't be too careful."

Orion winks. "G'night." He plants a soft kiss on my forehead.

A balmy July evening gets the rest of him. The staircase gets my sore feet and full belly and wine-flushed movements. Half-dimmed light greets me when I reach the flat. The outline of Cate in a fluffy robe draws me to the overstuffed sofa. A wineglass hangs between her thumb and forefinger and the TV drones.

Seeing me, she scoots then pats the cushion. Lowers the volume on the remote. "Want a glass? Spence is still out with some mates."

I snort and ease my aching limbs. "Another glass and the inn won't eat tomorrow. But thanks."

"Gordon trudged up a half hour ago. Knackered and stuffed. You were incredible today. Cooking and dancing and reminiscing were such fun." I nod and she says, "Flora working with you—she needs it." She flicks the crystal wineglass, makes it hum. "I know the truth about the ruined blueberry pastries. In your sleep you couldn't make empanadas look like those."

I flinch, then shrug. "Well."

"Lila." Cate's voice thickens. "What you did for Flora, more than bread or pastelitos or a business, that was what Abuela really taught you."

I drift into the words and the quiet—plus the wine, the friends and food. The electric pulse behind Orion's fleeting kiss on my forehead. The salt in my throat. This place I love and might have to lose. I close my eyes, giving in.

"I've seen you on London's Le Cordon Bleu website while bread bakes. It reminds me of Gordon, all wide-eyed when he studies grand homes and buildings. All the possibilities." A short sigh, then, "I want you to understand you always have a place here. Our guest room is yours as long as you need it."

I lift up, blinking away moisture. "Thank you. I really do love this inn. And all the England I've seen."

Cate toys with the tie on her robe. "You seem to especially enjoy the tea, here."

Oh, Cate. "I've become super fond of the tea here."

"We all think it's extra special. A rare blend. You can't find tea like that just anywhere. It seems to agree with you, too."

"Mucho," I tell her. So much. I shake my head. "Tell me. After you left Miami with Spencer, when did you stop missing it so much? Your family, your friends?"

She sips wine, then nods toward me. "Any minute now."

25

One day before Orion takes me to London to check out one school, I'm head instructor in another: Bread 101. After two weeks of basics, Flora is ready to knead today. We double quantities to prepare for my extra day off.

"Good, now a quarter turn," I tell her as we press the heels of our hands into the spongy white bread dough. She follows my every movement, adjusting pressure and minding my warnings to use only enough flour to combat the stick and keep fingertips out of her knead.

"This is kind of fun," Flora says. "Getting to push something around. Having it do what you want."

"Ha. Only if you know how far to push. Too much flour or handling makes the loaf all tough and chewy." Flora looks like a bona fide baker today. Her bobbed curls shoot backward over her ears under a blue bandana. Her apron's stained with cinnamon from the apple breakfast cake we made while the dough was rising.

"But you're right," I add. "When my ex-boyfriend and I had one of our blowouts, my family had bread for days."

"A better outlet for your rage than faces, though?"

I turn to her with a dramatic wink. "You should have seen me on prom night. The *neighborhood* got bread the next morning. Wait, do you have something like prom? A big formal dance at the end of your last year?"

"We do, except the ones at my school tend to focus on how much alcohol you can work into your evening. Flasks. Plonk hidden in the bushes, Alcopops," she says then stops to explain about the branded spiked lemonades and punches. "Loads of Tesco champagne before you even leave with your date."

I send her a wry, knowing look. "Actually, that's exactly like prom. Okay, time to flip." The dough smacks against the butcher block.

"What was yours like? You had time to knead and bake dough before you got ready?" She laughs. "If anyone would, it'd be you."

"Thanks. I think." My voice grays. "But I didn't actually go to prom. My ex had mono during his. And then he dumped me a few days before mine."

Flora's movements halt. "Does it get lower than that?"

"Long story, but it was one of the worst weeks ever. Pilar and I shopped way ahead for my gown. It was long and fitted, champagne colored, and had this amazing slit. Some subtle beading, too, and crisscross straps in the back."

"Was? You returned it?"

So real in my mind, Pilar clearing my bedroom of prom. The

beautiful gown, the matching gold heels. The chandelier earrings. She hid it all, then made it disappear when I gave her the go-ahead. I tell Flora these things as we start on the last two dough balls.

Flora says, "I think I would've gone anyway—I mean, I *so* get why you didn't—but I would've put on my stunning gown and gotten my hair fixed really nice and stepped out proud with my friends or something."

"I might've, but my grandmother died the month before."

"Oh. I see." Her words quiet a notch. "You talk about her a lot. But I didn't know she was gone. She really taught you *all* this? The cooking we did and all the baking?"

"That's only a fraction. My sister was really close to Abuela too, but they had more girl talks in the bakery office than the kitchen. My natural love for cooking and baking made me Abuela's shadow. My grandfather died when I was only three and she moved in with us. I was with her constantly. I just . . . wanted to be like her."

Flora nods. "My nan moved in with us, too. About a year after my mum was diagnosed. She was there two years until Dad got a caregiver to come help us."

Orion never told me this. "You were only about eight, right?"

"About. Nan tried to fill the gaps for me and Ri. Did my hair for school and such. But she never had time to make biscuits with me."

"Caring for your mother was a full-time job, I bet."

Flora turns her dough with me. "And then some. One of the symptoms of Mum's disease is constant movement. It was rare for her to just settle and watch a show. She'd walk the house, pacing and pacing. Upstairs, downstairs, picking up items, putting them down. She could never be left alone and only slept after we gave her powerful tablets. So yeah, there was never time." A sprinkle more of flour. "Mum broke her ankle about a year ago. That's when Dad realized we couldn't keep her safe at home anymore."

"The care facility." The home Orion wants to bring me to see.

"Yeah." Her eyes fog. "To go from that constant motion to nothing now. We knew it was coming but . . ."

"I'm sorry, Flora," I say, butter and sugar and yeast heavy in the air. "Is your grandmother still . . . here? Does she know?"

"Yeah, Dad told her this week. And she visits from Manchester a few times a year. But I've never really had the time with her like you did with yours."

The bread is ready to bake. I show Flora how to use a peel to slide the loaves into the oven. For a few moments, we stare into the heated space. What we make will matter to someone who wants to relax in the parlor with a newspaper and cup of tea.

"You could go visit your grandmother?" I suggest. "Take the train sometime and stay a week? Maybe she could teach you some of her favorite recipes."

"My nan is all right in the kitchen, but not like yours. Not like what you can do. But she's amazing at knitwear. I have lots of knitted scarves and beanies from her."

My smile pulls at the image. "You never know, you might be good at knitting too. You could make things for your friends."

"Maybe I could." The corner of her mouth quirks. "That gray cardigan of Orion's you're always wearing. She made that."

26

Later, I'm folding laundry when FaceTime pings, the icon window layering over Le Cordon Bleu's website on my laptop. I've watched the promo videos a hundred times now. It's Mami's account. When I answer, I meet the tight huddle of my family at our dining room table. Mami's face is flushed, and she clutches a well-used tissue.

"¿Qué pasó?" I sputter, panic rising. "Who died? Who's getting divorced? Or is it the panadería? Or is someone in the emergency room?" Was it Javi or Marta or our neighbor Chany or—

"Tranquila, Lilita," Papi says. "We have such happy, happy news."

Mami sniffs then says, "We have an early birthday present for you." As my heart settles she continues. "It's *Family Style*. The producer of *Family Style* contacted us and they are going to feature La Paloma at the end of next month! They got so many customer nominations for us, and another café had to cancel, so we were bumped up. Can you believe this? ¡No puede ser! Years of following this show and we are going to be on it. On TV."

All settling is gone. My parents' favorite Food Network show featuring the best of the best of small family eateries and shops? "Oh," is all I can say. My mind races with my pulse. The opportunity and exposure. The swarm of new customers and revenue and clout. La Paloma is going to be famous!

Pilar says, "We have so much to do to prepare. It's time to come home. We'll get your ticket early and you can even be home for your birthday and—"

"No." Air leaves my lungs along with the single, sharp word. *No* is my first thought, rogue and restless. New panic drops as England summer hangs behind my open window, dusk toeing over afternoon. I can't leave yet and how, *how* am I the same girl who begged for home only weeks ago?

But I am and I can't. It's too soon. I need more time with my new friends and I want to see the pastry school and visit London. Flora has come so far and . . . Orion. This cuts most of all and deeper than knives. I am not ready to leave Orion Maxwell.

"What do you mean, no?" Mami asks, and this starts the wave of liquid to my eyes, another kind of salt water. My sweet mother thought she was just lending me to England to give me a break and a chance to heal. Would she have ever sent me knowing I'd grow to entertain such traitorous secrets inside my heart? Another *no*.

"The inn," I spit out. "I can't just ditch Cate and Spencer and leave them without a baker after all they've done for me. Polly's not due back until mid-August."

"Ah, tienes razón," Papi says. "We didn't even think of that."

I nod. "Book my ticket for two weeks before the taping. That will be plenty of time for me to help get La Paloma ready."

Pilar says, "We need to find a color to repaint the showroom and figure out all the foods we're going to showcase."

"I can help from here. It's going to be awesome. Perfect." Excitement builds, humming. My family business, this precious thing that my grandparents started will grow and expand like never before. *Abuela, this is your legacy.*

We chat longer, catching up and plotting. When we finally reach goodbye, I don't even think about my next move. I'm already in motion, my hair in a messy topknot and the rest of me in a simple tee and cropped yoga pants. I slide into Chucks and bolt.

I'm panting when the front door opens. "Hey," Orion says, eyes blinking with surprise.

"I'm sorry. Sorry I didn't text." I glance left then right. "I just had to—"

"Don't be silly." He opens the door wider. "Come in. You're worrying me."

I shuffle inside the warm space as locks click behind me. "I know you just got off work."

Orion faces me, bracing steady hands on my shoulder bones. "No bother. Dad's at the shop late and Flora left from there to Katy's. I was about to heat up some leftovers of that incredible roast you made. Ropa?"

I sniffle. "Ropa vieja." Old clothes. A fitting name for the fragrant, shredded beef roast I served last night over black beans and rice, over a silly classic film and lots of wine. August seems so close and no one's going to cook for him after my plane takes off.

He leans in, eyeing me with concern. "Come," he says and leads me to the leather sofa. He sits closely, clasping all of our hands together. "What's up?"

I recap everything from the call with my parents, watching his features shift in tandem with the rise and fall of my words. We're silent when I reach the end, our eyes passing the incredible, terrible truth between us. Back and forth.

Finally he says, "I can't imagine what this opportunity means for you. Your place wouldn't have been chosen if it wasn't for all the work you and your family have put in."

"Yes." My family. "But the taping. I wasn't planning on two fewer weeks here."

"I wasn't either. But we knew all this. Each day we've had, we've lived it knowing full well it has to end," Orion says, his voice balancing on the thinnest wire. One wrong move and we both tumble. "We always knew you were going back to Florida."

"Florida," I muse. And then I just release it because I'm tired of the past eating through my gut. "Andrés called. Twice. Said he . . . wants to talk again. He's having second thoughts."

Air rushes from Orion's lungs. His eyes hood, dark and deep. He stands, rushing to the piano. My heart cracks when he angles away from me. "Well then." He speaks to his family photo from Ireland, to a time when this home held all of its hearts. "That should make it loads easier for you. Miami, your successful business, your boyfriend you were pining for. Your amazing future now with this galaxy ahead of you."

"Easier?"

"Lila, you're getting everything you dreamt of."

"No," I say for the second time tonight.

He shakes his head. "Andrés wants you."

"Orion, stop. Just because—"

"It's so simple. Part of the reason you're even here is him—"

"¡Me cago en diez! Will you bloody listen?"

This gets him. He turns, granite-jawed and blurry-eyed. No, he doesn't get to be hurt. He doesn't get to feel hurt about Andrés and the second this flashes across my mind, the answer beams, free and clear.

My smile breaks out in sheer relief before it remembers all the other hurts. I stand; we're a pace or two apart. "Do you want me to show you the time stamp from my parents' call? 'Cause you'll see there's not even five minutes between me hanging up, then knocking at your door looking like shit. What does that tell you?"

He scrubs his face, shrugging. "That you're as fucking fast on your feet as you ever were."

"Try again. I didn't go to Andrés with my news. Didn't call or message or even think about him. I can't be with a person who's a second thought. Yeah, I loved him for a long time, but I can't go back to him, Orion." My words tangle in a rush of oxygen. "He should be with a person who runs to him first. I didn't want to."

Orion absorbs this with a pinwheel of reactions. His wide-eyed jolt morphs into a jagged smile, ending in a messy, caustic laugh. "See, I told you. No motorbike, no deal."

I match his mess. "He hates tea with a passion."

"Oh, well, come *on*, then," he says and steps forward until he's going either to run into me or draw me into his arms. I get the latter—home. So very much at home. "Lila Reyes of West Dade is gonna be on television. It really is cracking news."

I fold myself into him and for a few moments, there is only me holding the star-named boy who dipped his finger into my cake batter. Weeks later, there's no part of my life he hasn't touched.

But time closes around us. He shifts but doesn't let go. Like this St. Cross house, we know we're just another home that can't be whole. "Andrés or no, you still need to return to Miami. Be there for your family, La Paloma."

"I am," I say into his polo. Meaning it. "At the same time, I don't want to leave anything here. Or anyone." Meaning it.

He pulls back. "Day by day. All we have." And this is all he says. *You could come back.* It rises, moving from his skin to mine. But would he ever voice it? Or am I just another impossible thing he'd dare not beg any God or universe for?

He thumbs underneath my eyes. "Stay and hang, okay? You can share my leftovers, but first, I can make us a cuppa? I refilled our stock here."

"Just what I need."

I wait on the couch, hugging my arms to my chest. Footsteps pad, then his soft gray cardigan drapes around my shoulders. Of course he has it near. I clutch the collar then say over the back of the couch, "You didn't tell me your grandmother knitted this."

"Not after learning you'd just lost yours." He winds around, then hands me a warmed cup. "Then I didn't think of it."

I sip the fragrant tea and maybe moan.

"Quite good, huh? All those puddings you feed me made me think of this variety now. Vanilla black."

I drink again, the flavors of two cities I love tangling on my tongue. "Orion, this one."

"What?"

"It's my favorite."

27

Orion's London is the streets and pavements and outsides of things. It's the vintage bookstores and secret neighborhood parks, the people watching with lattes in quirky Covent Garden. Then Neal's Yard with its cluster of brightly colored storefronts and the eclectic beat of Soho. His London is plunking our elbows onto the Embankment wall on a sun-bright Saturday, where we can get by with his short sleeves and my stretch jersey maxi dress.

The River Thames flows in front of us, winding through boroughs. Four hundred feet high, the white London Eye observation wheel twirls over South Bank, just across Westminster Bridge. Midday light glows off Elizabeth Tower at the edge of the monstrous Parliament compound. "Lots of tourists think Big Ben *is* the clock tower. It's actually the bell inside the tower," Orion says.

I stare at the blended landscape of medieval and modern so hard my eyes blur. "Never stop." I let the river have my words.

"Never stop what?"

"Telling me things about things."

He smiles and leads us toward Parliament and Westminster Cathedral. I link our elbows and ask him to show me Buckingham Palace.

"We should try to come back at least two more times before ..." He doesn't have to finish. "The British Museum is so cool. And the Tower of London. You'll love the crown jewels and all the armory, the weapons. And anything you want to see the insides of, we can."

But today the sun is high and the Mall leads us into a long thoroughfare with a fantasy palace at its foot. Union Jack banners flank our way, and when I get my Buckingham dreams fulfilled, he shows me the posh and manicured Mayfair borough and leads me into Kensington Gardens.

While I'm dreamy inside an Italian water garden, I remember the junior high plan Stefanie and I made to see London and Paris together the first time. Me, here with Orion instead of her, doesn't feel like a loss. It feels like a change. And there's always Paris.

Orion speaks more "things" into patches of my silence, like how in 1861, Prince Albert built this ornamental garden as a gift for Queen Victoria. We stroll around Italian urns and manicured hedges.

"It's been a whole five minutes since I told you a superstition."

My laugh hums; I thump his side. "Well, go on. You have to have one about gardens or flowers."

"About bees, actually. But we wouldn't have gardens without those guys. And this one's English in origin, so, also fitting," he says as we stare into one of the reflecting pools. "Beekeepers thought it was essential to good honey production to talk to their bees. So, telling the bees, as they called it, became a must. They'd tell them about any household events like births or marriages. And especially deaths."

My reflection leans its head against his shoulder.

"Most of all, when someone died and the family dressed for mourning, you had to dress the bees for mourning too. You had to tell them."

"How do you dress bees for mourning?" And here's a series of words I'd never say in my Miami life.

Orion's melancholy smile ripples through the water. "They'd usually drape their hives with black fabric, letting them know. Otherwise the bees would leave the hive or even die. As a penalty toward the family."

"Abuela would've loved you." My storyteller and teamaker and the boy who could nick and knife my heart, just for living under another flag.

"She traveled a few places, but she never went here or Europe. And I wish she'd gotten the chance to walk in a London park. I wish she'd seen Paris and Rome." Now I look at the real him, not the blurred face swimming with lily pads and lotus flowers. "Funny because it took us an hour on the train to get here. And the whole way, I was thinking that her flight from Havana to Miami was only about thirty minutes."

"Is that all, really?" We move along toward Hyde Park and the giant Serpentine lake separating the park from Kensington Gardens.

"Really. So close but a world away. She was only seventeen. My age. And so brave to leave her family . . . her country, alone."

"How did she?"

"A special opportunity through her church and a Miami parish—like an exchange student program. It's much harder now, of course. I'll need more than an hour train ride to get you through Cuban-American politics. But Abuela made it a forever exchange. She lived with her host family for years after the program ended and started La Paloma with my grandfather. My mother didn't inherit the chops to bake cakes, but she learned to decorate them early on. And still does."

"And your father?"

"He was in marketing. But when my parents married, he joined the business and freed up Abuela and Mami to have more time to create. La Paloma doubled in size and they bought the shop next door, expanding the whole place. Pilar is so much like him." We walk the footpath and watch Londoners and tourists row in pairs or trudge across the lake in pedal boat rentals.

I take three steps before I realize Orion didn't take them with me. I spin around; he's looking at his phone, texting and shaking his head in disbelief.

"What happened?" I say at his side. We're at the same park, but the whole landscape's changed.

"Bloody hell. Now they've done it. And I'm—"

"Who's done what?"

He flips to another screen and my stomach sinks. More graffiti. Only this time, both the side and back walls of Maxwell's Tea Shop have been tagged, and with more paint than we've seen yet. Much of the shop exterior will need refurbishing. Thoughts swarm like the bees in his superstition. Flora. But she promised. She *promised* me. And tagging her own business?

"Those fucking wankers," Orion says. "Hold up, Dad's texting me back."

My phone buzzes too.

Flora: I swear it wasn't me

Before I can even respond she messages again.

Flora: I was at Katy's the whole night. Her mum's name is Abigail and I'll give you her number and you can ask her yourself. Her parents took us to a show and Katy and I crashed in the living room after. It wasn't me

Me: I believe you

I write this because it's true.

Orion's forehead creases with strain. "Enough with waiting to catch those arses." He whips his head left to right. Checks his watch. "I'd never ask you to accompany me for this. I can drop you somewhere you'd love, like Fortnum and Mason, just until I handle this situation. But I'm going straight to Roth's place. Gonna make him admit it and repair my walls. Now."

"No!" My pulse beats ten steps ahead of my fear.

"What do you mean, no? They went too bloody far this time. They destroyed almost our entire exterior!"

My skin glazes with dampness. What can I say? I promised Flora I'd keep her confidence. "But what if you're wrong? What if it's really not Roth and his boys. What if—"

"Look, we've been dealing with that group and their antics long before you got here. We know it's them, and the town's sick of it. Sick of spending our time with scrub brushes and solvents." He brings up the picture again, swearing richly. "Sick of bullies, Lila."

"But look, it's two colors. Black and light gray and it's not any of the same symbols. And none of the other instances had so much damage. It's probably just some kid." Orion keeps shaking his head. "You don't know what Roth is capable of if you go over there, accusing him with no proof. You said he's a hot head. He could snap."

"Fine, I'll not go alone. Remy's off today. He can get here soon enough. He's got his eyes set on law school—becoming a solicitor. This will give him some cross-examination practice early on."

"But Orion you can't just—"

"I'd do it for him, any day. He'll come."

My breath quickens. Would Jules go for this idea? Worse images flash: Flora's trembling face and *please don't tell Orion*, and Orion getting *his* face smashed in, and this whole charade going on and on and . . . "Wait! It's not Roth. I . . . I know who's been doing the tagging—not this one, but the others." I hear myself, the words breaking free of their sentences, pelting me back in jumbled order. A gust between my ears.

The disbelief in his eyes tears me from face to foot. "What do you mean?"

"It's not Roth who did all those symbols, all those months. It's not them, Orion. Let it go."

"How can you possibly know?" he asks, his voice dragged across weathered brick.

I squint, rattling my head. "I . . ."

"Lila, I appreciate why you're trying to stop me. But I need to put an end to this and I'll handle myself just—"

"It was your sister," I spit out, hating myself. "Flora. I caught her tagging." *Forgive me, Flora.*

A ragged shock, then his expression hones to hard marble as he listens to the events from that night I jogged after Remy's pub.

"Please don't tell Flora I told you. Don't tell your dad. Just let it ride. She begged me. *Begged.* The damage to your shop from last night couldn't have been her. She has proof, okay? She told me she'd stop and she has." Tears well my vision. "Promise me."

"Promise you? Promise . . . *you?*" Heat rolls out in waves from him. "Christ, Lila, is this why she's working with you? Some kind of payment to buy your silence?"

"It's not payment. I wanted to help her. She's hurting."

"You don't think I know that? Me of all people? You don't think I know?" His hand dashes out. "Hurt aside, she still did wrong and she needs to be held accountable."

"I agree." I dig my fingers into my aching temples. "But Friday she told me she went and cleaned up the wall where I caught her. She's doing really well working at the inn. She's opening up. She was just desperate to be seen and heard. To be remembered. She was crying out—"

"That wasn't your choice to make." One step forward. "She's

not your sister. She's not your responsibility. This is *our* family. *Our* business. You made the choice for all of us."

Oh, the words. I have no more room, no place left inside to hold them. I get right up to him, setting my face into iron. "Flora's my friend. Doesn't that mean anything? All she wants is for things to go back to the way they were. I know how she feels, even if we're not going through the exact same thing." My hands slice the rancid air between us. "So yeah, I could've turned her in, but I didn't. I decided to give her a chance for something new, just like I had."

He half-turns, then points at me. "You never hurt people or their private property like she did. You didn't hurt your city."

"I hurt my*self*. And how is that any less?"

I spin on the ball of my foot and bolt. Not once do I look back. Fury fills my veins and hurries my steps down the path bordering the Serpentine.

Minutes later, I'm not even sure how far I've gone. There's so much green, so much open space to swallow the enormous rush of me. But now I slow and stop, dropping onto one of the many benches along the water. Why did I think my half-lying plan would be different just because I was genuinely trying to help someone? Today, there *was* no better choice, no winning door to walk through that leads to prizes.

Help Flora and keep her confidence, and Orion is hurt for my deceit.

Or tell Orion, like he said I should've, and Flora is hurt enough to maybe find another version of paint on a brick wall. Hurt enough to be more careful and maybe even more destructive.

And now it's done. I can't bake around it or add any more sugar to the sour, beating it into a win for everyone. I have to accept another thing I can't change. And then I have to go on and remember why I came here.

So I remember: school, skills, my passion. Even if it might not be in my future, one choice I made before even hopping on the train in Winchester, I'm still choosing, for me. I'm going to get across town to Bloomsbury and visit Le Cordon Bleu. I pull out my phone. I can find my own way there and, if necessary, find my own way back to Winchester, too.

"Lila." The voice behind my bench is full of dust.

Well. I tuck my lips inward, my face bent over the grass.

He sits beside me, farther than he's ever been.

"I never want to lie to you. I'm sorry," I say, then measure the next part as carefully as soufflé batter. "Do you think it hasn't been making me sick to keep Flora's secret? That it was some whim? Do you think it was *easy* to just push this away every time I was with you?" Right into his eyes.

Hearts are not meant to be ripped in two, split between seas and skies. Split between two people I care for and . . .

Orion shifts, only a few inches. "I don't feel that way. I didn't, even for a second." He scrubs his face. "But I'm losing her, Lila. She's barely around and she doesn't talk to me anymore. She doesn't even go to see Mum as often as she used to."

Losing a sister. Losing a mother.

"But I did some thinking back there," he adds and flattens his back against the bench. "The other day when I was with Mum and couldn't run with you, Flora brought home a loaf of fresh bread. She was so proud of it and that means something. I haven't seen Flora be proud of anything in so long."

"I know how much you love her. How you want to stay close and reach her. But she's starting to relax. She's fun. We have a good time even at the half crack of dawn."

"I know. And that means something too." A weighty sigh. "So I'll promise what you asked. The two of us will share her secret now."

Air leaks from my lungs in relief. "I'm not trying to fix her. I just wanted to be a safe place for her. Like someone else I know is for me."

"Safe." He balls his fist over his mouth, sucks in a rush, nodding. "And yet I said horrible things to you. I try to take this good and right view about my life. But that doesn't mean I always say the right thing."

I hold out my hand. He grabs it tightly.

"If you did, you'd be a tea-obsessed, history buff cyborg on a too-loud motorbike. Which sounds more like a comic book character than a person. You know you can be whoever you are with me."

"I don't want to be someone who hurts you."

"Yeah, but you will," I say. "And I'll hurt you. But there's the kind of hurting that happens between . . . friends that makes you human. You get past those hurts." I think of Stefanie, the ways we've hurt each other. Our future's still shaded, not steady and warm like the sunlight over my bare shoulders.

I scoot closer. "But there's also a dangerous kind of hurting between people. You run from those hurts."

"You ran from me. Back there."

"I needed to decide how I felt without unleashing my Reyes wrath."

His brow arches as he jerks his thumb sideways. "That wasn't your wrath?"

"It's funny you thought that was my wrath."

He laughs nervously, but he drops into gravity when he meets my face. "And how you feel now. Is there a part of you that's able to accept my apology?"

I nod. "All my parts do."

He cracks a smile and takes my other hand. "Do you want to go back to the inn? Or will you let me take you to Le Cordon Bleu? Show you around the neighborhood?"

"Let's go."

But instead of leaving, he rests his head on my shoulder. "I'm not the hurting kind of dangerous, Lila." We'll get up soon, but not yet. Right now, he's warm as sweaters and sure as stars. And every other kind of dangerous I know.

28

Flora stays when I offer to brew café con leche to drink with the guava pastelitos we made. She sags into a stool and cuts thick slices of the bread we also made, watching me pour Cuban coffee shots into fat mugs of steamed milk. "It's like a latte, then?"

"Pretty close." I study her. She worked hard today, making her first pastelitos on her own. And now she gets to eat them. But all through the mixing and layering and folding she was the kind of quiet most girls notice about other girls. I noticed but kept my mouth shut.

Instead I drag over mugs, sugar, and the plate of extra pastelitos we kept back for her family. I toy with the pastry—perfectly golden and flaky, with just enough guava filling peeking out from the sides and ridge-cut tops. In my head, I'm back in London on Saturday, staring up at a classic ivory and brick building locked into a row of attached brownstones. Le Cordon Bleu.

The school was closed, but its public café flanking the adjacent courtyard was busy with customers. We studied photos of students in their white emblemed chef coats over loose gray pants. Then we sat under a blue umbrella and shamelessly sampled four desserts and pastries. So light and airy, with carved chocolate shapes and delicate cakes filled with creams and fruits.

"Why this school?" Orion asked over a miniature lemon tart covered with tiny puffs of toasted meringue shaped like clouds.

"There's not much more for me to learn in Cuban baking. But there's so much out there—so many techniques I don't know. How to mold sugar and chocolate and countless other tricks." I pointed my fork at the layered torte we were sharing. How did the chef stack all those fillings so thinly? "I don't know how to make a pastry like this. It's artwork. Also, Abuela's sweetness philosophy was different from what many Cubans believe, which is add sugar to your sugar."

Orion laughed and finished off the lemon tart.

"By the time she opened La Paloma, she'd had some French desserts and noticed they were more rich than sweet."

Orion bumped me playfully. "That's how I'd describe your pastries for sure."

"Right. At home, I saw no reason to learn more. But being here and getting out of my little Miami corner changed all that. It's reminded me that the world is bigger than my neighborhood, and my skills could be bigger too."

"Like what you've been doing at the inn? Mashing everything up?"

"Yes, only better. Like taking an intricate French dessert but subbing out some Cuban flavors. Or British flavors. Of course, I'll always make my old recipes. But customers love eclectic pairings and interesting food. For that, I need help. Yeah, there are schools in the States, but not LCB caliber. London is the closest one where I . . ."

He snaked his fingers over my wrist. "Where you have people you're close to."

I nodded. "It's an hour from the inn, but back home, people who work in Ft. Lauderdale drive that long too, and in the most stressful traffic you can imagine. I could relax on the train. Read or message or make calls." Call my family? Call them while they stayed in Miami and ran my business without me? Again, there was no choice here that made everything all better. Another time, I'd have to decide who would get all the hurt. And either way, one of those hurters would be me.

"I was never specifically told to stay put, or to stay in Miami, but that's the pattern in my family. Most of my cousins lived at home until they got married. Some of them were pushing thirty."

"So this is the opposite of those unspoken ideals? Run off, not just away from your family, but to another country. Another culture."

"Another life."

Now, I leave that Saturday afternoon an hour train ride away, and catch up. Flora's got a pastry in one hand and buttered pan Cubano in the other. I tip my cup at her. "Be careful, girl, you're starting to turn Cuban."

She laughs, but it comes out weak, her eyes boring into the wooden island.

I dunk my bread in the milky coffee. "So, anything new?"

"Not really."

"'Kay." I break apart my pastelito, stealing a quick glance at the last small tray browning in the oven. Butter stains my fingers and pastry flakes stick to my lip gloss as I eat.

Gordon swoops in from outside, windblown, a knapsack hanging from one shoulder. "Ri said you're hiding extra tins of that vanilla pudding in the fridge."

I snort. "Traitor. But have at it."

Why it takes Gordon this much time and noise to get himself one ramekin of natilla, a glass of water, a spoon, and whatever else, is beyond me. He bee-buzzes into the pantry, then through another drawer, the fridge again. "Don't mind me."

We don't. The guava filling is too good. The coffee is better.

"Well," Flora says when the third wheel finally leaves out the back door. "Actually. Can I ask you something weird?"

"Besides baking at odd hours, weird is my other specialty."

She inhales, releases, then says, "Is it normal for a guy you're kind of chatting to and getting to know . . . I mean, is it weird that he asks about your friend a lot? Like too much?"

Ah, sí. "Not only weird, it's what we call a red flag at home."

"Same here."

I face her directly. "I think you know the answer."

Her next bite leaves a dab of butter on her chin. She wipes it clean. "So, yeah. Will. I'm afraid he's been using me to get close to Jules. Maybe to slide into our group for Roth's sake. Not mine."

My fifteen-year-old self aches for her. I look inside my heart, at my own truth. "Anyone who's lucky enough to hang with you needs to be all about you. You know, more thoughtful." I sip coffee and bite off more than flaky pastry. "Like, say, Gordon."

"Gordon?" She whips around with a look as blank as an English morning sky. "*Gordon?*" She actually laughs. "God, no. I've known him since I was in nappies. And he's a good mate and all. But not *more*." She shakes her head to seal it. "Could you imagine . . ."

I could, but I am no one's forceful matchmaker. "Okay, but whoever it is needs to make you to feel the most special."

"Now that, I'd like."

"And you'll have it. But really, there's no rush. Enjoy the friends you have now."

"I do have friends. But sometimes they just go along with things. So, if your sister heard about a guy like Will doing that to you, she'd probably get on you?"

I laugh, shaking my head. "So, so much."

"I was thinking, that time you told me about your prom. I'd like to have someone who'd go into my room, and *not* Orion. Someone who'd clear my space of a boy who'd hurt me. Clear out all the things before I saw them."

"I think Jules would do that if you'd let her."

"True. She'd throw out all sorts of shit from my window. Then she'd write a rager of a song about it."

"The ragiest."

We laugh, and then Flora whispers into the belly of her cup, "You'd be good at that too. Not the song part. All the other parts."

The oven timer chimes over my heart-ping. "Your turn."

Flora jumps up for the oven mitt. "Eww! What the devil?" she cries after shoving her hand inside. She pulls out a frothy white mess and licks her fingers. "Whipped cream?"

I'm already at the oven, killing the heat and using a thick towel to remove the pan.

Flora dashes to the sink. "Someone booby-trapped our oven mitts?"

A twitchy noise whips our heads to the swing door. It's cracked open, a patch of red hair curling around the frame. The door releases and hasty footsteps slap.

"Gordon!" we yell in unison.

Flora's brows drop as she points to the fridge. "He was in there twice for one dish of pudding?" She lunges for the stainless-steel door and pulls out a spray can of whipped cream. Holds it up.

I take the can, snarling. "I don't know what's worse, his prank and sneaking back around to spy on us, or that he dared to bring this processed, fake shit into my kitchen."

Our faces volley from the can to scheming expressions.

"I know his hiding spot. He's already out the front door, trust me," Flora says.

I plunk the can into her hands before we shoot onto the patio. "He has a head start, but we're smarter."

Flora's grin, her sunshine hair after the rain. "He's gonna look amazing in white." We run St. Cross like my cousins stealing bases.

29

Instead of Millie, we take Orion's dad's Volkswagen to visit his mother. We've piled backpacks and insulated totes onto the vintage motorbike many times. But Millie wasn't built to carry a huge white bakery box.

I bring scones, strawberry empanadas, and cheese pastelitos for the staff, fortifying myself with the lidded box like a makeshift shield. Isn't this what I always do? Hide behind bread and baking?

It's not that I don't want to come to Elmwood House. I want this crucial piece of Orion Maxwell. I want to see the part of his heart that lives down one of these blue painted corridors.

"Sara," Orion says to a receptionist behind the welcome desk. "My friend Lila made treats for everyone."

While the grateful clerk sends Orion to the manager's office to grab some paperwork, the staff swarms like humans usually do around sugar. Nurses appear, followed by a couple of medics and maintenance workers.

Waiting in this reception room with its potted plants and periwinkle wallpaper, I watch as family members are reunited by long-awaited visits, and once again separated by departures that come too soon. My heart tightens as one woman wipes away tears as she leaves.

But she can come back again. I can't stop the thought. *I will never visit Abuela in a home like this.*

Recipe for a Funeral
From the Kitchen of Lila Reyes

Ingredients: One grieving family. One coffin (it *must* be white like flour and sugar). One cathedral. One white apron. One abuela, gone, dressed in her favorite blue vestido.

Preparation: Sit between your boyfriend and best friend as they try to hold you upright in the pew. Clutch a white apron tightly on your lap. Watch your parents weeping one row ahead, and your sister leaning on your mother's shoulder. Look back once over the massive cathedral, marveling at the crowd that came for her.

*Leave out actually seeing your abuela laid out so lovingly in the white coffin. She is not *there*. Instead, cry, kneeling during the private viewing with your eyes secretly pressed closed.

Cooking temp: 100 degrees Fahrenheit. The coldest your oven goes.

Months later, no one knows that I never saw Abuela in her blue dress that March day. Is there some ancient Cuban mourning code I'd broken with this behavior? Probably. But I didn't care. For me, she had to rest where I could hold her forever, a heart-home warm and worthy of her. I decided to leave her where I found her. I left her where she found me as a toddler, at her feet with a clanging set of measuring spoons. I left her where she grew me. No, not a white coffin. And not a long-term care facility. I left my abuelita in the kitchen.

"Lila?" Orion's voice brings me back to this home, and this day. "Everything okay?"

I nod. The sweet concern in his eyes and his palm curled around my shoulder make it true.

I fortify myself with his hand threaded into mine as we enter the wide hallway. *Evelyn Maxwell,* the sign at her door reads. Before we enter, Orion takes a moment inside himself. He looks down and away and I wonder if he does this every time. Only a blink or two before he's back with a soft smile. "Don't be sad. I mean, for me."

"Okay," I promise. Pity, sadness, and grief are not what our visit is about and not what he needs from me.

A nurse in green scrubs exits before we enter. She types into a tablet then says, "Orion. Good afternoon, then. I'm headed to reception. Heard there's pastries."

He introduces me, the pastry chef, to Kelly and we learn his mom has just eaten an early supper and she'll go out to the garden after we leave.

Inside the cozy room, impressionist artwork hangs from pale

green walls and a window with floral curtains looks out into a courtyard. A wall-mounted TV is on, but the sound's muted. Then my eyes fall onto the neat single bed and a mother.

"Hello, beautiful," Orion says to the blond in a pink long-sleeved top. Someone has colored her lips with tinted balm.

She moves, shifting and stirring, but doesn't look at me or even her own son. We pull up two side chairs. He sits closest and reaches out.

"I always hold her hands or touch her face," he tells me. Then, straight into the blue eyes they share. "Mum, I've brought Lila today. The girl from Miami I've been telling you about. And she made quite the stir at reception, bringing treats for everyone. I really wanted you to meet her."

My heart balloons and he's right, sadness isn't the biggest emotion I want to feel. The room is full of love and quiet acceptance. Orion tells stories, bringing life here, pulling bright pieces of it from himself, from me, from music and motorbikes and friends. He pours living into her and fills her with a world she can't fill herself with anymore.

"Did you tell her about the batter bowl incident?" I ask.

"That same week. And how you got after me—God, your face." He smiles. "Figured she should know about that."

He slips into more updates about taking me to see my first castle and us romping around London. A few times, his mother mumbles or nods randomly. Orion notes and savors these sparks of reaction before moving on to more adventurous tales. Is this the room where my storyteller was born?

Soon, I feel comfortable enough to join in. "Flora's been learning to make bread. She loves kneading it the best because she gets to boss the dough around," I say, then I tell her more about how proud she should be of her daughter. No matter what, every mom likes to hear that. "And Orion's the best at knowing when you need a cup of tea or a really big hug. Well, it would actually take me until bedtime to tell you all the things he's the best at."

But as our visit lengthens and the sunlight thins, the world between Lila Reyes and Evelyn Maxwell changes. I find myself drifting then falling into full Spanish, letting myself tell Orion's mother things I can barely tell myself. Los secretos. She gets my secrets as her son splits his gaze between the both of us. I know she can't comprehend a word. But I don't give her my mysteries and heart puzzles to make her understand them. I can't understand them and speaking them is all I have.

So I do, until I've said all I can.

Suddenly too aware of myself and Orion, I turn to him, heat filling me. "Sorry. I kind of got carried away."

"No. Don't be." He kisses his mother's hand then takes mine. "If a Brit tells you not to be sorry, then you're really, *really* not supposed to be sorry, okay?"

My mouth jerks sideways. "Right."

"About what you said, I think I caught the words *sister, abuela, airplane, mother,* and *bakery.* And my name's the same, so . . ."

Not sorry, but still feeling like he can see right through me, I shift my gaze out the window. "Then you caught the gist."

✳

It's unspoken where we both want to go after Elmwood House. A few visitors picnic on the grass or throw balls to dogs on St. Catherine's Hill, but we settle inside the shady thicket. Plum-sky dusk bumps into the last stretch of afternoon. We spend ours on the fallen tree log bench, quiet.

"I've been watching you shamelessly and verging on creepily," Orion says after long minutes. "The way your face twitches all sorts of ways, and you move to speak then twist your mouth sideways. Is it about Mum, then?"

"Yes and no. My plane ticket came today, right before we left. I told your mother about it."

"Oh," he breathes more than voices. We're hip to hip, soul to soul. We both knew the date, but I can't stop seeing the official logo in the e-mail. *British Airways. LHR—MIA.*

"And I also told her—" Eye roll at myself. "Never mind."

His chin tilts, gaze narrowing. "Don't you know there's literally nothing you can't tell me?"

"Not this, trust me. It's horrible. Terrible." Desgraciada—I am wretched and wicked. "Don't make me say it."

"I'd never make you do anything. But I'm well used to terrible. I can handle yours."

Sadness isn't here, either. Rage taints my blood, reddens the words trapped behind my throat. I dig my fingers into the rough and rigid tree bark. "Fine. I wanted to know, okay? What's worse: Walking into your kitchen after school and finding your grandmother, your *everything*, on the floor in front of the sink. Already gone."

"Christ." His arm pulls me in. "I didn't know *you* found her. Bloody hell."

"Yes . . . so that, or loving a mother who's still here but not present. Watching her lose a little more each month, preparing yourself. I hate throwing your life into your face right now. And I still have my own mother. But . . . Abuela—I never got to say goodbye." I bury my head into his chest in shame. "And I don't know what's worse, not getting to say goodbye, or saying goodbye to a little more every year."

"The tidal wave or the hourglass."

"Yeah."

He threads his fingers through my hair. "Does one have to be worse? Or can't they both be the same amount of terrible? They change us and make us stronger, and we do our best to go on, all the same?"

"We do," I tell him, letting his words rise and swell into cracks. "And you're right. It's amazing the way you handle what life hands you, how you deal. But don't you ever want to fight back a little? Cheat the universe? Take a moment just for you and not wait for life to plan the rest of it?"

Glazed blue into my brown. "Or take it away?"

"Or that."

"Every single day."

"But you still . . . can't?" And I can't look at him anymore.

"Lila," he says, his hand clamping around my forearm so quickly, I flinch. "Am I such a total dolt that you have no idea of my feelings? For you?"

Do it. Look at him. Face him. I lift up and find another kind of storm—the longing of warm drinks and warm sweaters, but the coldness of being bare. "I feel them more than anything. And I wish . . ." I shake my head. "Does it even matter? Do we not get to do that anymore? Wish? On stars or for moments just for us?"

He fits his hands into both of mine. "What's your wish, then?"

"Um, no. *No.* Your superstitious self should know better than to ask for details. There's already enough in the universe fighting against my wish coming true." I straighten my spine, sniffling. "And if you don't already know then *I'm* the dolt at—"

Orion knocks my words aside, stealing my space with his mouth over mine. A low-toned oath strums the back of his throat. Holy. This is new and what are we doing? We do it anyway, figuring it out as we go, a chaotic mess of flailing movement—teeth scraping, noses bumping, loose-limbed and greedy.

He rips backward, breathing like a winded runner. "I was right, then. Same as mine, you know, if I was a wishing kind of bloke."

I make some sort of agreeable noise.

"But I can do better."

Dios, he does. *He does he does he does.* My cheeks caged in his hands, Orion looks at me like I'm the finest dessert I've made yet. He thumbs my jawline and slides his mouth lazily over mine. Takes his time like we have it to spare.

His hands travel down, down, and lower still until they're clasped behind me, lifting me onto his lap. He tastes of fruit and sugar. Then his smile—sweeter—before he dots his lips along my forehead and the rise of my cheekbones.

I drag him back down. Golden sparks from all the city lights we've seen tunnel through me, across all my avenues. I can't stop touching him. Can't get close enough. I push my body into his, the lean strength of his muscles and bones teeming around me.

Keep me? Another wish I can't even trust the stars with. What language do I use to wish for continents and cultures to bend? *Keep me impossibly.* I wish this with my hands, my nails marking a star-named boy with half moons.

Tonight, I kiss him under a beech tree canopy and learn the pattern etched across a twilight sky doesn't matter. Orion Maxwell is all the northern lights, the North Star—my true north—even when my legacy calls me southward.

Southward. Miami.

Clocks strike home at that, and phantom wheels touch the tarmac. We both sense the shift and ease away at the same unspoken moment. I'm still in his lap, wrapped around him like wool. My forehead tips against his with four thousand miles between us.

"When you first came here," he starts, his voice full of gravel, "your heart belonged to another guy." When I nod he says, "But even now, you still belong to another place. I can't even think of being with you in Miami for years. Not with Mum and Flora—"

"I know." I've always known.

"So much is goodbye and fleeting in my life. I'm losing people and I'm so tired of that feeling. And *you* . . ." The single word reflects in his eyes. "You couldn't be just some quick fling. See, I can't do that—weeks of summer shags—with an end date in my head. I can't and then put you on a plane, and only get to keep the memory of it. Of you."

My breathing staggers, understanding and knowing he's right. Hating his rightness. Loving him being all about me in this terrible-beautiful way. "We can't do this again, can we?"

Eyes glassy, he shakes his head. "It's just too bloody hard. For now, let our time here be our moment."

The moment we cheated worlds and lives and universes for.

They still win. Por ahora.

For now.

30

On the night of my eighteenth birthday, I'm told to wear my nicest dress and stay in my room until someone comes for me. I do have a new dress, a short wispy number Victoria at Come Around Again said was perfection a couple weeks ago. The price was also perfect, and so is the fit. Black floral chiffon skims just off my body and rises to a square neckline framed with thin straps.

I add finishing touches to my look while starting my packing. Two days left, but I'm focused on finding all the celebration I can, not fumbling over what, and who, I have to leave. To get myself through, I had to take a perfect, cheated moment with Orion in a twilight thicket, locking it in a treasure box inside of me. *For now.*

But Orion was not without other treasures and gifts. Earlier, I got more London for my birthday, this time, the inside parts. I spent all day ogling the crown jewels and dragging him through every floor of Fortnum and Mason's food hall and department store, fawning over gourmet ingredients and picking souvenirs for

Mami and Pilar. But my real surprise was Orion treating me to a splurge-worthy tea in Fortnum's Diamond Jubilee Tea Salon. We ate through the afternoon, surrounded by white tablecloths and robin's-egg-blue china. We drank their signature Royal Blend and stuffed ourselves with finger sandwiches, scones, and fancy cakes.

Then we took an early train back, leaving plenty of night in Winchester. But for what? I'm fastening the last buckle on my gold sandals when knocking sounds.

My someone?

"Oh," I say into the open doorway, then, "*Oh!*" Orion's showered and changed into a slim black suit, complete with a silvery blue dress shirt and matching tie. Tan guapo—gorgeous—and everything dapper.

He steps in, leaning to kiss my cheek. Even though we've been back to PG for the last week since St. Catherine's Hill, no one's bothered to tell our eyes. Am I staring like a fool?

His are large and ocean-deep enough to draw me in for drowning, his own siren song. This black-suited boy hugs me again. "You look beautiful," he says into my ear, my nose full of bar soap and wood-spiced cologne, the tang of styling gel.

My hands press down the smooth lapels of his blazer. "*You* clean up well, Maxwell. But you're a walking superstitious danger to yourself going out with wet hair." I gently ease my fingers over his washed and styled locks.

"Danger and recklessness and tons of alcohol are typical for a school dance night around here." He arches a brow.

"A what?"

He slides his other hand from behind his back and my heart jumps. He presents a clear domed box with a pink rose wrist corsage.

"Is that . . . ?"

"It is. We wanted to do something special for your birthday-slash-going-away party. Flora had a brilliant idea and you'll soon see what some elves have been up to while we were in London." He opens the box and sets it on my writing desk. "English roses for a Cuban girl. Come to prom with me?"

I nod rapidly as he slides the corsage onto my wrist, then I throw my arms around him. "Thank you. I spent ten minutes on this smoky eye, and I'm about to turn into a raccoon."

He pulls me closer, laughing. "No forest creatures. Just us heathens tonight. And I'll warn you, I'm an even worse dancer than cook, but we're going to dance anyway."

"Before we do, maybe you can explain these?" I reach toward the desk for the ribbon-tied set of teakwood mixing spoons I found on the kitchen island after London. I hold out the attached card.

To Lila, on the occasion of your birthday. I trust you'll use these to make many wonderful things back home.
Regards, Polly

PS. Your lemon biscuits and fig pastries and Cuban breads were quite edible.

"Quite edible," I repeat in my best British accent. "But how did she try my pan Cubano and all the rest?"

Orion takes the spoons, admiring them. "That's on me. Polly still comes into Maxwell's for tea. I've been sharing samples of the treats you send home the entire summer." He shrugs. "I guess this is a bit of a peace offering. A lovely gesture, as well."

I shake my head, smiling. "It is. I'll leave a thank-you note for you to give her." For when I'm gone—I don't say this part. I rest the beautiful spoons and grab his hand. "Now it's time to dance."

Steps later, I'm floating down on his arm, catching a few stray smiles from inn guests as we move toward the foyer. Orion hangs a left; the parlor doors are shut, a sign tacked over the entrance. *Closed for private event.*

He ushers me into a smaller, cozier version of the senior prom I never had. Cheers and greetings flood my ears as I try to take in everything at once. All our friends are here, even the Gold-line members, turned out in makeshift prom finery. Orion's dad and Cate and Spencer huddle by the big picture window. A strobe light throws bright fragments around the softly lit space. Hugs—everyone comes up. My arms are full of people.

Jules appears last, rocking finger wave curls and a black strapless dress. Layers of polka-dot tulle poke from under the tea length hem. She squeezes me tight, my words of thanks in her ear. "Aww, we had fun with all this." She grins. "Happy birthday, my friend. Come look, we moved all the sofas so there's room for dancing."

She and Orion lead me around the transformed space. Remy's parents brought platters of fruit, chips (and my favorite curry sauce) and mini sliders. All of the parlor tables are grouped near the buffet, but it's what's on top that has me staring in disbelief.

"Wait. Centerpieces?" And then I realize they're everywhere. Mismatched centerpieces, all colors and sizes, decorate tables and the bar area, even the fireplace mantle.

"Unfortunately, you can't take them home and make your mother's covert floral aspirations come true. We borrowed these from a bunch of local businesses. They need to go back tomorrow, but we thought . . ."

"Everything." He brought Miami to my English party. "You thought of everything. Thank you doesn't even work."

"Your smile does," Orion says.

Gordon leans in from behind. "Not an ombre carnation in sight. We made sure of that."

My night flows, sweet and dreamlike. Music pipes through and I dance with everyone, even Orion's dad and Spencer. But all my dancing parts are most at home with a prom date I didn't even know I was waiting for, on a milestone night I'd wished away.

Is there a superstition about things you let go of, only to be surprised later with a version of them that's so much better? I have the better now. But I don't want to ask Orion anything. I only want to do what I'm doing—dancing with him so closely there's no room for any holy deities between us. My head sinks heavy on his shoulder and his hands link into the small of my back. Song after song.

Sometime later, pictures and voices in my head creep over the soft ballad.

"You went all tense just now," he says.

"Before you knocked, I started packing and each item reminded me of something we did when I wore it. And I don't want to ruin this night, but I can't stop seeing the ticket."

He draws circles on my bare back. "I won't say any more about day by day because we only have two days left. But look, I didn't go to my prom either. And now I have this night. I left school thinking I wouldn't and now I do, Lila."

"So do I." And one cheated moment is better than an entire champagne-gowned life with another boy who was my yesterday, but doesn't fit into my now anymore.

And what about mañana? What and who and where fits into that? Orion fits *me* close, warm, and wanted into his today. But even after the way he kissed me, the way he honors me tonight, he still can't talk about tomorrow.

I find ways to snap back, to keep my celebration in focus. I hide my ticking clocks and impossibilities into centerpieces, drowning them in flutes of bubbly champagne. I study the faces of my new friends and try to memorize them. We'll have texts and FaceTime, but I want all the RealTime skin and bones of them, the hearts and little pieces of them. Enough to last.

Orion, toting a big plate of chips, finds me again. He turns me around as Jules and her Goldline friends group in the opposite corner. "More surprises."

"She's going to sing?"

The band members settle into a stripped down, acoustic rig of two guitars, keyboard, and a box drum. Jules grabs a mic that's been turned low for the inn. "Where's Lila?" She spots me through the faded light then grins. "Oh, there she is. So in honor of your big birthday, and well, just in honor of someone who is bloody spectacular, I wanted to debut Goldline's newest song tonight. It's called 'Sweaters,' um, not 'Jumpers,' because America and all. This one's for you." She blows me a kiss and I'm already teary.

Orion pulls me into his side as the minor chords strum. Remy videos as Jules comes in with her airy singer-songwriter tone. My heart breaks over beauty when she hits the chorus.

> *Sweaters for my shoulders*
> *Blankets for the cold*
> *You're painting stars where*
> *I colored black holes*
> *Your embers, my ashes*
> *Your sugar for this sinking sand*
> *You cover me again*
> *You cover me again*

It's like Jules took everything out of me—the bricks and building blocks of my heart— and set it to music. All these weeks she's been watching, writing my life with lyrics.

Orion has to hold me steady when the bridge starts. The guitar players grin, standing from their stools. Leah the drummer winks, then the chords, the beat, the rhythmic patterns change: Goldline is referencing salsa. Jules toggles between English and Spanish in the most unique bridge I have ever heard. It's not out of place, but a perfect mash-up like a Cuban pastry filled with English fruit.

"What?" I look at Orion and find his face split with a grin. "You knew about this?"

The music goes on and shifts back to the delicate minor progression. "Only that she was planning a song. She's bloody brilliant. The Latin groove in the middle slides in perfectly. Unexpected but not out of place." He kisses my temple. "Just like you."

When it's over, the band moves into more acoustic numbers, but Jules finds my big sandwich hug. "You're incredible," I tell her. "Thank you. I'll never forget this."

She draws back. "After that night we had in the kitchen, cooking and dancing, I just had to. I had the lyrics in bits but couldn't fit all the pieces together. Then it hit me. Maybe it was the Coke and lime." She laughs, but her eyes mist. "Can I come to Miami to visit you? I'm going to miss you so damn much."

I nod into her bare shoulders as we hug again. "Soon—please. Soonest."

And then, and not at all surprisingly, we decline as much as the party. Our chaperones head out. Wine and champagne and cider flow and so does sugar from the ice cream sundae bar Cate set up in lieu of cake (for the best baker in Winchester?).

Another not-surprise, the girls end up together in one corner for a bit, belly-down or crossed-legged on the carpet, shoes flung. Flora, darling in a plum lace minidress, licks her sundae spoon and cracks up as Jules entertains us with parody songs and bawdy jokes.

"What do you think it'll be like? Being on the telly?" Carly from Goldline asks.

"Terrifying," I say through a laugh. "But hopefully less scary after my sister and I spend about a week salon hopping. Brows and nails and highlights." My other life tugs—me racing around with Pilar in my Mini Cooper, barely dodging speeding tickets.

"Yeah," Jules agrees. "It takes a village to look like we do." She fluffs her hair.

My gaze hooks onto Orion, sprawled out across the room with his buddies. Bottles and shot glasses are lined up beside them. He smiles; it unravels loose and lopsided across his face. I chuckle to myself—he could be at any prom after-party I've ever heard about. Alcohol moves his limbs with the wobbling sway of marionette strings.

Back to my girls: Leah and Jules and Carly have moved aside, giggling between pulls of cider and bits of story. But Flora rests her back against the wainscoted wall, just watching me. I scoot closer.

"I'm still gonna do it. Keep baking like you showed me," Flora says.

I toy with my rose corsage. The only centerpiece I want to take home. "Your family will love that." I meet her eyes. She did a worthy job with gray shadow. "Even though I have to go back, you can FaceTime or call or text, anytime." I shrug. "If you have cooking questions or just want to talk. That's how I've been staying close to my sister."

"Yeah, I'd like that." She shifts to watch her brother for a few beats. "I'll make sure he eats right. When you're in Miami. I mean, you can yell at him over the line about his cheese toasties, but I can do more."

Oh, my heart. "You can take care of each other. And your dad, too."

A smile lands then lifts off her face, winged. "But I'll still miss us baking bread and dunking it into that really good coffee you make."

I have to close my eyes, throat burning. Hazlo—so clear what I have to do. So right. I remove my golden necklace, slide the precious dove charm off. I secure the bird to one of the corsage ribbons and drop the delicate chain into Flora's palm. "For you."

She lifts her hand, letting the links fall. "I can't. Your grandmother gave it to you."

"For me, it's more about the charm. I can get another gold chain at home."

Flora smiles. "Thank you, Lila." She lets me fasten the clasp around her neck.

"Add your own special charm when you find it. But wear this and know someone is always thinking of you." Not forgotten. Remembered.

Later, only two remain in the parlor and one wears pink flowers. The other's clutching the door frame for support after shooing out his last friend. I'm quick with my elbow hooked into his. "You. Couch. Now."

Orion utters a British noise of assent, teetering on my arm. "Beautiful. You were. Beautiful dancer."

I ease him onto one of the sofas. Help him out of his jacket.

"Mmm, that's nice."

I sit next to him and he's quick to lean against me. Even his skin reeks of ale and a bar cabinet of hard liquor. "You had quite the prom, didn't you?" I loosen his tie, pull it out from under his collar.

A low, breathy laugh before he slumps and drops his head into my lap.

"Oh. Okay, then. Hi." Wonderland or fairyland or dreamland, he's got a ticket to any one of them.

His eyes drift shut, his lips pulling into a smile then snapping back, and I get my introduction to the sleepy-drunk Orion his friends laughed over.

"We didn't," he mumbles, "do everything. So much more."

"So much." I bite my cheek and caress his.

He leans into my hand. "I like bookstores."

My watery smile. "Me too."

"Better. Don't have to. Give them back. Can dog-ear their pages and write in. Margins. Mess them up."

My stomach heats. I push a stray curl off his forehead.

"Better than. Library books. Can only borrow."

In the dim light, I borrow time and read his face. His strong jaw and knife-edged nose. I touch the little cleft at his chin, peering into the space as if it leads to forever. He snores faintly now, out cold. His eyelids tremble.

In the dim light, my forbidden truth writes across my mind. I dress up as myself, the Lila Reyes who sometimes doesn't listen to people or reason. Doesn't protect a damn thing like she should. Sometimes she runs too far and reacts too quickly and hurts herself and her sister when she's hurting.

In the dim light, I am still her. Just another flavor of the girl who came here weeks ago. She'll go home the same and different.

Sí, claro, I do these forbidden things. I'm reckless with words this time. I swirl them around my mouth and bounce them off my heart. I whisper them in English. I say them in Spanish. I put them into hands that feed cities and will hold Orion until dawn. "Te amo."

31

Two suitcases wait in Spencer's Range Rover after I've said goodbye to everyone but Orion. Down to minutes, we spend them on the church courtyard bench.

I yawn richly, headachy and bleary-eyed, wearing my dove charm on a silver chain I bought in town.

"The lady said she wanted to stay up all night and she did." He nudges me.

"So did you. At least I can sleep on the plane." To Miami. Home.

I was careful about my last day. I didn't want anything new. No new places or memories. I wanted hours of my old ones and the people I met and loved.

Recipe for Goodbye
From the Kitchen of Lila Reyes
Ingredients: One Cuban girl. One English boy. One English city.

Preparation: Give Polly her kitchen back and share a genuine smile, from one legitimate baker to another. Ride through the countryside on a vintage Triumph Bonneville. Walk through Winchester, all through town and on the paths you ran. Drink vanilla black tea at Maxwell's. Eat fish and chips and curry sauce at your friend's pub. Sleep in fits and bits curled up together on St. Giles Hill.

*Leave out future talk. Any form of the word *tomorrow*.

Cooking temp: 200 degrees Celsius. You know the conversion by heart.

At once, Orion gets up and paces to the fountain. Is this how it is now? Do we need to practice how to *be* apart?

"Flora," he says. "When I came in to brush my teeth she was covering dough to rise."

I rise too, keeping my distance. "I'll stay close. Talk to her as much as I can."

"She loves you." His hand balls, then lifts to cover a face still turned away. But on his next breath, he spins, jaw fitted as tightly as the stone walls. "You came here and you fed everyone. Not just me and not just sandwiches and pastries. You fed the guests at the inn, and people in town will ask where you are tomorrow. You fed Jules's music. You fed my friends and you fed my sister with skills and love and now you're . . ." He ducks his head.

I'm shaking at this, realizing the meaning. Today he fights

against worlds and universes, not accepting the boarding pass in my purse. Not accepting what he's powerless to change. Tomorrow, maybe he will. But not now.

"Orion."

He looks up, anguished.

"You all fed me back."

"That's the fucking hell of it isn't it? After all that, we're still starving." He scrubs his face roughly. "I'm sorry, Lila. It's not your fault. Your life was yours before you landed here."

Teeth clenched, I nod. "You're a bloody fool if you think I'm going to forget you, or lose you. Do you really think I'd let that happen?"

"Of course not . . . But don't promise any more now. You're going home to a great future."

What if my future falls underneath a different flag? Right now, I can't even allow this thought. Miami has to be my rightful castle today, not an English ruin.

He approaches. "Well then. Spencer will be calling for you. It might as well be now as it is in five minutes." Orion looks me over, head to toe. "Be safe. Ring when you land, no matter the time." He holds me close. Kisses each of my cheeks then nods once, bidding me home.

I touch my fingers to my lips, then turn toward the fountain. I won't watch him walk away. It's fitting that the water under the sainted statue rests still. I try to turn myself off too. This one time, I want math, need it like Pilar does. I make equations: The square root of *Family Style* plus flan divided by Miami rain minus South

Beach sand. I make more, repeating them until the cool gray of graphite covers all my heart and Spencer's voice calls from next door.

It's time to turn my feet around. Time to go home. But just as I reach the gate, I jolt at Orion blocking my way, jerking me toward him.

"I lied," is all he says before he kisses me. Full and long and richly dark. One last time, we feed each other before he pulls away. "Goodbye, Lila."

I still can't say it back.

32

There's too much heat in this city. My British summer body has to adjust like reptiles and amphibians do from shady coolness to the blistering scorch of rocks. I wake too early and even now, just ahead of dawn, air steams with the promise of a makeup drip-off day when clothes stick to skin and sweat gathers in inconvenient places. A Miami August always keeps its promises.

Yesterday my city put me into my family's arms. I cried and clung to Pilar like a little child. I told her she looked beautiful but needed a haircut. She told me I looked like a plane cabin disaster and absolutely perfect. I texted Orion and then slept off the emptiness of our messaged words and emojis. Then I slept some more, waking only to eat.

I will go to La Paloma today. See what's the same and what's changed. But now I walk West Dade with a big mug of café con leche before the gossip birds are up. Chany redid his landscaping and Susana got a brand-new Honda. Grace and Cristina and

Sophie left their trio of pink and purple scooters in their driveway.

I learn my house again too. Sí, the kitchen faucet drips if you don't really jam down the tap. The floor creaks just here and the walls smell like garlic and onions. And my room—my suitcases are a tumble of rummaging and half-unpacking—carries only the sound of Pilar's shower and the tick of an old clock of Abuela's. But even my hazed, jet-lagged eyes spot the package on my unmade bed. The yellow sticky note reads:

> *Sorry, I forgot because my sister is home.*
> *This came yesterday to LP. Sleep well?—P*

DHL Express? The return address shoots tingles up my arms. Carefully, I undo packing tape and box flaps and tissue paper. I let out a helpless sob when I lift out the softest, grayest, England-est, wooliest, Orion-est cardigan ever. I clutch it to me, breathing in a Winchester townhouse and rainy soapy spice. Breathing in memories of kisses and cobblestones, motorbikes and music. I pluck out a flat white card:

> *This was always meant to be yours.*
> *Love, Orion*

It's extra hard to text when your hands are shaking.

Me: I got it and you can't

Orion: Absolutely, I can

Me: But your grandmother

Orion: Will make me another cardigan. This one belongs to you

Me: I love it so much. Thank you forever

Orion: Keep warm and talk soon

Me: Goodnight, England

Orion: Good morning, Miami

I wrap the gray cabled wool over my tank top. There's too much heat in this city, too much for England sweaters. But this one warms a shivering heart.

"I'm a little scared for you to try this," Angelina says, offering me her pastelito de guayaba.

I bite into flaky, sticky goodness. Yes, deliciousness. I smile broadly. "Angelina."

"Really?" She places a paper napkin on my table.

"It's perfect." I'm parked at one of the two-tops at La Paloma. Rather, I'm forced to sit and look over the *Family Style* production details, finalize our menu choices to showcase, and greet all the customers who have been asking about me for weeks. "This is quality food and I know you've been doing it all summer. Thank you."

She smiles and readjusts a bandanna over her dark blond hair before returning to the kitchen.

They don't let me in to work today, only to poke around and bask in hugs and welcomes. In three days we will close to prepare for shooting. Showroom walls will get a fresh coat of the warm ivory I picked out with Pilar. Floors and surfaces will be scrubbed and shined.

Instead Papi gives me a throne by the entrance like I'm the panadería's lost prodigal daughter. Their fatted calves are cafecitos and sugary samples from the kitchen. My family means well, but don't they know I need to bake? I need to put my hands in flour, to feel like myself in this place again.

Instead I get up to look over items other employees have baked, milling around the big display rack piled with breads and Cuban rolls. Glass front cases burst with pastries, miniature desserts, and savory croquetas. Sweet and warm and inviting.

I stop at the wall where the framed *Miami Herald* article has hung for four years. An oversized photo in the Lifestyle section shows Pilar and me smiling over a tray of assorted pasteles. The headline beams proudly in block letters: *West Miami Teens Save the "Date" at Congressman Millan's Charity Fund-raiser.*

It seems only yesterday that the same reporter who'd covered the Millans' charity event was sitting here, interviewing Pilar and me. La Paloma grew exponentially because of my one choice to not cancel an order. To work overnight and command a kitchen at thirteen with my sister. So much change came from a single newspaper article. Now we're going to be on TV and I can't even dream of what will happen to this place once again.

But that same girl on the wall, printed in black and white newsprint, doesn't sit here with a black and white mind. I think in so many shades, on the edge of myself, balanced between yesterday and tomorrow.

Basta. Enough sitting and thinking, and enough of this storefront.

In the back, the kitchen rides on grease and yeast and sugar. I stand where I would usually stand and realize too many bakers are scheduled for morning shift. They don't need me today.

Marta whips mango mousse, alive with color. Gives me a taste with a spoon.

"Qué rico," I tell her.

She starts pouring the filling into individual molds. "So, for the show, will you do tres leches or the flan?"

"Both if there's time."

I wander more, peering into the deck ovens, winding through the storage bay. I finally land in Papi's office and stop short in the doorway. "What's going on?"

My family perches on the small sofa, a trio of love. Papi, with his work-weary eyes and dark hair sprinkled with salt, and Mami still wearing her apron. Pilar's in the middle, binding everyone together like glue.

Mami lifts her face from her laptop. "Why did you not tell us, Lilita?"

"What?" My mind reels. I sink into Papi's desk chair.

Their faces drop and Pilar's fingers fidget in endless combinations.

"Catalina sent the pictures she took at your birthday party. The prom they did for you," Mami says. "Qué linda."

"It was." Those pictures are in my e-mail box too. I haven't been able to open the file. Not yet. Orion's flowers rest on my dresser, drying out.

Pilar says, "We were waiting for you to say something. Nothing yesterday off the plane, but you were so tired." Her hand dashes aimlessly. "And nothing today, this morning over breakfast."

My palms turn clammy and my heartbeat thrums in my chest, and not from two cafecitos.

Papi turns the laptop, scrolling. Cate snapped my party but captured my truth. Pictures show Orion dancing with me, his eyes closed and his lips poised at the top of my head. My face rests against his lapel, dream-spent. Then me, snuggled into his side as Jules sings my song, and dozens more of me and my new friends.

Words fail. I'm stripped of more than my apron today, naked and bare. I have to cross my arms at my chest to keep my traitorous emotions from flooding this place we all built. The sobs start inward, rolling, but I hide them behind a storm wall, anchoring myself into my father's seat.

"We know about Le Cordon Bleu," Papi says. "Catalina had a lot to say about that. About your plans and how much you impacted Winchester. How you love the city and could bring our food there. But *you* have not had anything to say."

Say it? Give it actual words, ripping this little square office right down the middle?

Pilar scoots forward. "Don't let it be like before. Don't hold it all in."

The wall cracks. "Yes, okay? Fine." I'm flooding now, standing, ripping into myself. "It's true. England, the school, Orion—all of it. But Miami is my home and everything here is my home. My future. How can I just . . . leave? Just forget everything we are, everything we've been working for?"

"Lila, answer the simple things," Papi says. "Your sister told us about your Orion. Does this boy love you too?"

I close my eyes as inner snapshots flip. Orion Maxwell has never said the words, but he's also shouted them a million ways, a million times. "He does."

Mami slides her arm around Pilar. They cling to each other, faces wrestling with emotions until jagged smiles win.

"Bueno. And we looked at the pastry program. It's wonderful. Do you want to go to this school?"

"The tuition is so expensive. And so are the train passes, and I couldn't work for a long time on a student visa."

"Abuela's inheritance for you is enough."

How can I even think of this? Using the money Abuela earned at La Paloma for a future opposite of the one she prepared me for? "I want to make the right choice. The best one for our family. For our business and everyone."

"What happened to the best choice for *you*?" Papi asks.

For me. My legacy. My heart. My future.

But a piercing truth slashes like Tío's knife into corn stalks. I turn to my mother. "You didn't send me to England so I would choose it over our family, over Miami and La Paloma." Not the woman who lost her best friend to the same country. "If you'd known, you wouldn't have put me on that plane. But you did and now look!"

Mami stands and reaches for me, her hands twined with mine and her eyes like arrow points. "Did your heart find peace and some closure and something new to smile about in England?"

"Sí, Mami," I whisper. "So, so much."

Now she cries, a fat tear rolling down her cheek and the smell of her like honeysuckle. "That is exactly why we sent you."

Stuffed with pork and Cuban side dishes, topped with an extended family's worth of kisses and dancing and domino games, I sit on my bed. I'm stuffed with choices, too, pulled in too many ways. I trace the miniature colored pencil drawing of the Owl and Crow Inn, Gordon's birthday gift.

FaceTime pings from my laptop and the name flashing on the screen sinks into my stomach. But I'm ready. I accept the call.

Stefanie stares at me from across the world. "Lila." Her voice is small and I barely recognize this girl with a straw hat and no makeup.

"Hi." How do we start? What do we do?

"I'm sorry about—" comes out of my mouth right when she says, "I'm sorry I—"

We both laugh shakily and I motion for her to go first.

"I've had service for a few weeks now, since my e-mail. But you went to England and I thought you'd be busy . . . and I was a little scared to call, to be honest." I nod and she says, "I hate the way we left things. I didn't get to explain. Lila, for years all I did was watch you change entire rooms with your food."

"Stef—"

"No, listen. You would bring over croquetas or your flan, and people would just smile. They'd forget their problems or stress for a little while. And I've always thought that was your gift. Your magic."

My chin crumples. But I keep listening.

Stef glances down then back at me again. "I just wanted my own magic too, separate from us together. I wanted to change rooms and help people. And I didn't want to wait anymore. I'll go back to school, but later. I didn't know how to tell you—"

I hold out my palm. "Wait. I wasn't acting like the kind of friend you could tell. So I'm sorry. Sorry I made you run all those miles and tried to plan your life."

Her face softens. "We both messed up."

"Yeah we did." I breathe in then out. "Are you happy?"

Her nod comes quickly. "So happy."

She tells me about Africa and the work she's doing—saving lives, changing them. Her face gleams and animates well enough, but she doesn't go deep into adventures.

"I'm finally used to the climate and no A/C."

"When supplies are brought in, we fight over the dark chocolate bars."

"Hats and long-sleeved white tees are my friend."

Stefanie summarizes Ghana and the people and the skills she's learning as if she's reading her new life off a glossy travel brochure. My friend is holding back.

I don't know what to do with this. I shift restless legs, then burrow under my comforter. I can't get comfortable so I take my turn and talk about England. Only, talking about England is like knifing my heart from my chest. Held in front me, it drones a steady metronome beat, keeping me alive well enough. But this heart ticking between my body and Stef's face on the monitor is cooler and paler than hearts should ever be.

So I can't go deep. I hold back too and remain like the last-minute toppings of things. My stories are dusted powdered sugar and mango glaze. I can't tell my friend about the thick, bittersweet fillings of castles and vanilla black tea, or the rich, spongy cake of new friends and songs. I can't talk about the motorbike wind and green and stone I baked into crusty bread and into the baker. *Me.*

"It rains so much. Like more than Miami."

"You'd really love the accents. They're always apologizing for everything."

"It's so old. There can be a petrol station right next to a five-hundred-year-old building."

Stef wrinkles her nose. "Since when do you say petrol?"

Petrol—I didn't even notice. Telling her why I brought so much of another country back into mine doesn't work. Neither does my mouth when I try to tell her about Orion. Nothing. Nada.

I'm 100 percent unable to tell the girl who cried for hours with me over Andrés a single word about Orion. The way we were in England is mine; I'm not sharing. I can't even say his name or that I'm holding his sweater on my lap because if I do, I'll knife through all the rest of me. I have to lock him inside to keep myself together.

But isn't Stef my best friend? And then, what if there's an African Orion, or a dozen other stories beyond chocolate bars and straw hats that she's not telling *me*?

If this is true, it's okay. And because it's so okay, I realize we aren't the same and different in a new-old friendship. We are just different now.

So this is what we do when our talking funnels down to drip-drops and long stretches of silence. I don't have a recipe for this. I've never had a best-friendship ending before. We improvise.

"I think I'm going to extend my term here," she says.

Which I'd already guessed. "I'm proud of you. I'll always be proud of you," is what feels the most true.

"I don't know when we'll see each other again." From her.

Tears well, but my heart has gone back inside now and it's softly thunking away. Right where it's supposed to be. "I don't know when I'll see you, either."

Her eyes are glassy. "I'll always be proud of you, too, Lila."

"I'll keep track. Of everything you're doing. All the good."

She nods and smiles. "I'll watch you take over the world." Then she looks left and right. For seconds—too many—the quiet is thick and gray like clouds. "I have to go," she whispers.

She doesn't just mean from the call.

"I love you, Stefanie."

"Te amo, Lila."

The screen goes black. And a best-friendship doesn't die. Instead, it runs its own way now, miles over bridges and roads and desert sand. Without us.

33

Days later a *Temporarily Closed for Filming* sign hangs on the door. I'm here when the shop is dark and wants to sleep. I rouse it awake, forcing it to listen. I came back to have this kitchen to myself for just a bit before the world peeks inside.

I don't know why Pilar is here.

"You're in my territory," I say. Pilar Reyes, who nests in the office and hates the dusty stick of flour on her hands.

"How I knew where to find you." Only a few of the task lights shine. My sister is half mermaid, half math itself in her prim white blouse knotted at her waist and a flowy miniskirt. The hair we share—it needs its own zip code, we always say—riots around her face, waiting for our stylists tomorrow.

We meet at the butcher block island and do something Mami and Abuela used to scold us over. One, two . . . *up!* We scoot close and let our legs swing and dangle. I lean against the shoulder that's always been so very strong. Strong enough to hold these walls up, and mine.

"Why are you wearing your dove on a silver chain?" Pili asks.

I reach for the gold bird. "I gave mine to Orion's sister. Flora."

"You wouldn't surrender that necklace in a robbery."

"Well . . ." is all I can say. Two sisters: which one will get Face-Time Lila and which will get the RealTime me?

"I was thinking you should highlight one of the special variations Abuela made here. For *Family Style*."

"Sí. One more way to make her a part of it." Slowly, I take in all my grandparents built. "Remember how she always put currants instead of raisins in the picadillo? She loved the little burst of flavor, even though they were more expensive."

"And the special sugar, the one that sparkles, for the pastelitos for fancy parties," Pili adds.

"Pineapple or hazelnut or pumpkin flan for different holidays, or the extra syrups she added to cakes, and everyone wondered why they were so moist. And knowing how to play with ratios so they were the same dishes or pasteles but also, just *better* versions of the same."

Pili bumps my side. "Like you know how."

Because she taught me to change recipes. But only after I could make the original perfectly. In my head her teachings come alive, not from a white coffin, but from years of corn and flour and sugar. I hop down and mark the spots where lessons were learned.

To change recipes.

I stand in the middle of her life's work. I stand in the middle of her *life*. And then—

She changed her own recipe too.

I open my heart like a history book. Inside, there is a seventeen-year-old Cuban girl named Lydia Rodriguez who leaves a small Cuban farm. She boards a plane alone, no family, no friends. She crosses an ocean and a culture with a single suitcase. She joins an American host family. And instead of returning home when her program ends, she works through a hundred details to stay. She chooses a new life in a new country, building a business with the recipes her own mother taught her.

Not just food. Abuela changed her life recipe.

In my heart, Abuela tells me I've been wrong all this time. She never put a spoon in my hand and skills in my head to tether me to one place. She gave me knowledge so I could choose too. The place she built. Or the places I will build.

Yo puedo—*I can.*

I can keep the recipes she taught me and make them here.

I can go to school in England and learn to combine French artistry with my cooking.

I can stay at La Paloma and work side-by-side with my sister.

I can move under the same sky as a British boy.

I can be fully Cubana in Miami.

I can be fully Cubana in England, or Africa, or France, or anywhere.

I was brought up for this place, but I can change my life recipe too.

I can. And I will.

Pilar's feet pad behind me. She touches my arm and I turn. Miami tears rain from two clouds. "You're going, aren't you?"

"I'm going," I say for the first time. "Pero, hermana. You and me. Las Reyes . . ."

"Will always be who we are. No matter where we are." When my sigh comes troubled and heavy, she adds, "Go, Lila. This place will always be here. And come home for Christmas?"

I hold her tight. "And in the summer."

She holds me tighter. "And I'll go there and you can show me your England. I'll bunk at Catalina's with you, and Orion can find my favorite tea."

"You hate flying."

"I can be different too."

The box of new aprons shipped a few days late, but in plenty of time for the staff to wear for the *Family Style* TV shoot. Forty-eight hours now. In the La Paloma kitchen, I'm studying the new design of smart white and blue ticking striped cotton.

"It *was* Señora Cabral," Pili says on her way back from the shop floor, laughing. "Two weeks we've had the closure warning posted, but you knew she'd ignore it."

Which is why I froze a few things for her before we closed. I tip my head at Pili. "No TV show is going to keep that woman from her pan Cubano."

"I didn't even charge her. Why fire up the system for one loaf?" Pilar pulls the apron box toward her and gazes inside, lifting the striped fabric. "Qué bueno," she says before heading back to the office.

Two days now. I've barely been able to FaceTime Orion, but he gets it. All my hours have gone to food and menu prep, plus new haircuts for Pilar and Mami and me, plus manicures and brow waxing and family meetings and supervising the bakery facelift. I've even been too busy to think about how nervous I should be.

Again, knocking sounds from the front. What, did Señora Cabral come back for the pastelitos I froze too? "I'll get it!" I call to no one.

When I reach the shop floor, it's empty. Just as I'm turning back, I catch the glint of silver foil from the empty bread rack.

I wind around from the service area and before I can process the strange reality of the Maxwell's foil bag marked, *Vanilla Black,* I hear from behind, "It's terrible luck for the person who takes the last slice of bread to not kiss the baker."

Dios mío.

My heart in my throat, I turn extra slowly because this can't be happening. There is no way Orion is standing in my doorway, in my business, in my city. But he is and I'm already running.

Orion barely has time to get his arms up to catch me, hiding any greetings or explanations inside frantic kisses. He's warm— too warm—like we're kissing in the middle of a sauna. He's salt and sweat and steam, and I wouldn't trade him for the world.

Finally we part, just enough for me to take in the misted eyes of him—more blue and vibrant than I remember—then the damp, mussed-up hair and wrinkled black tee and soft, faded jeans of him. "How? What are—" I get these sounds out, but shock steals the rest.

He pecks my forehead and smiles at me, dimple deep. Then his face shades with gravity. "You left something in Winchester."

I launch into him again, burrowing my head into his chest. Soon, I'm giggling. "You look like . . ."

"Like a British guy's lost his first bout with a Miami summer?" His chest rumbles with mirth.

"*Well* . . . Did you jog here or something?"

He keeps me close but turns into my gaze. "I got off one bus stop too soon and thought I'd walk the remainder of the way. The app said I was only fifteen minutes away, but five minutes in, I realized my grave error. God, it's bloody volcanic out there."

"Bienvenido a Miami, Orion," I say over a laugh that fades into a little sigh of disbelief. "You're really here."

"About that," he says, brushing back my hair. "Dad was about to drown me in the Itchen. Said I was acting like a quote, 'miserable git.' I told him everything and that I needed to come here. Needed to say some things I should've said. But he decided it's been too long since we've taken a real family holiday. Just like that, my uncle came down to mind the shop and we landed today. Flora's already slathered in SPF 50 sun cream at the hotel pool, dying to see you."

I jerk backward, "Oh, she came too?" I cup his face then reach up onto my toes to kiss him again.

He moves into one of the café chairs and pulls me down into my favorite sitting spot—his lap. "Back in England, I didn't want to be 'that guy.' I couldn't ask you to leave your family, your business, your country, just for me." He rubs my shoulder. "So I wanted you to choose a future that's first and foremost yours alone. Not to belong *to* me. I want you to belong *with* me. That's the part I didn't say enough."

I lose my breath, then sputter across the next one.

"I still don't know how we can work it out with you here and me there right now, but I'm not giving up." His voice shakes. "I was wrong, too. Sometimes we have to want more than we're given. So, this is me, wishing for someone as impossible and otherworldly as you."

He ducks, but I don't let him get far. My hands force his gaze. "You were an award-winning tour guide, but you missed one thing."

He cocks his head on a resigned smile. "What's that?"

"Your constellation. So to fix that, I'm gonna need to see Orion's Belt on St. Giles Hill, with you. And it will be winter, so I'll be wearing your cardigan under the biggest, puffiest coat I've ever owned. And we'll probably stay out way too late. And the next morning, I'll be yawning the entire train ride to London." I make sure he sees me say the next words. "To school. For my future. My choice."

He sucks in a breath of disbelief but I nod my secret into him. "You're doing it? The winter term at Le Cordon Bleu?"

"For a start. I submitted my application and applied for a student visa this morning. Before you came, I was trying to think of some cool way to tell you over FaceTime later. But this is a thousand times better." I grin, clasping my hands behind his neck. "I'm not going back to England just for the pastry program, though. See, no other girl gets to make you Cuban sandwiches and lemon biscuits and ride Millie and run with you. No one but me."

He takes a moment, lets us both write my words into memory. Then he kisses me starstruck.

"Come see La Paloma and meet my family." I jump up and pull him with me. "Prepare yourself for three Cubans to faint, or at least pretend-swoon with extra drama."

He follows me into the vast kitchen. "About that, your family *might* already know I'm here." When my eyes spring wide, he adds, "I've, um, been talking to Pilar. She helped me pull off my little surprise. Made sure you were here and all. And apparently, there's some huge supper being planned for my family after the taping is over. At your uncle's house with all your relatives?"

My family and his family—my heart smiles. "Warning, don't eat for two days."

He laughs, and after he cleans up in the staff bathroom, I show him around the place that grew me. Equipment and old photos and some of the prepped pastries and cakes we'll display on TV. The spot where I kneaded my first loaf of bread.

Orion arcs his hand, sobering. "All of this. Can you . . . really?"

Yo puedo. "I can and I'm ready. Not gonna lie, it's going to hurt." My eyes well again. "Some days more than others and at weird times with no warning. I'll need tea and extra hugs then."

He loops his arms around me. "I'm told I'm the best at those."

From the back, Pilar yells, "Lila! Are you done snogging off Orion's face yet?"

"No?!"

They come out anyway. In ten minutes, Mami falls in love. Pilar and Orion settle into an easy banter about music and the London scene she's dying to take in; I catch her blooming pink at his accent and natural charm.

But we all hush when Papi leaves then returns with two glasses of Coke, lime wedges hinging off the rims. He offers one to Orion and motions him toward the storage room hallway.

Orion winks at me and goes with my father, edging just ahead of him into the back office. Papi lingers for a beat. A father turns to the daughter who will leave his home in three months. He nods once, his eyes damp and heavy with endings and beginnings.

Todo está bien. All is well.

Mami and Pilar press me into a group hug then follow to their own spaces, leaving me alone in mine. This week I will show La Paloma to the world, and order a winter coat, and bake bread with Flora in this kitchen. I will tell a star-named boy I love him in front of my great uncle's corn plot—not in secret—but under a wide-open wish across a Miami summer sky.

But before tomorrow happens, I have to do one thing today. I pull Abuela's apron from the butcher block island. All the bakers' hooks line the wall, her framed memorial picture smiling above the one where she stowed the white cotton cloth every evening.

"Gracias, Abuela. Te amo," I whisper and place a single kiss on the embroidered script *L*. I hang up her apron for the last time. Then I move to the cardboard shipping box filled with white and blue ticking stripes.

And pick up my own.

Acknowledgments

When I began this project, I wanted to honor my mother's journey from a small Cuban farm to the United States as a teen exchange student just before Castro assumed power. Most of my relatives followed over the next few years. By the time I came along, my extended family had grown into the loving, vibrant network I know today. My family history became the scaffolding for a story featuring another brave and vibrant teen girl, layered with many of my own teen experiences. Soon into drafting, I lost two of the beloved relatives who inhabit these pages. What started as a book became a tangible way for me to hold them close. Their spirits fill these scenes. I can think of no better place to keep them until I see them again. If you have come here after reading Lila's story, you have experienced many anecdotes I witnessed as a girl, watching and listening, eating and cooking with my beloved Cuban relatives. Thank you to all of my tíos and primos, for all the ways you fed me.

To my brilliant editor Alex Borbolla, from day one you showed such a genuine understanding of me and the unique aspects of this story. Your love for this book and the history behind it touched me. And your skill and guidance inspired me. Partnering with you has been one of my greatest professional experiences. It is my honor to work with you.

To my agent Natascha Morris, thank you for taking this book you always call a "big hug" and working so faithfully to manage and place it. I couldn't ask for a better cheerleader, confidant, and advocate for my stories and my career.

To my critique partners and trusted friends, Joan Smith and Allison Bitz, Lila's story would not be what it is today without your faithful insight, editing, nudging, and wisdom. I love you both so much.

To art director, Karyn Lee, and illustrator, Andrea Porretta, thank you for envisioning and designing one of the most beautiful covers I have ever seen. You have brought Lila and Orion to life so masterfully while showcasing the perfect mashup of Miami, Cuba, and England.

To Clare McGlade, Tatyana Rosalia, Shivani Annirood, and the entire team at Atheneum, thank you for your tireless efforts in bringing this book to the world.

Thank you to my early readers and sources who helped with everything from careful beta reads, to checking those wily Spanish accents, to making sure my British rep was solid. Alexandra Overy, Marlene Lee, Ximena Avalos, Beth Ellyn Summer, Susie Cabrera, and Yamile Saied Méndez, I could not have done this without you.

To my Las Musas hermanas, thank you for your friendship, support, and our fabulous community. I am so honored to be a part of this beautiful organization.

I'm so thankful to God for the opportunity and grace to be able to write this book, and to you, reader for opening it.